UNCOMMON HOMECOMING

The ferrequus rumbled on. The train was like a gigantic metal worm wrapped around the low, curved hill. In the front I could see the stately Ionian columns of the locomotive; behind was an area where the slaves shoveled wood into the great burners; the chambers of state followed. Directly behind the attack car on which we were standing was a temple on wheels, a sort of Doric parthenon with a marble roof. I was about to say something about the herd of buffalo we had passed when a horn began to blare out an alarm.

"What's the matter?" Papinian asked.

"Dust storm, General, sir!" a centurion said.

"That's no dust storm," I said. "We're being attacked!"

It was unmistakable now. I stared out at the northern horizon. Several hundred horsemen were attacking the Iron Horse; I could hear their war cry *"Huka hey!"* punctuated by the pounding of hooves. My heart sank. Lacotii do not fight Lacotii. I had come all th~~is~~ to get involve~~d~~ the wrong side!

By S.P. Somtow
Published by Ballantine Books:

THE AQUILIAD
Volume One: *Aquila in the New World*
Volume Two: *Aquila and the Iron Horse*

STARSHIP & HAIKU

THE AQUILIAD

VOLUME II
Aquila and the Iron Horse

S. P. SOMTOW

A Del Rey Book

BALLANTINE BOOKS • **NEW YORK**

A Del Rey Book
Published by Ballantine Books

Library of Congress Catalog Card Number: 87-91854

ISBN 0-345-33868-5

Manufactured in the United States of America

First Edition: May 1988

Cover Art by David B. Mattingly

dedicated to
Eleanor Wood, who made a very convincing
case for frivolity;
to the mighty
Greg Bear, the SFWA's equivalent of the
Dimensional Patrol;
and also to the precocious
Joshua Levy, whom I'm grooming to be
my replacement.

CONTENTS

PRIMA PARS:

ROMA

CHAPTER
I

ANDROCLES AND THE LIONS

IDON'T SUPPOSE YOU WOULD HAVE PICKED UP THIS weatherbeaten old papyrus if you had not previously read a memoir written by my bumbling, bubblenosed stepfather, General Titus Papinianus. My stepfather is somewhat decrepit these days. He was a boy during the reign of the Emperor Nero, when the territories on the other side of the Oceanus Atlanticus were just being opened up, and when General Pomponius Piso the Elder first battled the indomitable Lacotii braves on the banks of the Flumen Pulveris. He was a general when Domitian ruled and when the giant chickens, potatii, tobacchii, and coecolactae of Terra Nova had lost their faddishness and became staples even in the lifestyle of the plebeians of Rome.

My stepfather became procurator of Lacotia during the reign of Domitian, and, whilst searching for the fabled land of Chin under instructions from that emperor and the Emperor Trajan, discovered instead a number of significant wonders: the Sasquatii, lost tribes of Israel who were mutated by a green pig from a parallel universe and condemned to live northwest of the Roman

3

territories; the empire of the Olmechii to the south, with its hot-air balloons and flying saucers; the were-jaguars from the future, who keep our age free of paradoxes by means of their Dimensional Patrol. Recalled to Rome, he had a thousand copies of his book made and distributed to the various libraries all over the empire. They are not good clean copies; I went down to the copying room while it was being done, and I saw several scribes doubled over with laughter, one drunk and flat on his back, a third interpolating bizarre obscenities. It was generally considered an amusing fantasy, though not up to the suppressed *Satyricon* of the late Petronius.

It was perhaps fortunate that my stepfather was not believed when he published his memoirs for most thought either that he had lost his wits, or that he had merely composed a romance in the manner of the writers of *scientifictiones*. In fact, however, he told the truth— oh, he stretched it a bit here and there, to aggrandize himself a bit more or to hide an embarrassing moment— but the truth more or less as his limited intelligence was able to perceive it.

Nevertheless...

I have decided, at this juncture in the story, to step in myself as your humble narrator for the remainder of these adventures. You see, for one thing, my stepfather isn't quite himself anymore...for reasons which should become apparent by the time I'm done.

For another, there's the matter of my real father— Aquila the Magnificent, the noblest savage of them all, distinguished conqueror of the Parthians (although my stepfather took all the credit) and power-behind-the-throne during my stepfather's entire régime as procurator of Lacotia...my real father, who, you may recall, was elevated to the Dimensional Patrol at the end of Papinian's memoir and who now roams through the time-lanes with his glorious compatriots from the future.

I, Equus Insanus, am the last of Aquila's twenty-odd

children—sired, they tell me, on some Roman patrician's daughter. Personally, I prefer to think of myself as
wholly Lacotian. It wasn't by choice that I was adopted
into General Titus Papinianus's family; but after my father was snatched into the sky by a flying saucer, what
could one do? Not that the general was unkind to me. He
was, indeed, lavish in his love for me. I had no objec-
tions to the gifts: the bags and bags of silver sestertii, the
use of the second-best chariot, or the presence, within
the procuratorial villa, of lots of slaves to do my bidding.
All that was fine and dandy, and I ought to say at the
outset that I do feel a certain amount of gratitude to the
old fool.

But there was one thing that General Papinian was
determined to do with me when we returned to Rome; it
was to cure me of my savage nature—to inculcate within
my breast a love for the finer things that Rome had to
offer—in effect, to civilize me.

The money, chariots, and slaves were some of the advantages of civilization.

The disadvantages—

Well, the clothes for one. The toga praetexta, which
was worn over a tunica which in turn covered a stifling
loincloth, was made of thick wool, and was not a particularly wonderful garment in the muggy Roman summer
which had just begun when we got off the ship from
Terra Nova. Not to mention the various cloaks and
things you had to throw over the toga "because you
wouldn't want to ruin that fine wool, would you?" Right.

Then there was the food. They didn't have any of this
killing your own—none of the thrill of stalking and hunting and felling the wild aurochs, and plucking out its
steaming liver and dining on it right then and there—
which is the proper way to eat, by Jupiter Vacantanca!
Oh, they had the odd hunt now and then—or "vena-
tion," as the patricians airily term such things—but having caught whatever it was they were hunting, did they

eat it? Never! It was just "sporting, eh what?" as my stepfather would comment whilst the carcass was left to putrefy in the horrid Roman sun.

No—instead, I was forced to eat such things as pea-cocks' brains and unborn dormice dipped in honey... while the Greek tutor my stepfather had purchased for my edification lectured me on the sterling qualities each of these rare viands was supposed to elicit within my oh-so-patriotic Roman breast.

Then there was education—countless Greek and Roman verbs to be learned, the exceptions noted, the endings to be recited ad nauseam—and, coupled with that education, the assiduous application of the flagellum to my quivering arse.

The Romans, in short, believe in pain. Not the momentary—and ennobling—self-torture of the sundance, but pain just for the fun of it. There isn't a single lesson, they feel, that can't be learned more efficiently with a bit of assistance from the lash. My stepfather, who, though stupid, has never been a particularly cruel man, thought nothing of the daily floggings that took place down at the slaves' quarters. As for me—by adoption scion of one of the most noble families in Rome—my name meant nothing to Androcles, the bearded, wizened, mincing, carping, pedantic pederast who was the head magister of the school to which my stepfather entrusted my education. If a day went by without a stripe or two upon my buttocks, it was, as Androcles opined, a day wasted.

It was, in fact, while I was splayed out on Androcles' whipping block, my tender flesh anticipating the descent of the magisterial rod, that I first had the idea of writing a book that would not only continue the adventures of the Papinian family, but also rectify some of my stepfather's more glaring omissions.

Just as the idea occurred to me—in a brilliant flash that momentarily dispelled my thoughts of the impending pain—the lash descended. I screamed.

"A decent Roman doesn't scream when he's beaten!" Androcles said, bringing down the flagellum with more might than you might imagine for a man with so withered a physique. "Now, once more—the correct version of the Battle of the Flumen Pulveris!"

There were about twenty other pupils in the chamber, and all of them had gathered around to enjoy my discomfiture. They all held up their wax tablets and their styli, ready to reel off the true facts that the magister was trying to get me to divulge. "Aquila the Magnificent held off ten cohorts of cavalry with only twelve braves!" I said, all in one breath.

The lash descended yet again.

"Wrong!" said Androcles. "Would someone care to enlighten young Papinian?" (For that was how I was known: as Titus Papinianus the Younger, much to my embarrassment.)

I waited for another welt, but the master paused for a moment. I could imagine all the eager hands going up. But I could not see my fellow sufferers, for from the whipping block, my buttocks exposed and my head pushed all the way down, all I could see was an upside-down view of the Via Vacantancae, which led to the Forum Lacoticum, which borders a slum—often called Little Lacotia for short. One side of this narrow street was the new Temple of Vacantanca—a newfangled, mystical religion brought over from the New World, which bore almost no resemblance to the true worship of the Great Spirit. The other side was a high-rise insula of some three or four stories, crammed to bursting with Lacotian immigrants who had come to Rome in search of a better life. Many, instead, had fallen victim to the lure of Roman wineshops.

I could see several Lacotian children playing a game of knucklebones in front of one such wineshop. They were not wearing the ridiculous garments of Roman aristocracy, but simple loincloths; one of them sported an eagle feather in his long, dark hair. A paunchy Lacotian elder watched them with one eye while guzzling from an enormous amphora. As the children yelled out insults to each other in the Lacotian tongue, I could not restrain myself. I thought of my childhood—of the buffalo hunt, of stealing horses and fighting noble wars—and the tears welled up and began running down my cheeks. I could see them dripping onto the imported marble floor of Androcles' schoolroom, and I knew that this would incite him to further flagellation. I was right.

"You spineless barbarian!" Androcles shouted. "Weeping, indeed, at so minuscule and deserved a helping of pain! You still do not see the virtues of Roman fortitude and stoutheartedness—despite the fact that you belong to a defeated people, Titus Papinianus the Younger!" He paused for a breath—having been belaboring my behind with all the fortitude and stoutheartedness his tiny body could muster—and said once more to his pupils, "And now, which among you is going to correct our ignorant savage friend's error?"

By now, my arse was scored with welts, and there were a few flies buzzing around it, so I was glad that one of the pupils answered the magister, distracting him for a moment.

"If it please the magister," said a weasly little voice— I knew, immediately, that it was C. Livius Prato who spoke, painstakingly and superfluously translating each Latin name into Androcles' native Greek, the preferred language of all intellectuals, in the hope of earning extra points—"Pomponius Piso was heavily outnumbered by the savage tribesmen. Having been driven from the Flumen Pulveris or Powder River, the forces met at the Parvulum Magnum Cornu, or Little Big Horn, whereupon the chief known as Taurus Sedentarius, id est, Sitting Bull, in a demonic vision, drove the Lacotians into a frenzy similar to the 'berserker' madness of the German tribes—"

Prato continued in this vein for quite some time, and I
could hear murmurs of approbation from the other pupils
as well as the grunting of my tutor. The only virtue in his
recitation was the respite it afforded from the pain.

I wanted to scream out the truth, but I must confess
that I didn't think that the truth was worth the discom-
fort. Instead, I gazed, from my topsy-turvy angle, at the
Lacotian children playing in the street outside, heartily
wishing I were one of them rather than the adopted son
of a preposterous patrician.

At last, Prato stopped prattling. Androcles said,
"Well, we have all had a most cogent and concise retell-
ing of the events that led up to that historic battle of the
early campaign for the conquest of the New World.
Would anyone care to add anything? Perhaps a brief
summary of the geographic and historic points that we
have learned up to today?"

Prato went on—always too eager—"Terra Nova is di-
vided into three parts, the easternmost being Iracuavia,
with its capital at Alexandria; the second Lacotia, the
largest province in the Empire, with its seat at Caesarea
on the fork of the River Miserabilis; the third being
lumped together as Terra Incognita, but containing such
lands as Algonquia, Apaxia, Sasquatia, Seminolia, Co-
manxia, and the mysterious Empire of the Olmechii ...
and, of course, the as-yet-undiscovered China ..."

"Get to the point, young man!" Androcles said.

The point was only reached after another twenty minutes of discourse, by which time my wounds were all
scabbing over. Androcles had not yet ordered me to return to my seat, though, so I was still doubled over,
buttocks up, head tucked under and enjoying an upside-
down view of the slums of Rome.

At last I heard a welcome voice—that of Lucius Vinicius, who in my weeks at Androcles' *schola* was the only
one of the boys who ever deigned to speak to me.

"If it please the magister," he said, "haven't you left

Papinian dangling for an awfully long time, what? If he's going to be up on the block, you might as well beat him some more."

A fierce growl—the sort of lion-about-to-devour-a-criminal sound that is so thrilling to hear in the circus—escaped Androcles' throat. I thought Lucius was as good as gone himself, but for some reason Androcles didn't order him up on the block.

"Just because you're the Emperor's nephew doesn't mean—" Androcles began, then stopped himself short.

"I understand they've had a fresh delivery of lions last kalends," Lucius said. "All the way from Africa. My uncle had them brought into the palace for a little, ah, private entertainment at his last orgy."

Androcles didn't sound much like a lion as he turned to me and said, "You may rejoin the others." I left my post and returned to my wooden tripos, wincing at the splinters on my arse.

"Thank you," I whispered to Lucius.

"It was the least I could do," he whispered back. "I mean, what with you trying to defend the honor of your people and all that. I'd have done the same, old chap."

"Still, the old man's a lunatic—he might have decided to beat the living daylights out of you, and the Emperor be damned."

"So what?" As I have said before, the Romans actually seem to thrive on pain—both the giving and the receiving thereof. "Anyway . . . I'll meet you after school, all right? Same time, same place."

"Yes, of course."

"Oh. Back to the Greek verbs—I think the old fool's looking our way."

At that moment, the rodentlike C. Livius Prato stuck out his tongue at me, but Lucius Vinicius hit him over the head with a wax tablet, and we were soon down to the next order of business . . . specialized uses of the second aorist tense in classical Greek rhetorical devices, with special reference to the Odes of Callimachus. Important stuff to learn for those who must one day be procurators, consuls, and assorted other rulers of the known world.

It was not very interesting, and I was soon daydreaming about my childhood once again.

CHAPTER
II

THE SLAVE MARKET

I RUEFULLY RUBBED MY BEHIND AS I AND MY TUTOR-cum-bodyguard, Thersites, left Androcles' school. It was still several horae until nightfall, when my father was scheduled to return from the baths; it was up to me to find some pretext for getting rid of Thersites so that I could meet up with Lucius Vinicius.

At the corner of the Via Formosa, I finally confided in Thersites that I had left an important scroll behind at Androcles'. "It's Father's favorite," I said, "a Latin translation of some apocryphal Homeric epics—of doubtful authenticity, but he does so love spectacle. We'll both be in for a severe thrashing if we don't bring it back."

"Oh, dear," Thersites said, rubbing his beard dolefully. Being a Greek, he wasn't quite as fond of pain as the Romans are, so he said, "Well, we'd best go fetch it."

"I can easily get home from here," I said. "You go."

"But, young master—"

"—Or I'll tell him it was all your fault."

Thersites dissembled for a few moments. I knew what

a coward he was. He was a cheap sort of slave, having once belonged to a household of one of the nouveau riche, a mountebank merchant who had become rich by selling a potion reputed to enhance the size of the male member; he had not only been that merchant's children's tutor, but had also doubled as a cook and gardener, so you can see what sort of people they were.

Before he could really come up with a suitable rejoinder, I slipped into an alley. Several wineshops fronted on the Formosa. Rows of enormous jars, each tall as a ten-year-old boy, stood soaking up the heat. I ducked behind a fat woman who was ladling some Lesbian wine into a cup. Thersites walked bemusedly by, and I saw that he was heading back toward the schola. I ran around to the front of the wineshop, ascertained that it was indeed his pudgy form waddling through the throng, and set off in the opposite direction.

The heat was stifling, my buttocks itched, and the fact that I was wearing the full dress of a young Roman aristocrat, and that everyone scuttled out of the way when I approached, didn't really cheer me up at all. If Lucius Vinicius were here, it would all be different...but, as I reached the appointed place, it didn't seem as though he had been able to get away from his tutor.

I was at a corner of one of the little forums that were built to commemorate our victories in the New World. I stood in the archway of a little temple of Isis, trying to avoid the attentions of a temple servant who was trying to get me to subscribe to the summer season of weird rituals. He smelled of embalming fluid, so he probably doubled as some kind of assistant mummifier.

The boy kept following me and I kept popping behind another column. Finally I noticed a slave auction going on at the other end of the square—nothing terribly exciting, just your run-of-the-mill Nubians and what have you, with the odd dwarf thrown in. Of course, we never had slaves in Lacotia before the Roman conquest, but that was long before my time. There was a small crowd gathered for the auction, but the bidding was slow. Nevertheless, it had a kind of fascination, and I was worming my way through the throng, trying to get a better view, covering my nose with a fold of my toga to ward off the foul stench of peasants, rotting vegetables, and sour wine.

Right now there were a couple of children on the block—Lacotians, I realized—and the auctioneer was listing their virtues in a bored, boring voice. "Lot number LXVII! A matched pair, citizens! Perfect as house slaves—train them while they're young—or as companions for your own children. They'll do anything, and I mean anything—a perfect gift for that randy uncle who has everything! The bidding starts at a mere fifty sestertii . . . a trifle . . . two for the price of one, and I'm practically giving them away . . . who'll give me fifty?"

A fat, bald man put up his hand.

"Surely we can do better!" the auctioneer said, surveying the crowd. I knew that children seldom go for high prices unless they are extremely beautiful or at least capable of some bizarre sex act; these were decidedly in the worst condition, scruffy and covered with sores. I pushed myself forward for a closer look. There was one of each sex. They were about ten years old—only a few years younger than I. They wore breechclouts—which must have been a sight more comfortable than the ridiculous Roman garb I was in—and the boy had an eagle feather in his hair. I wasn't close enough to determine how it was notched, so I didn't know if he had actually taken a scalp or whether he had been the first, second or third to touch the slain enemy. In any case it was remarkable that so young a child would display such a trophy. So absorbed was I that I completely forgot that I was supposed to be on the lookout for my friend Lucius Vinicius.

In any case, I soon noticed that the boy was staring

me down. He didn't have his eyes downcast, like most slaves. I was somewhat taken aback at his insolence.

Then he called out to me: "*Chiyé! Chiyé!*" which is to say, "O frater meus!" in the Lacotian tongue. And I was shamed, stung to the quick. Of course he had been staring at me. For all my fine clothes, I was a Terra Novan. I would never be a Roman, for all the welts old Androcles cared to inflicted on my hapless arse. And yet—for a while—I had seen him as a slave boy and myself as somehow superior to him. The boy was quite right to call me brother. I was among aliens, by Vacantanca!

I blurted out, "One hundred sestertii!" before I had a chance to think. That was at least two months' allowance. Perhaps I could pawn my collection of aurochs skulls.

The auctioneer brightened. Evidently they weren't worth nearly that much. He cheerfully waved me forward for a closer look. I squeezed forward. The heat and the stench were overpowering.

"Terra Novan yourself, are you?" he said with an obsequiousness that thinly disguised his prejudices. "Need to hear the old native lingo about the house, I'd imagine, young sir."

"I am Titus Papinianus the Younger," I said, to put him in his place, though I didn't much enjoy invoking my stepfather's name.

"Well, well, well! I very much enjoyed your father's most recent *scientifictiones*. The one about the little green men who—"

I didn't bother to tell him it wasn't fiction at all. I had a more pressing problem: backing out of the deal before being made a fool of.

"On closer examination," I said, "I don't think I quite like the merchandise. The boy's awfully sallow, don't you think? And the girl...well, you know how loose those people are. I'll wager she isn't even a virgin—"

"How dare you impugn the goods, sir—" the auctioneer began. He was cut off by the braying of trumpets and the pounding of drums. Everybody turned around and I saw the auctioneer bowing reverently at the approaching entourage.

An enormous motorcar was ploughing through the muck, churning up streams of mud, old vegetables, and excrement from the street. Since there were only half a dozen such vehicles left since the time that the Emperor Nero wrecked them all in the arena during a day of massive spectacle almost fifty years before, and the secret of their manufacture had been irretrievably lost with the death of the mad inventor Epaminondas of Alexandria, it was clear that the new arrival was someone of the utmost importance.

When the auctioneer fell to the ground with his arms upraised, I realized that it had to be someone very close indeed to His Imperial Majesty—

I had no idea who it was. But when the curtains of the motorcar were drawn aside, and the steam from its engine ceased puffing, I saw, sitting on a gilded chair between two miniature Corinthian columns, an old fat man wearing the senatorial toga praetexta, whose jowls quivered and whose nose extended outward like an eagle's.

"I say, what!" the old man said, as a Nubian hastily got out and lay down in the mud so that his master would not sully his feet in stepping from the motorcar. "Surely these aren't the Neronian Baths, are they?" He squinted.

I knew from his nearsightedness that he must be C. Lentulus Fortunatus, one of the richest men in the world, highly favored of the emperor, widely believed to be about to receive the combined governorship of Lacotia and Iracuavia. That would make him just about the second most powerful man in Rome.

"My Lord—" the auctioneer panted, "if you had but turned left on the Via Neronis—"

"What? These aren't the Neronian Baths?" Fortunatus blinked several times but still appeared to make no sense of his surroundings. "But didn't I come here for a rubdown and a massage?"

The crowd was silent; no one dared contradict him. Presently one of his slaves came and whispered in his ear. "Oh," Fortunatus said, "a slave market, is it? Well, I am so terribly forgetful, ha, ha. Well, I'll take them."

I looked down at the brawny Nubian, who was desperately trying not to move in case his master should slip off his back. Mud matted his hair. His face was buried in a pile of offal. I had rarely seen anyone look so pathetic.

"You—you'll take them?" The auctioneer asked, dazed.

"Of course I will!" Fortunatus said. "Didn't you hear me the first time? Just send along the bill."

"Of course, my Lord," said the auctioneer, unshackling the two children—for whom I would have spent two months' allowance!—and waving them in the direction of their new master.

"Jolly good," Fortunatus said. He blinked a few more times, then added, "Now where's the hot water?"

The boy looked at me with big, round, doleful eyes, filling me with an unconscionable sense of guilt. "Save us," he whispered in Lacotian. "Save us, *chiyé*."

"I—"

Before I could respond, someone poked me in the ribs. Instinctively I turned and swung with my fists. There was no one there. I lost my balance, tripped, and sprawled into the mud. When I got up, the two children, the ostentatious motorcar, the Nubian slave and the corpulent Fortunatus had disappeared; and in their place stood my companion in mischief, the Emperor's nephew, Lucius Vinicius himself.

"Sorry I'm late, but it took me awhile to get me tutor drunk enough to give him the slip. Come on, get up," he said, kicking me a few times.

I did so. "I've just seen the most extraordinary thing," I said, and told him all that had just transpired.

"Wine?" he asked, throwing me a jug. I took a deep swallow as he began lecturing me about Fortunatus. "Had a stroke several years ago; his mind's completely gone, I'm afraid. He's always buying things by mistake. He goes to the senate and thinks it's the baths and starts taking off his clothes; he goes to the baths and starts cheering the gladiators. That sort of thing."

"I really wanted those slaves."

"Oh, slaves. I'll give you some of my extras if you'd like." Lucius was nothing if not generous. "Mother always clutters up the house with more than we can ever use."

"They were Lacotians, though."

"Lacotians." Lucius sighed. "Ah, Lacotians. Like you. By Jupiter, I wish I were one. Imagine doing nothing all day but hunting aurochs . . . wearing beautiful warpaint instead of these hot clothes . . . scalping and raping just for the fun of it. What a fine life! Instead I'll have to be a procurator when I grow up. Or even higher."

It was the first time he'd ever mentioned it to me, but everyone at school knew that it was true; the emperor was fond of Lucius, and it wasn't inconceivable that he would formally adopt the boy and ensure him a place in the line of succession. That Trajan had had Lucius' father poisoned only the year before was irrelevant.

"Forget the slaves, Equus Insanus," he said. He was one of the few who ever called me by my real name, and that was another reason I took pleasure in his company. "What are we going to do this afternoon? There's only a few hours left before sundown. Teach me some more about stalking aurochs . . . or one of those crazy Lacotian songs . . . or how to use a bow and arrow."

That was what I liked best about Lucius. Sure enough, he could affect the languid airs of his class well enough—and sure enough indeed, he always came to school immaculately groomed, clothed, and perfumed.

But he dreamed of the wide open spaces of Terra Nova. As I did.

"Let's get out of here, at any rate," I said. "Slave markets are depressing places." I thought of Fortunatus and his new acquisitions. And of the Lacotian boy's last words to me.

"You know, old chap, it was absolutely splendid the way you refused to give in with old Androcles flogging away today. Half the class was talking about it. I think you'll find that you're the most popular boy in schola tomorrow."

"But they all turn up their noses at me for not being a real Roman."

"Rubbish! Everyone knows that the number of lashes you can endure without screaming is the most vital indication of status in Androcles' little schola."

It was an unnerving thought. I didn't want to think about it anymore, so I tugged at Lucius' arm, trying to steer him away in the direction of the Temple of Isis.

Just then, however, the auctioneer started up again, and I couldn't help but turn around to look. . . .

"Lot LXVIII! An Egyptian mage—a magician— scholar—mystic!"

"By the maidenhead of Isis," I said. "I know that man!"

The Egyptian was thin, spindly-shacked, and scowling. He was chained hand and foot, but that didn't prevent him from wriggling and squirming like an angry octopus. He was cursing, and when the auctioneer tried to ennumerate his finer points to his putative purchaser, he began to complain bitterly.

"You're not fit to tie my sandals, you son of an incestuous she-camel! Let alone ennumerate my virtues. Don't you know who I am?"

"Let's go," said Lucius.

"Wait!"

"Who will give me five sestertii?" The auctioneer was throwing up his arms in disgust. "Four?"

"Who on earth is that?" Lucius asked me.

"Why . . . that's Aaye the Egyptian. Scholar and mountebank. He came with us on our travels across Terra Nova. He was there when we discovered the land of the sasquatii . . . when we visited the citadel of the green men from the future . . . when we battled dinosaurs on the island of temporal anomalies . . ."

"Venus, Mars, and all the gods," Lucius whispered, openmouthed, his eyes bulging out of his sockets. He started waving and shouting out, "Five sestertii!"

"Wait!" I said. "You don't know what trouble that man is. He nearly got us killed a dozen times. He's the most cantankerous, argumentative, bloody-minded, pig-headed ass you're ever likely to encounter. Anyway, what's he doing on the auction block? He must have been up to no good."

"Yes, but he was with you on those adventures! He actually knew Aquila!"

"So did I—he was my father, remember? Why don't you just give me the five sestertii and I'll go and bet it on the races or something?"

"Do I hear six?" the auctioneer called.

"You didn't even hear five!" I shouted.

"You again!" the man shouted back. "Always trying to interfere with decent businessmen—" He was probably regretting the loss of the hundred sestertii on those two kids; after all, Fortunatus would probably forget to pay his bill, and one doesn't send dunning letters to the second most powerful man in the empire.

"Five sestertii!" Lucius Vinicius said again, pulling the five silver coins from a pouch. Under his breath, he said to me, "And what's more, you can have half of him, if you want."

"Sold!"

Aaye the Egyptian, gangly and withered in his chains

and linen loincloth, came down the platform toward us.

"Aaye!" I cried out. "What have you been doing since I saw you last?"

He looked at Lucius and then at me. At last he seemed to recognize me. I had, after all, grown a few cubits since I rescued him and all the other explorers from crucifixion and a brontosaurus several years before.

"Well, it's about time," he said at last. "Now hurry up and feed me, will you? And then take me back home."

"Wait a minute!" Lucius said, taken aback. "We own you, Equus Insanus and I."

"Humph! Nobody owns Aaye the Egyptian!"

And that, it seemed, was that.

CHAPTER
III

THE EGYPTIAN

THE THREE OF US SET OFF MORE OR LESS IN THE DIrection of the Capitoline Hill, with Aaye the Egyptian complaining endlessly about the heat and about how we weren't paying enough attention to his comforts.

"But we just redeemed you from slavery!" I protested, regretting the whole thing more and more.

"I'm hungry."

Lucius said, "Look, there's a wineshop. Let's feed the poor bugger and then dump him by the wayside before his chattering drives me crazy."

We turned a corner. There was the wineshop on the Via Formosa, where I had lately abandoned my tutor. "Food ho!'" Aaye said, and charged inside before we had a chance to reconnoitre the premises.

"Oh, no!" I whispered.

Smoke was everywhere. The front of the shop was hung with strings of sausages. It was through this sausage curtain that I beheld Thersites, sitting at a table with Diogenes, the tutor of Lucius Vinicius. They hadn't seen us yet. "Ignore them," Lucius said. "They're drunk."

Sure enough, I could see that they were arguing away in Greek, their voices slurred by wine. "The nature of the one—" one would begin, and the other would finish, "is subject to the one of nature," and other such meaningless paradoxes.

"Bloody Roman adolescents," Diogenes said. "Illiterates. Boors. Couldn't tell Sophocles from a hole in the ground."

"Couldn't give you the second aorist of a deponent verb to save their souls."

"Bloody Romans. Masters of the fucking universe, what! Boors. Peasants."

Lucius shrugged. "All Greeks are alike," he said. "Think they're better than us, somehow. Think that we're inferior just because we happen to speak Latin."

"But you're not speaking Latin," I said.

"Well, of course not! One only speaks Latin to the servants."

This was another peculiarity of the Roman aristocracy; so besotted were they with the culture of the Greeks, whom they had plundered into abject servitude, that they had all but abandoned their native language. Oh, the peasants and the military and such spoke it, of course; but you'd never hear a word of Latin at a respectable dinner party. Lucius, whose blood could hardly have been more blue, even affected a Greek accent in his Latin, and would frequently pretend to forget some commonplace word just so he could use the Greek. It wasn't surprising that he failed to see the irony of my remark.

In any case, our tutors were so absorbed in their arcane argument that the three of us slipped right by them. I asked the mistress of the shop for a private cubicle, and she pulled aside a curtain and led us into a dank room that stank of piss and sweat. A lone torch burned in a bracket in the wall. There were no windows, and so much smoke that we could barely see each other's faces.

"Six or seven sausages," Aaye demanded, "and a jug of wine—any kind. And perhaps one of those calf's brains omelettes?"

"I wouldn't mind a sausage or two myself," I said.

"Do you have anything more...more...gentlemanly?" Lucius asked the woman. "Larks' tongues in aspic, peacocks' brains, that sort of thing?"

"Get stuffed," said the serving wench, and marched out of the cubicle.

"Well, a sausage, then," Lucius called after her.

While waiting for our victuals, I thought we might as well find out why our charge—whom I had last seen as co-proprietor of a small Platonic academy in the Imperial Seat of Caesarea-on-Miserabilis, back in Lacotia—had ended up on an auction block in one of the tawdrier sections of town.

Aaye sighed and began: "Well, as you well know, there were three of us academics running that schola. Nikias, alas, passed away. Abraham bar-David, the Hebrew sasquatch, left to find his fortune in Rome; I was left alone in the New World. The only employment I could find was with a traveling merchant who made a living selling *mniwakan*, that is to say, intoxicating liquor, to the natives. He also had a unguent which, he claimed, was guaranteed to enlarge the male member, and which he sold for two sestertii the jar to half the inhabitants of Terra Nova. Well, how was I to know that this wonder ointment was nothing but a foul concoction of aurochs excrement and pulped pemmican? And when that mountebank abandoned me in Cansapolis, surrounded by irate customers whose virile members had not enlarged themselves by so much as the breadth of a single camel's hair—"

"You were hauled before the procurator for fraud!" Lucius said, laughing.

"And sentenced to be sold into slavery—my civil rights as a Roman citizen suspended—ah, sorry was my fate! I don't think this is very funny, young man."

I didn't laugh. I had not been told that Nikias, my stepfather's aged tutor, who had accompanied him on every one of his wacky adventures, was dead. I sat there, gulping down the hideous Falernian wine, all teary-eyed and nostalgic for the good old days.

"But how did you come to be in Rome?" Lucius asked at last, when he was through laughing. The sausages, by then, had arrived, and Aaye continued while endlessly stuffing his face.

"Well, my first master commanded me to bring his dead wife back to life, for, as you know, we Egyptians are an enigmatic race, and even the lowliest of us knows the secrets of life and death—"

"Your big mouth!" I said, amused at last.

"Well, for some reason I cannot figure out, my spells failed to work. I was then purchased by an Iracuavian farmer who wanted me to control the weather. Upon the first drought, I was sold to a naval captain; he ordered me to minister to his sick galley slaves, but through no fault of mine, all succumbed to an apoplexy—"

"Driven mad by your chattering, I bet!" Lucius said.

"And so, upon our arrival in Rome—"

We paused for a while to eat. Now and then, fragments of our tutors' philosophizing drifted into the room. "We can't very well keep you," I said at last. "My stepfather would have a fit."

"And my mother...doesn't much care for Egyptians," said Lucius. "The last one we owned tried to embalm our cats."

"Cats are sacred!" Aaye said. "They are supposed to be embalmed."

"They weren't dead."

"Well, I am sure he had a good reason. The wisdom of Egypt, O Romans, is not something easily fathomed by your puerile minds, for we are an ancient race."

"Well, there's got to be somewhere we can dispose of you," I said hastily.

"What about that sasquatch friend of yours? The one, you said, was back in Rome now?" Lucius asked. "Do you know where he lives, Equus Insanus?"

As a matter of fact, I did. My stepfather still kept in touch with Abraham bar-David, that hairy member of the lost tribes of Israel who had accompanied us on our adventures in the New World. He was chief librarian in the archives of the Temple of Jupiter Vacantanca, that composite god, created by political expediency, of Romans and Lacotians alike, and he had a little house not far from my stepfather's mansion.

"This rather ruins our whole afternoon, though," I said. "I was hoping we could go down to Little Lacotia and fool around there . . . and I was going to teach you more Lacotian stuff."

"What!" said the Egyptian. "You have here an unparalleled opportunity to learn at the feet of Aaye the scholar, and you'd rather spend your afternoon slumming with savages?"

"Yes!" Lucius and I exclaimed simultaneously.

Aaye huffed and pouted until we agreed to take him to the dwelling of the most learned megapus, id est, bigfoot. When the serving woman returned, Lucius grandly told her to send the bill to the Vinicius house; the woman, startled and profoundly impressed, bowed and backed slowly away, for all the world as though my youthful friend were already emperor of the known world.

In the front of the wineshop, our tutors had both collapsed in a drunken stupor. Doubtless they were both afraid they would be flogged if they couldn't find their precious little charges by sundown.

"I'll send a slave from the house to roust them and see them safely back," Lucius said. He threw the serving woman a silver coin to keep her from whining.

"Pythagoras' metempsychosis," Thersites mumbled in his sleep.

"Those upstart Greeks!" Aaye said. "They always think they know everything. We were building pyramids when they were still running around in loincloths! Begging your pardon, Equus Insanus—but I see they've done a fine job civilizing you."

As we walked farther uphill, I could see the Capitoline ahead, the marble monuments gleaming, the cypresses tall, the hot Roman sun streaming down on us as we sweated. Civilization, indeed! The streets swarmed with merchants, slaves, centurions, peasants, and the odd patrician on a litter. We passed the Neronian baths, their elegant façade decorated with a frieze that showed the Emperor Nero being greeted by braves from all the corners of the western empire: Lacotii, Iracuavii, Manhatii, Cansae, Delavariae, and countless other tribes in their ceremonial togas and warbonnets.

A very familiar-looking motorcar was parked outside, guarded by Nubians. I wondered whether the two Lacotian children were inside. Fortunatus was not there; presumably he had finally stumbled on his intended destination.

Lucius noticed it, too, and he read my mind.

"As soon as we're rid of this silly old man," he whispered in my ear, "let's cook up a plan to rescue them."

CHAPTER
IV

THE WORLD'S GREATEST INVENTION

"WELL, IT'S ABOUT TIME," AAYE SAID AS WE staggered up to the house of the Sasquatius. "My feet are tired, and I'll need someone to massage them. And, I think, more food."

A stucco wall, covered in graffiti, hid the house from the street. The porter admitted us, and we waited in a vestibule that looked out over an atrium, with cool fountains and a pleasing arrangement of flowers and shrubs. The colonnade was particularly high, for the Sasquatii are tall, and cannot easily be accommodated in the houses of regular people. One feature that always amazed me was that there were no statues and no paintings at all—and though the floors were beautifully inlaid with tiles, the mosaic represented only various religious symbols; there were no pictures of chariot races, orgies, or mythological scenes such as any other house might have.

"It's a rather *dull* house," Lucius said in my ear.

"It's just like this in Judaea, I'm told," I said. "No pictures."

"Of course not!" Aaye said, anxious to demonstrate

his superior learning. "The Sasquatii, being members of the Hebrew persuasion, are not allowed to possess any kind of representational art. Rather silly, if you ask me, but there it is."

At that moment, our friend crossed the atrium and came toward us. My stepfather's book describes him as of terrifying stature, and completely covered with hair; in fact, his appearance never ceased to amaze me. He was wearing flowing white robes, and held a scroll in one hand; in the other, he toyed with a bizarre scientific instrument, all cogs and wheels and spokes and spikes and spirals.

"*Shalom aleichem*," he said.

"Salve," I said.

"Rejoice," said Lucius. Aaye didn't speak at all; clearly he expected the Sasquatius to burst into a torrent of joy upon recognizing him.

Instead, Abraham bar-David peered at us. "It's my declining eyesight," he said at last. "I could have sworn I saw that intransigent Egyptian rogue Aaye—but no, that's impossible. It's just a bad dream—some imbalance in four humors—some apparition sent by the gods of sleep. I have been laboring too long at my experiments."

"By Isis and Osiris!" Aaye exclaimed in a rage, "do you not recognize me? Intransigent rogue, indeed!"

"It *is* you," Abraham bar-David said ruefully. "What do you want, and why aren't you back in Terra Nova fleecing the natives?"

He clapped his hands, so that the slaves would bring us refreshment—some delicious, flaky pastries that surrounded nuggets of spiced lamb, and an amphora of fine Lesbian wine—and invited us into the triclinium, where we were able to recline at last.

"I need a hot bath," Aaye said. "Have one of your slaves draw one for me, will you? That slave market was a most tiring experience. And perhaps you or someone you know could petition the emperor for the return of my civil rights. After all, it's simply a miscarriage of justice to have someone of my qualifications being herded around like a common criminal."

"Have you thanked these young men, by the way, for saving you from servitude?" Abraham asked severely.

Aaye did not seem to notice, but continued to prattle on about his experiences, his brilliance, and the injustice of the world.

At length, Abraham said, "Come, Equus Insanus and your young friend. I have something very exciting to show you."

We left the Egyptian talking to himself and followed the sasquatch into his laboratory.

"What's he going to show us?" Lucius whispered.

"Probably some arcane experiment."

An entire wing of the house was devoted to scientific studies. There was a model of a motorcar, all its parts labeled and marked; there were vials of bubbling fluids, and bizarre surgical tools that bore a remarkable resemblance to instruments of torture. This side of the atrium was right next to the hill, and received little sunlight. Oil lamps glowed in odd corners of the room, and the smell of dust was everywhere. The unnaturally high ceilings, put in so that Abraham wouldn't have to stoop, made me feel I was in a dark and hellish cavern . . . I had not felt that way since my childhood, when my father Aquila took me into the Montes Negri so that I could set eyes on the most sacred places of the Lacotii.

"Now, where was I?" said Abraham. "Ah, yes! The greatest invention since the time of Epaminondas of Alexandria . . . where did I leave it, now?"

We went through another doorway into an even more dimly lit chamber. The stench of cow dung greeted me as we stepped over the threshold. There was a white heifer, chained to a post, in the middle of the room. The creature was mooing and farting as it grazed on a small pile of hay.

"That's the greatest invention since—?" Lucius began, and then he couldn't stop laughing.

"Shut up!" I said, fearful of offendiing the Sasquatius in case he should make us take the Egyptian home with us.

"Not the cow, you silly children! But I might as well introduce you . . . Voluptua, this is Equus Insanus, also known as Titus Papinianus the Younger, the son of that Roman general I was telling you of . . . this is Lucius Vinicius. Be very nice to him; he might be emperor one day. Lucius, Titus . . . Voluptua, the prize cow of the Temple of Jupiter Vacantanca . . ."

"Sacrilege!" Lucius said, appalled at the impiety. "That creature's supposed to be under heavily armed guard in the temple—it's going to sacrificed next month in my uncle's honor! There's not a single blemish on her."

"Indeed," Abraham said, "but the cow is here by the command of His Most Puissant Majesty the Emperor Trajan. And I will tell you why. The Emperor is about to embark on a most ambitious campaign on the eastern front, against the Parthians or some such, and of course, there must be sacrifices; and the augurs, by examining the entrails of the sacrifices, will predict the outcome of the war. But what if there were a way to second-guess the augurs—a way to examine the entrails of a beast without leaving a mark on it—to ensure that the predictions will be, shall we say, politically correct?"

"That's impossible!" Lucius Vinicius gasped.

"Impossible for you, perhaps! But to the properly scientific mind—" Abraham chuckled. "Shall I explain the theory behind it?"

I sighed, found a low bench by the wall, and sat down beside Lucius to await the inevitable lecture.

"Imprimis," began Abraham, "there are certain substances to be found in nature which exude a certain *transcendental humor* or radiation, which, unseen, can nevertheless affect the nature and lives of mortal men, as witness the power that flows from the stars and is the basis of your everyday astrology. Grant this and it follows that certain lumps of stellar matter might produce the same energy. Whilst exploring the wilder parts of Terra Nova, I discovered a certain rock or ore which indeed seems to possess this celestial energy. Since the power resides in the heavens, I have dubbed this mysterious substance *uranium*, or more properly, in Greek, *ouranion*, after Ouranos, the god of the sky. But what use, may you ask, is such a depository of divine force?

"Ha! You are silent, dumbfounded! But I will tell you. The transcendental humor passes through all living things, but cannot penetrate dead objects such as stone or bone. But it is particularly attracted to silver, since silver is sacred to the moon, and the moon is that object which separates the realm of the sublunary, or impure, from the celestial or quintessential, which is of absolute perfection . . . it follows that, when the transcendental humor strikes a sheet of iron that has been coated with silver that has been dissolved in aqua fortis, an image will be formed—an image, however, that reverses the dark and the light, just as the terrestrial is the negative image of the celestial. It follows, secondly, that, should this heifer be placed in between the irradiation and the metal sheet, and be fed with a special hay that contains certain pulverized rocks to give the food a certain quality of deadness . . . that the position of the cow's entrails should be clearly visible upon the plate for study—days before the sacrifice is to take place! And if the animal is found wanting . . . well, you see the political advantage of such an invention! That is why Trajan has asked me to keep it top secret."

"Why are you telling us?" I asked dubiously.

"Because it's so exciting, my boy, that I just can't

keep my mouth shut!" He was trembling with excitement.

"Well, it all sounds very impressive," Lucius said. "But let's have a look at it. The plate, I mean."

"Promise you won't tell?"

"We swear by the graves of our mothers!" I said, forgetting that Lucius' mater was still very much alive.

Abraham thought for a few moments, keeping us in almost unbearable suspense; then he led us to yet another chamber. This was a cramped, damp room, and it took him a moment to light the lamps. But there, lying on a table cluttered with human skulls, Hebrew texts, and strange rocks, was a thin metal sheet upon which there was, indeed, a sort of an image. We crowded around it, and the sasquatch began pointing out various details of anatomy.

"The liver, as you see, has a slight deformity here . . . I would say that the campaign will have some difficulties, perhaps in the western region of Asia Minor."

"How can you be so precise?" Lucius asked.

"Well, I am not the actual augur, so I don't have to worry about being executed if I'm wrong," Abraham said.

I couldn't see very much—it all seemed very shadowy and incomprehensible—but Abraham seemed to know exactly what he was talking about as he pointed out various problems with the heifer's heart and intestines. "All in all, I'd advise against using this particular beast," he said. "That's the message I'm going to send to the emperor."

We were much relieved to have deposited Aaye at the house of the Sasquatius. Both Lucius' house and mine were farther up the hill, and it was almost sunset by the time we reached the intersection where we had to bid each other good-bye.

"What an extraordinary day!" Lucius said. "Rude

Egyptians, a garrulous Sasquatius, a top-secret invention—"

"I can think of a lot more interesting ways to use that thing," I said.

"Yes. I wonder if it'll capture an image of a woman through her tunica . . ."

"Your sister!" I said. For Lucilla, a year older than we were, was the most desirable creature I had ever seen.

"But we never made it to Little Lacotia," Lucius said, turning down the pathway lined with olive trees that led to his mansion.

"Our tutors are probably being flogged at this very minute," I said, feeling almost sorry for them.

I set off alone up the left fork in the road. The evening was muggy, and it was fast getting dark. Presently there came a slave boy from the house, carrying a torch; I gathered that my stepfather had sent him to fetch me.

I could see all of Rome beneath me, vast and frightening, from the slums and the insulae of poor to the palaces whose gold glinted in the last rays of the sun, from the market places to the many-arched Flavian amphitheater . . . and my buttocks still ached from the day's dosage of civilization. I thought of the Lacotian children I had almost saved from bondage, and I knew that I would find a way of rescuing them, regardless of cost or personal danger.

But for now I would have to banish my memories of the wide open spaces . . . of the great plains and the feathered countenances of my ancestors . . . of the herds of aurochs that roamed the wilderness of Lacotia. I had a terrible ordeal to face—in some ways even more painful than the lash of old Androcles.

It was time for dinner.

CHAPTER
V

TITUS PAPINIANUS SENIOR

I NEED HARDLY DESCRIBE DINNER, EXCEPT TO MENTION that it was all I expected, and worse. My stepfather was busy dictating the second volume of his memoirs to a scribe as I came in. Handmaidens were plying him with food and drink, and the scribe was dutifully setting forth his words verbatim, belches and all. There were a couple of dinner guests, who were politely listening to Papinian's ramblings, stifling their yawns as they stuffed themselves with bizarre tidbits.

Our house on the Capitoline Hill had seen better times. Our adventures—mostly undertaken at the command of the parsimonious Emperor Trajan—had depleted the Papinian fortune to the bare minimum necessary to maintain the house, the country estate near Neapolis, and a couple of hundred slaves; the murals were peeling, the mosaics had more tiles missing than not, and my stepfather was constantly inveighing against the rudeness of the help. Indeed, he was doing so as I entered and took my place at the table.

"Your average savage," Titus Papinianus said, the gravy dripping from his lips to his beard, and thence to his weatherstained toga, "is a boor, nothing but a boor. He lacks any of the good Roman virtues—discipline, hard work, the ability to withstand pain . . ."

The scribe scratched away with an old reed.

"Ah, there you are, old thing," my stepfather said to me. "Sit down."

"What's for dinner?" I asked.

"Exotic viands from the west!" he said. "Braised giblets of Terra Novan giant chickens topped with a sauce of pulped cranberries . . . hummingbirds' brains in an intoxicating paste of cocoa leaves . . . a ragoût of *fungii peyotuli*, upon which—no, you idiot! That's not part of my book!" He clouted the scribe on the side of the head with a little flail he kept tucked into his toga.

"I'm terribly sorry, Excellency . . . it seemed so relevant, and you *had* been discussing the flora and fauna of the New World but a few sentences before."

"I won't eat it!" I said.

"Won't eat it? Won't eat it, my dear boy? Do you realize that thousands of Nubians, Lacotians, Germans, and Gauls are starving?"

"And why are they starving, my good stepfather? Could it not be because you Romans are taxing the life out of them so you can enjoy your hummingbirds' brains?"

"You're a Roman, too, now, young man," Titus Papinianus said, "and I trust you will behave in a dignified Roman fashion." He belched, and more gravy dribbled onto his clothes.

"Dignified!" I said.

My stepfather looked ruefully at the gravy, then said, "Don't even say it, my boy! You and I have earned the right to stuff ourselves with these fine delicacies because we are the conquerors of the world. You can't possibly compare your native Lacotian, in his primitive tipi, slobbering over his raw aurochs' liver, with the highly decorous, civilized debauchery that we Romans practice."

"I won't eat it."

"You ungrateful little savage! Was it not I who saved you from the prairies of your homeland and brought you here to Rome?"

"You bubblenosed old fool—was it not I who rescued you from the Time Criminal and his ravening brontosauruses?"

Evidently my stepfather didn't want to be reminded of our old escapades. I am sure that, deep inside, he knew he wasn't the real hero of most of them. I think he was about to slap me when he noticed that the scribe was still taking down everything we were saying. That hapless slave received the blow intended for me, and fell, cringing, at Papinian's feet.

"But my lord . . . I thought what you were saying was most apposite to the subject at hand, namely the congenital inferiority of non-Romans . . ."

Papinian allowed him to gibber a little longer, all the while quaffing his Chian wine, each mouthful of which was worth, in the open market, approximately two such gibbering scribes.

I toyed with my hummingbirds' brains, arranging them in a little pyramid on my plate.

"Don't play with your hummingbirds' brains, young man," said my stepfather.

"I say, Papinian, what," said one of the guests. "Go easy on the poor child. He's only been a-civilizing for, what, two or three months?"

"What did you learn in school today, young man?" asked another.

I knew he was trying to deflect my stepfather's ire, but all I could remember was my fury at Androcles' revisionist history. Quite unmindful of my manners, I started shouting, "Androcles was telling us a bunch of lies about the Battle of the Flumen Pulveris! But I got up and told the truth and I don't care! And you can try to civilize me all you want, but I won't be civilized because my father was Aquila, not some bumbling, incompetent, pretentious, bigoted, slow-witted maggot of a Roman general!"

"Remove him!" my stepfather said, and several of the house slaves grabbed me forthwith by the shoulders and dragged me from the triclinium. "To bed without any supper!"

"To the vomitorium with your hummingbirds' brains!"

I could hear the guests laughing uproariously as I stood in the vestibulum. I didn't think they were laughing entirely at me.

Several hours later, I was lying in my room. The full moon shone through the high, open window. At the head of my pallet was the chest where I kept my treasures: a leather shield, a peace pipe, and two of my father's favorite scalps, as well as a jade were-jaguar that I'd received as a gift from the Time Patrol before they had departed in their flying saucer.

I lay tossing and turning, not quite asleep.

Suddenly I was aware of someone else in the room. Breathing deeply and drunkenly, somewhere above my head.

"Get out," I said.

"I brought you some food, old chap." It was Papinian. "No, not hummingbirds' brains...it's something I've been saving for you."

I sat up. He handed me something. "Pemmican!" The smell of dried buffalo and crushed berries filled my nostrils. I almost wept.

"It's the closest the cook could get," he said. In the moonlight he seemed a strangely forlorn figure. I knew he could not help being such a fool, and I suddenly felt sorry for him.

"Stepfather, I want to apologize for—"

"It's all right, old thing," he said, patting me on the head. "But you really mustn't lay into me in front of the guests. It just wouldn't do, you know, to have them think I'm an ineffective paterfamilias; it's just, well, un-Roman."

"Are you going to beat me now?"

"I've half a mind to."

We didn't say anything to each other for a while.

Then my stepfather said, "You miss him, don't you?"

"Yes."

"So do I," he said. "That wily old scoundrel."

"I want to go back to Terra Nova."

"Maybe you do," he said, "but your father's been snatched away from us now, and we live or die by the emperor's will; and I'd appreciate it if you wouldn't embarrass me at my own dinner parties."

"I'll try."

I finished half the pemmican and wiped my mouth on an old centurion's cloak that I used as a blanket. Then I put the rest under my bed for midnight consumption.

My stepfather slipped away. I felt a bit guilty for upsetting his banquet. Perhaps, in his own way, Titus Papinianus loved my father, too. Much as I despised this Roman civilization, I could not entirely blame him for being the way he was. Not all of us are lucky enough to be born Lacotian . . .

I was having yet another dream of wide open spaces when someone shook me awake. He started pulling me out of bed. "Lucius!"

"Quiet!"

"How did you get in?"

"I climbed over the wall. Then, up the olive tree, across the rooftop, and . . . through the window."

"But the guard—"

"I gave him a sestertius."

"What are you doing here?"

"There's some kind of weird Lacotian festival going on in Little Lacotia. I decided to go. Thought you might want to come along. Translate for me, give me a few pointers and whatnot."

"But I'm supposed to be asleep."

"Now who's civilized? Besides, I figured we might be able to rescue those Lacotian children of yours."

I rubbed my eyes. Lucius was wearing a muddy cloak; his hair was tousled. He wore a sort of a headband. He had covered his face with strange patterns— astrological signs and numerals.

"What's all the makeup?"

"It's war paint, stupid! I wanted to look inconspicuous."

I started to laugh.

"Come off it, old thing! I had to raid my mother's cosmetic box. It was the closest I could find. And I don't know what war paint is supposed to look like."

I opened my chest of precious possessions. He stared at it in awe. "Wipe that stuff off," I said. "Let me show you how a *real* warrior paints his face."

I found my supply of pigments, and showed Lucius how to apply it himself, using a knife as a mirror. Then I started to do my own face. I winced when I touched my short hair; this Roman fashion seemed somehow so unmanly. Then I stripped to my loincloth and bade Lucius do the same.

"What if it gets cold?" he asked.

"Cold? *Winyan yelo!*" That is to say, "mulier est iste."

"I take it you're insulting me?"

"Calling you a woman," I said.

After we finished painting ourselves, we sat around preening for a few moments. Then I said, "We might as well go now.'"

"Wait." He looked around anxiously. "What about provisions? I mean, I'm hungry. Got any hummingbirds' brains or something?"

"You can eat this." I tossed him the last hunk of my beloved pemmican.

He grimaced hideously as he tried to chew it. "Is it real leather?"

"How dare you! If you really want to emulate us savages, that's what you're going to have to eat."

"Oh, very well." Manfully, he swallowed the entire thing. He was almost choking. "Is there any wine around?"

"Oh, quiet. Let's go before someone catches us."

The moonlight beckoned to us from the window.

CHAPTER
VI

BIG TROUBLE IN LITTLE LACOTIA

W E STARTED ON THE WALK TO LITTLE LACOTIA, Lucius somewhat self-conscious in his Terra Novan finery, I feeling more at home than I'd felt in a long while. It was dark and there were few people about, and I imagined myself in the forest, stalking deer perhaps, or about to sneak up on an enemy encampment to steal horses.

As we reached Little Lacotia, we heard more and more signs of activity. A distant drumbeat from behind a temple façade. And the throaty wailing that is Terra Novan music. I could almost catch the words... *akichita*...that is to say, warrior...we crept closer now, until we reached an alley that led straight into the Lacotian quarter. The drumbeat was louder now, and I heard many voices. Orange, flickering light played on the walls.

"Look!" Lucius said, pointing.

There was a small crowd in the street...aristocrats in their litters...merrymakers on their way home from some orgy or another. We crept up behind a nobleman's litter. Its curtains billowed, and there was a girlish giggle

42

from within. "What are they watching?" I said. But my heart responded to the pounding drum.

A bonfire had been lit in the middle of the square, beneath a triumphal arch that honored the conquests of Pomponius Piso. Around it old men danced. They were paunchy men, their bellies distended by too much wine and by the cheap grain the imperial government handed out to the poor; and their hearts were not in the dancing. A little Lacotian boy in a silly, gaudy parody of a plains Terra Novan costume scurried through the crowd selling scalps. "The genuine article!" he was shouting, "only half a sestertius apiece!"

"I want one," Lucius said with a catch in his throat. I shared his longing for Terra Nova . . . but I was disgusted at how he had been taken in by this mockery of the truth.

He stared at the dancers. Perhaps he saw what I saw in my mind's eye. I shook him. "This is just tourist nonsense," I thought. "I can't believe my people would descend so low."

"But the dancing—"

The bodies of fat men glistened with sweat. They were absurd specimens of Lacotian warriors. Was this what it had come to? Could this be the reality behind the memories of my early childhood? I found myself weeping suddenly, and didn't even try to wipe away my tears when I noticed Lucius Vinicius staring at me strangely.

"It's very un-Roman of me," I said apologetically.

"Quite all right, old bean," he said, patting me on the back.

Suddenly I discerned a familiar face among the curious bystanders. "C. Livius Prato!" It was indeed that ratlike boy, and he was once more thrusting his tongue out at me from the other side of the street. "I'll beat him to a pulp!" I screamed, furious that he had witnessed my sorrow.

Prato came up to us. "That was jolly brave of you today," he said to me. He didn't show a shred of the disdain he usually showed in class. "I couldn't have done it."

Lucius had an I-told-you-so look on his face as Prato continued, "We've all decided that you're not such a bad sort after all. For a savage, that is. I mean, we're all one empire now, aren't we? Pax Romana and all that, eh? In fact, we're all sort of fascinated by you people."

I noticed that several of the other boys from the schola had shown up. "Don't your parents know where you are?" I asked.

"Of course not!" Prato said. "Father's at an orgy at court and mother's in bed with the Vestal Virgins. Or is it the other way round? I can never keep our parents' debauchery straight."

"My dad's in bed with some filthy little Greek of indeterminate gender," said another boy, "and my mother's gone to a secret meeting of one of those weird oriental cults—Adonis, or Christ, or someone."

"I told you you'd become a big hero after today's thrashing," Lucius said, and I sensed that he was proud of me and of our friendship. Uncertain what to make of this about-face in my peers, I watched the dancing. The old men were leaping now—well, staggering about, anyway—with lances upraised, and women were moving slowly in a circle, their eyes downcast. They were dancing on the scalps of the fallen enemies—except that there had been no war, and the scalps had doubtless been purchased off some entrepreneur, hovering, vulturelike, at the circus, waiting to strip the dead gladiators and criminals as they were hauled out through the Gates of Death.

"Ho, there!" Prato had cornered the young Lacotian scalp-vendor and was buying one. "Give me a nice fat juicy one." For some reason he sniffed at a couple of different ones until he found the right one. He paid for it—it was on a little stick—and wedged it into his tunic. "Bring me luck, eh?"

"This is all nonsense," I said. "Fantasy. It's not like that at all, in Lacotia."

The other boys fell silent and looked at me expectantly. To my astonishment, I realized that I had become their leader.

"Well," I began uneasily, "for one thing . . . we don't just run around wild, raping and killing and all that. We have to have a purpose . . . a sacred purpose. A matter of honor, that sort of thing."

"Like freeing those Lacotian slaves that you were supposed to have bought!" Lucius said, and quickly explained the situation to the others.

"And we don't usually kill people at all . . . it's much more prestigious to whack them with a coup stick."

Prato said, with deep feeling, "I'd like to whack old Androcles with a coup stick!"

"Or better yet . . . that old fart Fortunatus!" Lucius said, laughing.

"Then it's agreed!" Prato said, his nostrils quivering in anticipation.

"Agreed?" I asked.

"We'll raid his house, count coup, free the Lacotians—" Lucius could scarcely contain himself. "*Huka hey!*"

At the sound of the rousing Lacotian war cry, the emotion overcame me too. "*Huka Hey!*" I cried out, and soon all the other boys of Androcles' Academy were screaming it, too . . . indeed, we were making far more noise than the dancers, who continued, in their desultory fashion, to prance and stagger in the middle of the street.

Suddenly I realized we were the center of attention. A huge litter, borne by eight or ten of the burliest Nubians I had ever seen, was bearing down on us, and the curtain was being drawn aside, and an extremely irate man was glaring at us and shaking his fist.

"O merda! It is my father," Prato cried. "He must be

coming home from his orgy. I'm going to catch it if he catches me—"

"After them!" Prato the Elder was yelling at his litter-bearers, having at them with a riding quirt.

"Quick—an alley—any alley!" I shouted. Instinctively they all followed me. I elbowed my way through the throng. I knocked over an amphora, slipped in a basket of fruit, slammed against a wall. Then I found myself climbing up a tree, with four or five other boys clambering behind me, making the branches sway, and Prato the Elder's litter-bearers jogging full tilt down the narrow street, knocking down plebeians and storefronts as they came.

I stood on the branch, tottering—

"Jump!" It was a voice, so low that only I could hear it, and it came from the other side of the wall.

I looked down. There was someone down there. It was an orchard. I could smell oranges. It was dark and I couldn't exactly see who it was, but the voice was so familiar . . .

The figure was bathed in a cold, greenish light. It was an old man in the toga of a Roman senator, yet on his head he wore an eaglefeather bonnet, and in his hand he clutched a war-lance crowned with strings of scalps and feathers . . .

"I'm dreaming . . . I'm dreaming . . . it can't be . . ."

But the apparition was already wavering as I leaped down from the tree, and when my feet touched the humid earth I could see no one at all. One by one the others jumped down beside me. We squatted together beside the wall, and we listened to Prato the Elder cursing away at the gate: "Porter! Let me in, I tell you! Don't you know who I am? I don't care whose house this is. I'm a consul, and I'll have the lot of you in irons!"

Finally we heard the voice of a porter roused from slumber: "My master doesn't see anyone. You are being most disorderly, sir. Perhaps you'd care to present your petition in the morning?"

"Petition? Petition be damned! My son's in there, and

I want him out so I can give him a good hiding, by Mars!"

"The High Priest of the Temple of Capitoline Jove cannot be disturbed, O Consul."

"High Priest? Oh, I say."

C. Livius Prato whispered, "He'll be home in a trice! What a stroke of luck that we've landed in the High Priest's house. My father is so superstitious, he lives in terror of someone jinxing the entrails at our family sacrifices..."

"Entrails..." Lucius looked at me.

"Sasquatii!" I said. Both of us laughed. No one else, of course, got the joke.

"The fact remains," Prato said, "that we're stuck here and we can't get out. We couldn't possibly be in a worse position—"

"Oh, yes?" Lucius said. "Listen!"

Sure enough, there were footsteps in the orchard. Putting my ear to the ground in the manner of my forefathers, I could make out two distinct gaits. One was a simpering sort of walk, the other that of a huge, lumbering person. We could see lights now; they were carrying torches, though we couldn't quite make them out.

"Who dares disturb the High Priest of Capitoline Jove?" came a high, wheezing voice. It probably belonged to the simpering walk.

"It is nothing, O Pontifex! Shall we return to our... ah, discussion?" A deep voice...deeper, perhaps, than human.

"The sasquatch!" Lucius said, barely stifling himself.

The torchlight shone right in our faces.

"Ha! What have we here? A gaggle of insolent young boys, by the gods!" We were looking into the face of the High Priest himself—in full sacerdotal regalia, and looking most displeased. "The consul was quite right to come banging on my doorstep. We don't tolerate trespassers here. Shall I flog you now, or shall I leave that pleasure to your . . . ah . . . fathers?"

"Please sir, don't—" Prato was practically weeping, and the other boys were trembling in terror.

"Think of something, Equus Insanus! It was your idea to jump into this orchard," Lucius said in my ear.

But it hadn't been my idea! It had been the apparition —a trick of the moonlight, perhaps?—a ghost that reminded me so much of my father Aquila . . .

What would Aquila have done? I had to think quickly.

"O Pontifex," I said, "if . . . if you, ah, tell on us . . . we'll be forced to publicize the fact that you're using weird machines to examine the entrails of sacrificial animals in advance and . . . ah . . . rigging the results of the augury . . ."

The High Priest paled. I had hit the nail on the head. "You—you hairy monstrosity!" he shouted at Abraham bar-David. "I knew I should never have trusted a Jew!"

"We'll not say a word, O Pontifex . . . if you'll agree to let us go without telling our parents . . . and if you'll fulfill a few other conditions besides."

"Blackmail! This is sacrilege!"

"Sacrilege my arse!" Prato said, emboldened by our apparent victory. "And what about you and the Vestal Virgins, your High-and-Mightyship? Isn't that sacrilege?"

"Blasphemy!"

"Forget the Vestal Virgins," I said, as the Sasquatius secretly gave me a thumbs-up signal above the priest's head. "Just give us a few concessions. In the matter of auguries, that is." For I had a secret plan which would involve the boys of Androcles' Academy in a thrilling adventure and satisfy my honor in the matter of the Lacotian children besides. Blackmailing the pontifex into collaborating was the final ingredient to make our coup-counting night a night of spectacle that none of these lily-livered Romans would ever forget...

It was almost dawn when Lucius and I staggered back up to the fork in the road where our ways parted.

"Friends for life, old chap?" Lucius said, and embraced me like a brother. "I'll never forget the pontifex's face! Why, he was jolly well shitting himself! I'd never have talked my way out of it."

"I inherited my father's quick tongue," I said.

"And the way you set him up for our coup-counting expedition—" He couldn't go on, he was laughing so hard.

"I hope it works." I wondered whether I should tell him about the apparition I had seen. Could I really trust him that much? Or would he laugh at me? Maybe I *had* been dreaming, but if not, then Aquila had returned to our world in some guise or another... and he was still watching out for me... he still cared for me!

I watched Lucius disappear around the corner.

Then I looked up at the sky for a long time. The day was breaking. But there, at the zenith, that streak of light... was I imagining it, or was it—could it possibly be—a flying saucer?

I could barely contain myself. So powerful was my excitement that I quite forgot to sass my stepfather over breakfast, and devoured my leftover hummingbirds' brains without complaint.

CHAPTER
VII

FUN WITH ENTRAILS

T WO DAYS LATER IT WAS TIME FOR THE SACRIFICE.
The Temple of Capitoline Jove was crammed with
celebrities for the big event; they flocked to fill the new
wing, built by the Emperor Flavius to accommodate the
fifty-cubit statue of Jupiter Vacantanca, which shows the
god astride a white buffalo, with a Roman sword in one
hand and a Terra Novan tomahaucum in the other. By
the time my stepfather and I arrived, we had great diffi-
culty finding a spot to park our litter, for the area in front
of the great marble steps was a sea of litters, and
hundreds of bearers squatted on the grass. There were
four or five motorcars, too—I knew Fortunatus wouldn't
miss an event of this magnitude—and a long procession
of priests and acolytes, in their white robes and long
beards, was already winding its way uphill from the sacerdotal compound.

As Titus Papinianus the Elder and I started up the
steps, I was forced to listen to the old codger regale me
about the might and majesty of Rome. "My son, you are
about to witness the sort of thing that makes Rome great
—the pomp and circumstance of the empire at its most-

50

magnificent—the richness of the present illuminated by the austerity of our ancient Roman values—" and other inspiring sentiments sprang in an endless torrent from his lips. I puffed up my chest in a convincing demonstration of patriotic pride while Thersites, walking a couple of steps behind us, fussed with my toga praetexta, trying to make the purple border go straight all the way around.

"What a tiresome business this toga is!" I said, for the heat was, as always, scorching, and the wool made my back itch horribly.

"One day, my son, you won't have to fiddle with the border of your toga . . . you will become a man, and don the toga candida, which has no purple border . . ."

"Unless I become a senator," I said, "in which case it's back to the toga praetexta." I always used to wonder why only children and senators are allowed to wear the purple-bordered toga. Then I went to a senate meeting once, and it became quite clear to me. You see, among the Lacota, old men are treated with great respect, and their opinion as tribal elders is much valued, and I had always thought that the Roman senate was supposed to be the same thing. When I sat in on a session of that august body, however, I saw a bunch of doting, idiotic yes-men, quarreling with each other like children. At last the emperor showed up, and they cringed in their seats as if they had been caught doing something naughty. I never wondered about the togas after that.

We got to the top of the steps. There is a huge portico, a floor all in polished marble, and there were already hundreds of people gathered. I caught sight of Lucius Vinicius, who had come alone, being the senior male of his family. By alone, I mean that he had his tutor and half a dozen other retainers, of course, but no one that he himself would have considered people.

I waved to him. He was scarcely able to contain himself at the thought of the forthcoming spectacle, but somehow we managed to squeeze into the temple without splitting our sides laughing.

"Come on!" Lucius whispered. "Give them the slip!"

He tugged my hand and pulled me away from my stepfather. Although the temple is normally well ventilated, there were so many people, and the Roman summer was so sultry, that we could hardly breathe. So I was panting heavily as we elbowed and shoved. A veiled matron—a Vestal Virgin, perhaps—wagged her finger at us, but Lucius ignored her.

Presently we were right up against the wall. "Give me a leg up," Lucius said. "See that ledge?"

"But—"

"Come on!"

I looked around nervously, but everyone was so preoccupied with the imminent arrival of His Imperial Majesty that no one saw two adolescent boys climbing up the walls of the temple, precariously stepping from ledge to ledge, until we were far above the throng, perched on the scrolls of two Corinthian columns. The flowery tops of the columns were such that you could wedge yourself in between folds of the marble, and the acoustics were incredible; you could hear every word of what the various priests were saying.

"There's this ledge right next to the roof," Lucius said, "and we can sort of crawl along it and it'll take us right between the eyes of the statue of Jupiter Vacantanca."

I looked at him curiously. "It's all right. I do this all the time," he said. I decided to follow him.

Soon we were actually inside the head of the god. There was a small chamber about where his brains would have been. Two round windows looked out over the altar area, where priests were even now muttering prayers. The room was well-appointed, with a couch, a low table, and even a silver platter upon which reposed a half-eaten meat pie. "Wine?" Lucius asked, pulling a jug out of a cupboard.

"This place is certainly well stocked," I said.

"It's sort of a family secret," he told me. "All the imperial children know about it; it's sort of a clubhouse, I suppose you'd call it." He sniffed at the pie. "Nightingales' tongues," he said, "I think." He tasted it, pronounced it a shade gamey, then went ahead and devoured the entire thing anyway.

I crept up to Jove's left eye and looked down. "The emperor's arrived!" So remarkable was the resonance within the statue every word the great worthies uttered was crystal clear.

"Bloody nuisance, these sacrifices," the emperor was saying to the pontifex in charge of the augury. I noticed that Abraham the megapus was hovering around in the emperor's retinue. C. Lentulus Fortunatus was there, too, huffing and puffing under several layers of silks, damasks, and gold. His costume was considerably more ostentatious than that of the Emperor Trajan. That was only to be expected. The pontifex was nodding sagely, but I could see him, now and then, twitching nervously and glancing back at the sasquatius for reassurance.

"You've checked out the cow? Quite thoroughly?" Trajan asked the pontifex.

"Well, Your Majesty, the vagaries of this inexact science—"

"Splendid!"

The pontifex cringed. He looked up at the face of the god. I waved at him. I don't know if he could see me, but he certainly seemed taken back. I took another slug of wine. I was feeling quite lightheaded. It wasn't just the wine; I think it was the altitude, too.

At length the crowd gave way so that the prize heifer could be led in. Priests were chanting on either side of her. It was really quite impressive. From somewhere outside one could hear the slow pounding of a sacred drum, and a dozen bucinae and tubae were blaring away from each corner of the hall. The cow must have realized what was going to happen, because it started mooing and kicking the priests. One sprawled onto the marble floor and was carried away.

There was a consultation among the other priests, and then they led the cow out. The music started all over from the beginning.

"What's going on?" I asked.

"It's a rule. If there's the tiniest error in the ceremony, they have to start all over again from the beginning," Lucius said. "I hope they don't make too many more. In the days of the Emperor Claudius, my dad told me, they'd do the same ritual ten times over and it used to take all day."

"Get those buggers to hurry up, someone!" the Emperor said.

The pontifex whispered in someone else's ear, who whispered in another's who whispered in another's... and presently the entire ceremony proceeded at double time. The priests pranced, the trumpets were going so fast they missed half their notes, and three or four of them were pushing full tilt at the cow's arse, and being baptised, for their pains, with the fruits of the hapless creature's terror.

Presently the animal reached the slaughtering site without any more mishaps, and they chained her to the posts, and the pontifex hacked away with his ritual axe, and then came the business of the entrails. The old priest slit the cow's abdomen—his robes and beard were covered with blood by now—and started pulling out various steaming organs.

"Excellent heart," he said. "No deformities... the campaign will be highly successful..."

"Shit!" Lucius said. "He's not going to go through with the bargain."

"The four stomachs are well formed," the pontifex

said, hoisting aloft a mass of dripping guts, "and bode well for the future of the empire . . ."

"Do something!" Lucius said.

"What?"

"I don't know." Suddenly I had an inspiration. "The wine! Give me some more wine!"

"This is hardly a time to get drunk, old chap. Besides, I was hoping to guzzle the last dregs myself."

"No, no, no—" I grabbed the jug from him before he could quaff it. Then I went over to the right eye of Jupiter Optimus Maximus and starting dumping the wine out of the eyehole.

"What the . . . brilliant!" Lucius said, as a cry of consternation went up from the assembled throng. "Quick thinking, what!"

"Jove himself is weeping!" cried someone in the emperor's entourage, who promptly fainted.

"Tears of blood!" a fat, bald priest shouted, pointing.

"Damn! I'm out of wine!" I said.

"I know!" Lucius said. Without further ado, he crawled over to the god's left eye, unfastened his toga, lifted his tunica, pulled his pecker out of his loincloth, and began to urinate copiously onto the heads of the priests below. "You'd better do it, too," he said. "Whoever heard of a god weeping out of only one eye?"

The die was cast. "Bet I can hit the emperor," I said, undoing my clothes and following suit. "Bull's eye!"

Trajan, a look of wild surprise on his face, was rubbing the crown of gold leaves that covered his thin gray hair.

Lucius was holding back howls of laughter. Suddenly he couldn't control himself anymore, and a highpitched squeal escaped his throat. It echoed through the god's head and resounded through the entire chamber. By the time the sound had gone around and around several times, it had become quite terrifying, for, as I have said before, the new wing of the temple had excellent acoustics. Everyone down there was panicking, and paunchy old senators were actually trampling each other in their haste to escape the wrath of Capitoline Jove!

"Do something!" the emperor said. "Or I'll have the bloody lot of you crucified . . ."

The High Priest went into paroxysms on the spot. Only the sasquatch appeared in command of his wits, so I tried to attract his attention by banging the wine jug against the hollow of the god's cheek. Each clang was amplified by those selfsame acoustics until it sounded like the very hammer of Vulcan. Abraham bar-David finally looked up and, I think, saw me, for he gave a quick thumbs-up sign and went over to the emperor.

"Your Magnificence," he said, "I think there's a slight problem with the entrails." Then he walked over to the gibbering priest, kicked him until he stood up again, and whispered something in his ear.

The pontifex bent over the carcass of the cow once more and finally pulled out another bleeding organ. "Your Majesty . . . this liver . . ." he said. "It resembles the liver of a human in the advanced stages of the illness brought on by the ravages of drink."

"And that means?" Trajan asked, on the verge of losing his temper.

"The portents are perfect—well, almost perfect—except that—well, I think this liver is telling you to loosen up a bit, if you know what I mean, Your Magnitude. I mean, you can't go off to war without at least a little bit of home-style debauchery! It's telling you you must throw a huge banquet—to appease the gods—live it up a little. Before you depart on the grand campaign. If you know what I mean. Ah, that's why the god is weeping." He was improvising wildly now, since the tears had never been part of the bargain. "Almighty Jove is sad and he, ah, needs, ah, entertainment, you see. A banquet in his honor. A small price to pay for victory, Your Most Sacred—"

"Our Majesty never throws banquets!" said the emperor.

"He's falling for it!" Lucius whispered. We had been counting on the Trajan's notorious stinginess.

"Never, never, never!"

"My lord, the portents—" said the pontifex.

"We're just going to have to find someone to host the banquet for Us," the emperor said.

"And pay for all the food!" said Lucius, laughing. "That niggardly old bastard never forks out for a banquet if he can get one of his minions to squander money in his place."

"I say! Fortunatus!" Trajan cried out, summoning him with a crook of the finger. "Fortunatus, would you mind doing Us a teensy weensy little favor?"

"A million sestertii down the drain," Lucius hooted, clapping me on the back—

"Shut up! They'll hear us!"

The emperor pricked up his ears. "A million sestertii, eh what? My, the gods are specific these days. I do hope you can afford it, Fortunatus old thing. I mean, it's not that big a price to pay for the governorship of Lacotia, is it?"

So it was true! That slug was going to be sent to the New World, to rule over my people! I was more determined than ever to get the better of him. I began pissing in earnest now, as the crowd ran amuck and the priests stared openmouthed at their god's supernatural grief.

CHAPTER
VIII

COUNTING COUP

THAT FATEFUL EVENING, MY STEPFATHER LEFT FOR the banquet, as did the parents of most of my schoolmates, pausing at the gates of our mansion just long enough to tell me to go to bed, have pleasant dreams, and be ready for schola bright and early in the morning. I smiled, as did my schoolmates in their respective mansions, gave Papinian a dutiful peck on the cheek, as did, et cetera, waited until the coast was clear, and went straight to my room to put on my war paint. I wanted to look perfect for the night's adventure, so I spent a long time deciding on which pigments to use. In ancient times, before the Roman invasion, the Lacotii used only natural dyes, but of course the new technology had brought not only such innovations as the horse and the tomahaucum, but designer war paint—brilliant colors from Greece, Egypt, and Asia.

I thought about the past a lot as I sat by my chest of Lacotian objects glaring at my face in a mirror of polished silver. I settled for only the earth colors: I daubed my cheeks with yellow and red, my chest and arms with the same colors, adding some ghostly circles of white. In the end I couldn't resist the appeal of the new colors, so I painted a pair of cerulean lightning bolts on each cheek —after all, wasn't Jupiter, Lord of the Thunder, just another aspect of the Great Mystery?

I didn't want to appear too conspicuous, so I threw an old soldier's cloak I'd been using as a blanket over myself. Then I climbed out through the window and into the night.

The streets of our district were mostly empty; now and then there would be some nobleman coming home from a party, with his torchbearer running in front. The moon wasn't as bright as it had been last week, but the night air was just as muggy and stifling. As I descended the hill, I saw people sneaking about, covered from head to toe in robes. They had to be in disguise— probably going off to a meeting of some weird religious cult or another. I was surprised that there seemed to be devotees of banned religions even in our very rich, exclusive neighborhood. As I reached the bottom of the hill, though, they were everywhere.

Our meeting place was the little Temple of Isis where I had first seen Fortunatus. Lucius was already there. He was doing a ridiculous wardance while Prato pounded on a wine jug. When they saw me coming they stopped. There were a good half dozen of them, painted and ready for mischief.

"All right," I said. "Enough silliness. War is serious business, and if we're going to make war on the house of Fortunatus, we have to get a grip on ourselves first." They sobered up a bit, and stood straight while I inspected their war paint. "Not incredibly authentic, Prato"—the lad had drawn pink flowers on his cheeks— "but I suppose it'll do. Lucius Vinicius has obviously studied the faces of genuine Lacotians." Indeed, my friend, having taken my instruction to heart, could not be told from the genuine article. "And now, let's get our wild animal cries straight."

"Wild animal cries?" Prato asked. "What's that got to do with—"

"Patience!" I said, and began imitating a series of forest creatures, trying to find one that they all could do passably well. At last we came to a decision.

"Right. As I understand it, old thing," Lucius said, "to hoot like an owl means to retreat, to growl like a wolf is attack, to quack like a duck means the coast is clear, and to moo like a cow is—"

The other boys listened with profound seriousness to this catalog of signals and their meanings. When he had sufficiently rehearsed these noises, I then had to teach the crew how to creep silently through the streets—not an easy talent to acquire in a few minutes. Then Lucius, as I'd asked him to, produced some rods, which he handed out to us.

"These are coup sticks?" I asked, examining mine, a highly polished, pointed wand, with some distaste. "I suppose they'll do, but—"

"They're manumitting wands," Lucius said, shrugging. "You use them to free slaves—you know, smack 'em over the head while reciting a ritual formula. It was the best I could do."

"All right, all right. Now, the first person to strike the enemy will receive the highest honors—the second and third to touch him are entitled to honors also." Then I taught them the Lacotian war cry, to be uttered at the moment of attack to strike terror into the enemy's breast.

"Now," Lucius said, "who knows the way to Fortunatus' house?"

The mansion of Fortunatus was at the bottom of the Palatine Hill, as befit his position as the Emperor's personal toad. There was a guard of Praetorians at the front gate. "Shall we jump them?" Prato asked, a bit fearful now that danger was indeed close.

"No," Lucius said.

"How else are we to get in?" I asked. "They're drunk, anyway, and won't give us any trouble."

"Why waste our strength? I have a better way," Lucius said, and marched boldly up to the door.

"Stop, ho!" It was a centurion, twice our height and armed to the teeth. "Get off the Lord Fortunatus' property, you riff-raff!"

"Oh, come off it, Licinius!" Lucius said. "Don't you recognize me?"

"Oh, it's young master Vinicius," the centurion said. "What, pray, are you doing out of bed? In that peculiar barbarian costume?"

Lucius turned and winked at me. "I know all the Praetorians," he whispered. "When I was little, they'd always get to babysit me and let me play with their weapons and stuff."

"Oh, it's just this native dance routine," Lucius said to the guard. "We're part of the entertainment. It's sort of a surprise for my uncle. You know, the emperor?"

"No one said anything about a Lacotian dance routine," the guard said.

"I told you it was a surprise," Lucius said.

The guard scratched his head for a few moments and then let us in.

As we stepped inside, we could hear the sounds of revelry going on across the atrium.

An old steward came out to greet us. "Jugglers and gymnasts to the right, dancers and sex acts to the left," he said officiously.

"Come off it, Demetrius! Don't you recognize me?" Lucius said, laughing.

"Oh, I see. A thousand pardons, O noblest of patricians. You're late, young masters—most of the food is gone, and most of the guests have retired to, ah, private chambers to, ah, indulge in, ah—"

"Yes, yes," Lucius said, in a manner so imperious

that it occurred to me he had all the makings of a future emperor. "We'll take care of ourselves, thank you. It's a surprise, you see. No need to announce us. And my uncle, he is here? Or has he gone off?"

"Things are a little confused, Excellency, but if you will permit me to guide you—"

"Just tell me one thing, steward. The two Lacotian slaves that Fortunatus purchased recently...where are they?"

"In the bedroom, Excellency. Fortunatus favors children as pillows; they are so much softer than feather-stuffed cushions, are they not?"

"Leave us."

The steward bowed, and we followed Lucius Vinicius into the atrium. So vast was this mansion that the atrium actually contained within it three or four fountains, a profusion of shrubbery, and all sorts of trees. "Now that I've got us inside," Lucius said, "let Equus Insanus take the lead."

As warchief, I made sure that the other boys knew the meanings of the various hoots and calls. Then, each of us clutching his makeshift coup stick, we crawled on our bellies toward the sounds of debauchery.

Although this atrium was hardly an untamed forest of Lacotia, imagination filled in the lacunae; I could see, in the shadows, the movements of deer and wolf, and hear in the trickling of the fountains, the whispering of clear, cool mountain streams. The smell of peacocks' brains and larks' tongues in aspic was transmuted into the odor of roasting aurochs, and I could almost see, in the dining room on the other side of the atrium, the distant fire surrounded by the triangles of the enemies' tipis . . .

We crept closer. We were at the edge of the triclinium now. There were several couches with their backs to the atrium, and we hid behind them, peering through a forest of the legs of humans and furniture.

There weren't very many people in the triclinium, and

what remained of the food was piled in heaps on the
floor—the carcasses of pigs, ostriches, peacocks, giant
chickens, camels, and other creatures. My stepfather
was fast asleep, wrapped in the intestines of some animal. The faces of the guests were covered with divers
sauces, and their wreaths were on crooked, and I could
see already that many had been unable to make it to the
vomitorium, for the marble floor was covered with re-
gurgitory puddles. Most of them were asleep. The emperor was listening raptly to what appeared to be a
scientific discourse from our friend the Sasquatius, who
was demonstrating a model of what looked like a cross
between a motorcar and one of those oriental merchants'
caravans.

"It is called the Ferrequus, or Iron Horse," the megapus was saying. "Using steam power, the locomotive
is capable of pulling a large number of carts, which might
contain soldiers, travelers, or merchandise, along this
iron railway." I sat up, peeking between the heads of two
snoring revelers, and I saw the model device he was
demonstrating. The motorcar was your typical ostentatious vehicle, with the Ionian columns in the front and a
statue of some goddess on the prowl; behind, however,
was a cart full of logs. Behind that was a sequence of
what appeared to be elongated chariot cars. The whole
thing moved along a track about the width of a human
hand, across a table on which some scaled-down scenery
had been built, showing some of the more famous monuments of the world: the pyramids, the Flavian amphitheater, the marketplace of Trajan, and suchlike.

The emperor asked, "And, pray, what is the use of
such a device?"

"Why, Your Majesty, it would link the far-flung cities
of Lacotia and Iracuavia far more efficiently than our
present roads; it would transport goods; military maneuvers could be effected; and, most of all, it would save
time, and therefore money! Imagine moving an entire

cohort at the amazing speed of twenty mille passuum per hora—day and night, without sleep!"

"Twenty miles an hour!" the Emperor said. "And saving Us money besides..."

From somewhere beyond the chamber came the sound of cymbals. The steward came in and prostrated himself. "May it please Your Magnificence and His Guests," he said, "the thirty-seventh course is now served: crocodiles' tongues, lightly basted in a sauce of honey and ostriches' blood, and topped with a delicate garnish of braised hippopotamus knuckles."

"Oh, how boring," the emperor said. "Thank the gods I'm not paying for it . . . where is Fortunatus, anyway?"

"He stepped out, my Lord," said the steward. "Perhaps the vomitorium . . . shall I fetch him?"

Trajan waved him away. There was a flourish of bucinae, and slaves came in bearing aloft the new dish on a gold platter the size of a palanquin. Nobody woke up as the slaves began ladling generous portions of this culinary gem onto the guests' plates. A couple of dancing girls came in behind the food and slithered between the couches, hips undulating, mouths pouting, but no one seemed remotely interested.

"Let's make our move," Lucius said.

"Be patient!" I said, putting my ear to the marble floor to see if there were any people about that we should be warned of. All seemed still. I quacked like a duck.

"What does that mean?" one of the boys asked. "I forgot."

"I think it means attack," Prato said.

It was out of my hands. The boys shouted, *"Huka hey!"* and ran into the dining room, their wands upraised.

"Help, ho!" the emperor shouted. "We're being attacked by savages, what!" His Majesty got up to summon the guard, tripped on the platter of crocodiles' tongues, and went sprawling into a pool of vomit. He was out cold, and several of the boys darted forward to touch him with their coup sticks. My stepfather came to and tried to wriggle free, but was too entangled in intestines to do anything. The slaves went on dolling out portions of food as though nothing was going on.

We ran around the room, striking the guests at will. Most of them didn't respond. The dancing girls were screaming at first, but when they saw what we were doing they giggled and joined in. Suddenly I heard the trampling of soldiers' feet outside. "The guards!" I shouted. "Quick, into the act!"

We fell into formation into the middle of the room, Prato began banging on a drum, and we all began capering wildly around, ululating and waving our coup sticks. The dancing girls, getting into the swing of things, leaped back and forth between us. It wasn't very authentic, but how was anyone to know? The Praetorians piled into the dining room, gazed at the spectacle for a few moments, shrugged, and left. Then we went back to beating up the guests.

"Come on, Lucius," I said. "While these fellows are having fun, we might as well go and set those slaves free."

Lucius followed me through an archway into a corridor. The walls were painted with scenes from mythology: Jupiter seducing Leda, Jupiter seducing Ganymede, Jupiter seducing Io, Jupiter seducing Callisto—all in the most graphic detail.

I flung a door open. A foul stench assailed us. It was the vomitorium. I slammed the door and went on to the next. A storeroom. The third door was the bedroom of Fortunatus.

Upon the bed, beneath a painting that showed himself sitting on a throne, Fortunatus, naked, was strenuously thrusting in the throes of passion. His massive body was covered with sweat. A single torch burned on the far side of the chamber, and the face of his lover was concealed in shadow. Chained to the upper end of the bed were the two Lacotian children, who were indeed being used as pillows. The little boy, seeing us, immediately recognized me, and shouted out, *"Chiyé! Chiyé!"*

Fortunatus turned around. He scrutinized us, his jowls quivering. "What are you savages doing here?" he demanded.

Lucius and I rushed at him and pinned down his arms. "I want those children freed," I said, "or your scalp will be dangling from the end of this coup stick, by Jupiter!"

"Wait a minute," Fortunatus said. "You're not Lacotians at all. You're that Papinian boy, aren't you?"

I pulled my scalping knife from my breechclout and held it against his forehead, delicately teasing one of his wrinkles.

"All right, all right," he said. "I'll free them in the morning."

"Do it now!" I thrust the coup stick into his hand and released his arm just enough for him to reach the two children. "With us as formal witnesses."

"I see you've come prepared," he said, and, touching each child lightly on the shoulder with the staff, said, "Ego te manumitto." Then he said, "Now let me go."

At that moment, the woman, who had coyly draped herself in a sheet at our approach, peered out from her concealment and said, "Fortunatus, dear, send these people away and let's get on with the ars amatoria, shall we?"

Upon seeing the woman's face, Lucius was so shocked that he let go of Fortunatus' arm and backed away. In fact, he was so horrified that, although he was ordinarily the most urbane of people, he forgot to speak Greek. "Sacra merda!" he exclaimed. "Illa mea mater!"

"Your mother?" I said, astonished beyond all measure.

"Mother, how could you?" he cried, regaining his composure enough to return to Greek.

Lucius Vinicius' mother burst into tears.

"Now look what you've done!" Fortunatus said angrily. "Be off with you at once."

At that moment, the Praetorians stormed into the chamber and we were under arrest.

An hour later, my friends and I were spending the night in a dungeon somewhere on the grounds of the imperial palatium. It wasn't that uncomfortable, mind you —after all, we *were* patricians, and could not be imprisoned among common thieves and murderers. Our cell was abundantly appointed with straw, and there were several platters full of leftovers from Fortunatus' banquet. There was even a window—barred, of course, but affording a view of the night-shrouded city.

"What are we to do?" Prato was wailing.

"Do you think they'll throw us to the lions or something?" said another of my companions.

"I'd rather be in school than in prison!" said a third. "Flogging's a jolly sight better than being eaten by lions."

"Oh, what rubbish," Lucius said. "We had an absolutely splendid time, thanks to Equus Insanus here. We painted our faces, we counted coup, we made war, we rescued slaves—we were as happy and carefree as the tribesmen of Lacotia. It was a perfect evening, and I don't regret a thing."

"It might be the last evening we ever have," Prato said disconsolately.

"I don't care," I said.

"All very well for you to say," said Prato. "After all, for all your civilized airs, you are a savage."

"And proud of it!" I said angrily.

"Come on, let's not quarrel," Lucius said. "I'll talk our way out of this in the morning. If I can't, no one can. Why don't we get some sleep until then?"

I lay on the straw, looking up at the window. Just as I

drifted off to sleep, I saw Aquila's face looking down at me, suffused with the same green radiance as in my previous vision. He was clearer than before. His white hair streamed behind him, and he was holding something out to me . . . something shiny, metallic.

"Father!" I whispered.

He smiled at me. And then, it seemed, he pointed upward at the sky. Against the starfield I saw a glowing object move. It had to be the flying saucer! I struggled to keep my eyes open, but tiredness overcame me. I slept like a baby. Everything was going to be all right.

CHAPTER
IX

AN AUDIENCE WITH THE EMPEROR

DAWN HAD BROKEN; A SHAFT OF RUDDY LIGHT
played over my sleeping friends as I came to.
"Lucius," I whispered, turning on my side so I could
shake him awake. "Lucius, what are we going to do?"

Lucius wasn't there.

What had they done with him? Had he somehow gone
to the emperor, and was even now tryiing to save our
skins by concocting some wild story? Perhaps he had
even taken all the blame. As I looked around me, the
other boys were rubbing their eyes and sitting up. The
cell seemed smaller, danker that it had been last night,
and my companions all seemed disenchanted with their
great adventure.

"I'm really going to get it when my parents find out,"
Prato was saying. "Striking the emperor! They'll probably put me to death."

"Don't worry about that ... he was unconscious anyway," I said. "It's the scandal about Fortunatus and
Lucius' mother that bothers me."

"Who cares about that?" said another youth. "She's

already slept with half the Praetorian guard and three quarters of the gladiators."

"Shh! Someone's coming."

The cell door was unbarred and we were let out under armed guard—two or three guards for each of us. I thought it was overdoing it a bit, but decided not to say anything when I saw one of them cuff Prato on the side of the head.

We were led through tunnels and passageways and up stairwells, and eventually we were dragged into the throneroom of His Imperial Majesty Marcus Ulpius Trajanus Augustus Caesar Great White Father and so on and so forth, who was sitting, robed in purple, on a golden throne. To my horror, the high priest was sitting at his feet, and my stepfather, twiddling his thumbs, was occupying a couch to the emperor's right. Fortunatus was there, too, resting on some plump cushions on the floor. He scowled at me as we came in.

Lucius Vinicius was standing next to Trajan, whispering in his ear. My spirits lifted. Assuredly he had used his nimble wits to get us off the hook.

In front of the emperor was a huge table, on which was erected a tremendous diorama of a Lacotian scene: rolling hills, tiny clay aurochs, a cluster of tipis, a Roman city by a river. The model was nothing to remark on, except for one thing: Running alongside the river were tracks of iron, and puffing up and down these tracks was the very Ferrequus that we had seen demonstrated at the banquet the previous night. In the daylight, against the miniaturized scale of the diorama, the Ferrequus was indeed impressive—a kind of mobile Greek temple, and each of the carriages like a moving slice of the Forum Romanum. Standing over the model, beaming proudly, was Abraham bar-David; beside him was the Egyptian Aaye, who was fussily rearranging tipis, tiny human statuettes, and trees, and generally ruining the verisimilitude of the landscape.

At last, Trajan looked up and saw us. He clapped his hands, and the diorama was wheeled out of the way. All the Roman boys performed an elaborate series of genuflections and prostrations, the latest in court ceremony. I tried to do what they did, but I ended up tripping over my own ankles.

With a crook of his finger, he beckoned us to crawl abjectly forward. We prostrated ourselves once more. Lucius Vinicius came down the steps of his uncle's throne and whispered in my ear, "I'm sorry—it was your hide or mine—don't be angry at me, old thing—there was nothing I could do—" and then ran off, his quick footsteps echoing and reechoing along the marble halls. I realized that all was not well. I would be lucky to escape with a couple of hundred lashes.

"So this is the savage who has been corrupting the youth of Rome!" the emperor said grimly. "Well, I've half a mind to have you crucified on the spot—"

I shivered. Crucifixion is not a pleasant fate to contemplate. Sometimes they use nails, and you die a bit faster, but even so it takes days.

"But, unfortunately, I can't, because you've somehow acquired the rank of Roman patrician—I don't know why—and we don't crucify real people, only slaves and barbarians."

"Your Majesty—"

"Perhaps the lions?"

"Your Majesty doesn't have any games planned this season—surely it would be rather extravagant to put on an entire spectacle just to have me eaten!"

"I suppose you're right, eh, what?"

"Perhaps a miserable worm such as myself is so beneath your notice that you might as well let him crawl away?" I said, seeing a glimmer of hope. After all, it would cost money to punish me, and the emperor hated to spend money.

"Don't mock me, young man. Those poor, innocent

Roman boys, so utterly unaware of the traitorous serpent in their midst!"

I didn't know what kind of story Lucius had told, but it was obvious that I was being made the scapegoat for the whole thing. I looked around, but Lucius was nowhere to be seen. Frankly, I didn't want to die. It was not a good day to die at all. Not here, not amid all this ugly architecture and among these mindless conquerors who had turned the whole world into a source of revenue. Just as I was considering all the hideous ways I could be killed, however, the emperor said, "Of course, we could be persuaded to be merciful."

"By all means, Your Majesty," I said.

My stepfather glared at me, and, when the emperor turned his gaze upon him, cringed in so unmanly a fashion that I was glad he was not a member of my race.

"You see, Papinianus Junior, We consider the presence of your entire family in this fair city to be a source of constant embarrassment to Our Most Divine Person. It's not just you, it's that bumbling, bubblenosed father of yours, too. Obviously, the farther you are from Our Person, the better. Now, exile is all very well, and the more remote an exile the better, but We may as well put you to some use in the process, mightn't we?"

"I suppose you're right, Your Divinity," I said, trying, for my stepfather's sake, to appear reasonably humble.

"Although, on the other hand, why should I exercise any clemency whatsoever to a boy who actually pissed out of the eye of Jove? That alone is worthy of the death penalty . . . and yet . . ." He beckoned me to crawl up even closer. I ascended the steps of the throne on my hands and knees. The high priest scrutinized me with an expression of disdain or constipation, I wasn't sure which.

When I reached the foot of the throne, the emperor said, "Jolly funny, actually. Keeps the priests on their toes, what. Used to hide out in the clubhouse meself, before the, ah, the terrible burden of kingship descended upon Our shoulders. Pissing out of the eye, though! We never did that. The best We ever managed was spitballs."

I started to giggle, but he shot me a baleful glare. "Silence, child! This is a serious misdemeanor of which you stand accused." Then, so that I alone could hear, he went on, "Besides, I need an excuse to get your silly stepfather out of the way."

"Frankly, I don't blame you, Divinity."

"None of this un-Roman lack of respect!" He reared himself up for an announcement. "Now listen while I pass sentence! All you young men will be returned to the custody of your respective paterfamiliases for appropriate flagellation. Nevertheless, in the case of young Papinian, it seems that Rome has failed to civilize him. It behooves Us to separate his foul savage influence from the youth of Rome, especially from Our nephew Vinicius. Fortunately, We were just about to send your stepfather on an exciting new mission, videlicet, the construction of a railway that will link together the principal cities of Terra Nova—"

"Oh, thank you, Your Majesty!" I almost burst into tears right then and there at the thought of once more returning to my native land. What did it matter that my stepfather's career was in ruins? It always had been.

"—and We hereby appoint him Special Procurator of the Railways, with authority to requisition slave labor and levy supplies all over the New World. His position will be directly under that of the Procurator of Lacotia, to which office We hereby name C. Lentulus Fortunatus."

Fortunatus let forth a gleeful cackle from his lips. I could see that my stepfather was not going to have an easy time in the New World.

Trajan went on to name Abraham bar-David as chief engineer.

"We'd be only too delighted to accept," Aaye the Egyptian said, bowing ungracefully in the direction of the throne.

"And who might you be?" the emperor asked, raising an eyebrow.

"Don't mind him, Divinity," said the Sasquatius, "he's just a cantankerous old Egyptian mystic. Every scientific expedition has to have one. He can be our mascot."

The Egyptian fumed, but said no more.

"As for the matter of the Lacotian slave children," said the emperor, "even though their manumission was carried out under duress, it nevertheless has the force of law; We therefore command that they be taken back to Lacotia—at your expense, mind you, young man—and repatriated."

"Oh, thank you, Your Majesty!" I said.

The other boys were being led away, presumably to be beaten by their fathers; I was the only member of our war party that remained. I backed away from the throne, my heart beating madly because I would soon be among my own people. I knew that Papinianus the Elder, for all his talk of how subhuman Lacotians were, would not mind being far from Rome, for he had narrowly escaped several of the emperor's purges. I knew that our old friend the sasquatch would be traveling with us, and the Egyptian would probably be coming as well, which wasn't so pleasant, but we'd always managed to tolerate him before. Was the emperor punishing me or rewarding me? I couldn't tell. I suppose that's what being an emperor is all about. Keep them guessing.

There were only one or two flaws in this whole rosy picture: One was that we would still have to contend with the hideous Fortunatus; the second was that I would have to leave my new friend Lucius Vinicius behind.

What friend? I asked myself angrily. He had just sold me out to save his own miserable hide, hadn't he? When all was said and done, he probably still thought of me as a savage—a romantic, noble savage perhaps, but still innately inferior to a high-and-mighty patrician like himself. A Roman is a Roman is a Roman.

What I fool I was for thinking we could be friends.

LACOTIA

CHAPTER
X

THE OCEANUS ATLANTICUS

THE STEAMSHIP IS, AS EVERYONE KNOWS, A MIRACLE of modern engineering. Only the Romans have the know-how to propitiate the right gods to send such a device across the vast and treacherous Oceanus Atlanticus. Unfortunately, with such feats of technology, there is also tremendous expense. Marcus Ulpius Trajanus, Pater Maximus Candidusque, Pater Patriae, et cetera, et cetera, was, as we have seen, a miser. It followed that only a single steamship was provided for Fortunatus and his entire entourage, including us, General Papinian's Railway Division. Naturally, Fortunatus ended up with the steamship, whilst the rest of us lower orders were forced to make the crossing by trireme, a journey of some months, heaving over the side all the way.

I had never traveled in such a transport before. There were seventeen ships in our fleet. The one in which we sailed also had a full sized Ferrequus locomotive tied down below decks, in the galley slaves' headquarters. How all the oarsmen managed to squeeze in beside it I do not know.

We ourselves had elegant cabins—the Egyptian and

the Sasquatius in one, my stepfather in another, and I, amazingly, had one to myself. The only luggage I had brought with me was the chest of Lacotian mementos.

By day I watched the sea, pausing occasionally to puke. I was supremely grateful that our ship's store of provender included no nightingales' hearts or rhinoceroses' feet or other typical Roman gourmet delights; instead, our diet consisted entirely of pemmican and wine. Though Papinian and the ship's officers complained heartily, I ate more in those months than I had in all our time in Rome.

By night I lay on my pallet and dreamed dreams which became more and more vivid as we neared our destination. I dreamed of my childhood . . . and most of all, I dreamed of Aquila. In my dreams we would be standing together on a ledge, on a towering precipice, and I would feel the wind of the sacred mountains on my face. And I would fling off my toga praetexta, and I would see it flapping in the wind, twisting and turning as it transformed itself into an eagle. Off with the chafing, suffocating garments of civilization!

In the dreams my father and I would smoke the peacepipe together, something we had never done, because before he left the earth I had been too young to be admitted into the sacred councils. But when I looked into his eyes, I could see that he was troubled. And invariably, just before I woke up, I would see him dimly, through a veil of mist, standing in front of the flying saucer that hovered just over the prairie, waiting to take him back to his newfound people, and he would be about to say something to me; but his words seemed to be in an alien language, or else I would wake up before I could hear what he said.

And when I awoke, it would still be night, and I would wander up and down the decks. In the night the only sounds were the songs of distant whales, the whining of the wind, and the whistling of the lash as it descended on the back of some hapless galley slave below, for our sea-captain trusted more the hortator's drum and the flagellum's coaxing than he did the sails.

I would stand and stare at the sky, watching, hoping for a flying saucer to appear. But I was always disappointed. Until, one night, almost at the end of our voyage...

I had had another of those dreams, a particularly vivid one. I sprang out of bed. "He's got to appear to me—he's got to," I told myself, struggling to hold onto my father's apparition. I paced the cabin awhile, couldn't get back to sleep, and finally went out for my inevitable midnight stroll.

There was no one on deck at all. From the scientists' chamber I could hear low voices: doubtless the Sasquatius and the Egyptian were having one of their academic feuds. From Papinian's palatial cabin came only the sound of snoring. It was unnaturally quiet; there wasn't even any whipping going on below decks, for we were traveling entirely by sail for once.

It was as I was standing in my accustomed place, beside the prow of the ship, which was sculpted in the image of Ptesanwin, the White Buffalo Woman who is revered amongst the Lacotii, that I heard a familiar high-pitched whirring in the air. I looked up at the night sky and saw a convoy of the flying saucers moving across the face of the moon. I was so excited I could hardly contain myself. I ran to my stepfather's cabin and pounded on his door, but he did not respond.

I went to the academics' door and shouted, "Come quickly, the saucers are coming!" But they, too, could not be roused, and I could no longer hear them arguing. Apparently it was something only I was meant to see. I went back out and watched. One of the saucers broke ranks and moved slowly towards the ship. At last it hovered directly overhead, and a portal opened in its belly.

Silently the door disgorged a metal staircase, whose bottom step came to rest only a few feet from where I was standing.

I waited. What was I going to say to my father now? I knew that it would be unseemly to display too much emotion, but my excitement had already driven me to the verge of tears. This was the moment my dreams had been preparing me for, I was sure of it.

A greenish cloud emerged from the saucer's hatch. It was vaguely humanoid. Wisps of green smoke tendriled about as the figure descended the steps. The suspense was unbearable. "Father!" I shouted. "You're back, you're back."

The figure reached the deck, waved at the flying saucer, and watched solemnly as the metal steps seemed to melt into the night air. Somewhere overhead a seagull screeched. Perhaps land was near. Still swathed in the green mist, the creature walked slowly, stiffly, toward me. Its gait was uncertain, as though it had not set foot on terrestrial soil for many moons.

I couldn't stand it anymore. I rushed toward him, threw my arms around him, and cried, "*Até, até*, father, father." As I embraced him, the fog began to clear, and I suddenly realized that fate had played a very cruel trick on me indeed.

"I say, what!" said Lucius Vinicius, stepping out of the mist and standing there in full Roman military uniform, helmet glittering, plumes flying. "Getting a bit carried away, eh, old thing? When we parted, I didn't think you were going to welcome me back, but I suppose absence does make the heart grow fonder, doesn't it, old thing?"

"Get lost!" I screamed. "You traitor—you perfidious piece of rancid elk dung—you—" I was both furious with him for turning up and dying of jealousy because somehow he had managed to wangle a ride on a flying saucer.

"Wait, old chap. I got you where you wanted to go, didn't I?"

"Just a by-product of trying to save your own miserable hide!"

I rushed at him and tried to push him overboard. We got into a tussle, rolling around on the deck and punching each other in the face. At last, Titus Papinianus came wandering out of his cabin, an oil lamp in one hand and a flagellum in the other. "I say, what! Calm down, you fellows . . . oh, it's *you!*"

We got up and stood to attention. "What are *you* doing here?" my stepfather asked Lucius.

"If you please, sir, a flying saucer brought me."

"And how does a decent young man like you get mixed up with flying saucers and such? Answer me! I thought your uncle would have kept you under lock and key after that pissing on the priests escapade."

"Well, you can't very well send me home, can you, sir? I mean, unless I swim. And I'd probably drown before reaching the other side of the Oceanus Atlanticus, wouldn't I? And then I'd be dead, and you would have killed me . . . not a nice thing to do to the emperor's favorite nephew."

"I suppose not," Papinian said.

"Well then, General, how about some food? You wouldn't believe the junk they feed us in those flying saucers . . . nothing but a green gooey gunk they call 'enhanced seaweed.' Apparently, a million years from now, everyone's going to be eating it instead of real food. They have sort of a metal machine that pumps out little patties of the stuff in a thousand flavors—they even had nightingales' tongues—but damned if they didn't all taste exactly alike! And then, when I complained, I had to listen to a lecture about how my senses were insufficiently refined to distinguish between the different flavors and how I was just a pathetic, pitiable savage from the remote past and why were they even bothering to cart me around . . . do you know, they had to make a 're-fueling stop' on Mars before they could drop me off? Mars is the most unlikely place I've ever seen. It's a real slum."

"Wait—let me catch my breath—" my stepfather said. "Do you mean to say that the august breed of little green creatures, that heroic time patrol from the far future, headed by the enlightened were-jaguar V'Denni-Kenni, actually condescended to pick *you* up in Rome and bring you all the way here?"

"Actually, it was Aquila's idea."

"Aquila—!" Papinian and I exclaimed at the same time.

I was not at all pleased at this turn of events. "Liar!" I said, without much conviction, knowing that not even Lucius could concoct so outlandish a story. I was particularly angry that my father had chosen to communicate with this traitorous monster rather than with my own self. "Why would Aquila contact you, of all people?" I said. "After what you did to me? And what are you supposed to be doing here anyway?"

"Oh, that. Well, a few weeks after you set out, I was puttering around in the atrium at home when a beam from the sky pulled me aboard the alien craft . . . there was this funny old Lacotian fellow in a loincloth. He looked perfectly human, except he was all green. That's why I didn't realize who he was at first. He yanked me aboard and took me on the bridge of the flying saucer, where an enormous green lobster asked me if I was hungry. I said, 'Who are you?' and the green Lacotian said, 'Why, I am Aquila, of course.' I was so stunned that I fell on my knees gibbering in front of him. He just laughed. Then he said, 'My son will need a friend on his new quest. Ah, there is so much peril, so much anguish he will have to suffer.' And he looked away into the distance—from the windows of the bridge you could see over the whole earth—and sighed. It was as if he had already seen the future."

"They do see the future," Papinian said, "those who travel down the lanes of time. To them, we're the past, actually."

"Well, he sure picked the wrong friend," I said, still sulking. "I don't plan to take you on any quest." I wondered what my father meant, but I didn't want Lucius to have any more of an advantage over me than he had already, so I pretended I knew exactly what he was talking about.

"But I've been practicing!" Lucius said. "Your father's been teaching me all sorts of stuff . . . stalking the aurochs . . . war dancing . . . he even gave me a personal song, which he said would bring me bona medicina."

I just stood there, fuming with envy. Aquila had never given *me* a personal song. And this fellow wasn't even a Lacotian—he was, by Jupiter Optimus Maximus, a namby-pamby, debauched, degenerate milquetoast Roman aristocrat!

"I can even speak Lacotian now!" he said. "Listen! *Toki ya la hwo?* That is to say, 'quo vadis?' I even know a few dirty words. *Onze wichahupo!*"

Which I will not deign to translate.

"Anyway," I said—my last fling at discrediting Lucius' story—"my father is not green. He happens to look perfectly human."

"Everyone who travels in flying saucers for a long time turns green eventually," Lucius said.

"What nonsense," I said.

"It's true! The green lobster explained the whole thing to me. It's something to do with the speed of light, the transtemporal refraction of the spectrum, and it's a sort of permanent Doppler effect of light seen through the dimensional quadrature of—"

"You don't know what you're talking about," I said.

"Well, no," he said, "I'm just repeating what they told me."

"Well, I suppose we can't very well send you home," my stepfather interjected, sighing, "especially in view of your . . . ah . . . military rank."

"What are you talking about?" I asked.

"Haven't you noticed?" Papinian said, as Lucius strutted about, flapping his cloak and making the feathers on his helmet roll about impressively. I had to admit that he was a handsome-looking, if somewhat diminutive, figure of a Roman. "Our young friend seems to have been made a tribune. He outranks almost everyone in our entire expedition. Except, of course, yours truly, who is a general, in case you'd forgotten, so shape up!" My poor stepfather. He is such an idiot, it is easy to forget that he has actually led armies into battle.

"Oh, that," Lucius said. "My uncle thought it was about time I became an officer—thought it would build character, you know. I got this the day after you fellows left. It was supposed to make me forget about you, you know."

"How touching," I said.

With all this emotional turmoil, I noticed only now that it was getting light. The sun was rising, and in the distance I could swear I saw—

"Land ahoy!" someone shouted somewhere. "The port of Eburacum Novum!"

We stopped arguing and looked out . . . far to the west . . . where a thin dark strip of land was visible now. We were getting closer and closer. Already I could see several small islands. Eburacum Novum, the northern capital of Iracuavia, is a city built upon an island, named after Eburacum in the province of Britania, which is called by the natives York.

"Look!" Lucius said, pointing excitedly. "There's the Colossus of Iracuavia!"

And now I could see it, too, a towering image of the

god Dionysos, who is the patron god of Eburacum Novum, silhouetted against the glowering sky. The god held aloft a beaker of wine. At his feet danced drunken satyrs. The three of us gasped at the wonder of it, for it was far huger than any statue in Rome.

I had often heard of this great symbol of the New World, but I had never seen it before, for when we left for Rome it had been from the southern port of Alexandria. Because one of the other names of Dionysus is Liber, meaning the freedom that comes from the imbibing of too much wine, the monument is usually known as the Statua Libertatis. An appropriate symbol for the wildest, craziest region of the Roman empire—a drunken god staring wildly at the sea! In a way—even though I could not help but hate what Rome stood for—I was profoundly moved by the magnificence of it all. For now we could see past the Statua Libertatis, to the island of Manhattium, where temples, amphitheaters, insulae, and hippodromes rose from the mist; we could see dozens of triremes, their prows displaying gods both new and old, moving majestically up and down the channel.

"Wine!" my stepfather shouted. "Wine and more wine!" He clapped his hands and slaves came forth with amphoras of the vinegary piss that passes for wine on ships of the imperial fleet. We started drinking. And drinking. And drinking. By the time we entered the harbor, we were too far gone to worry about Fortunatus or the railway or anything else.

CHAPTER
XI

SPECTACLE IN ALEXANDRIA

WE STAYED AT EBURACUM NOVUM ONLY LONG enough to watch a few chariot races, for my stepfather, upon breathing the air of the New World, seemed to acquire a new energy. At the local garrison, using the authority vested in him by His Divinity the Emperor, Papinian requisitioned two cohorts of cavalry to escort us south to Alexandria, which is, in the summer, a hideously warm and muggy city, not unlike Rome. It rests on the banks of the River of Pluto Maximus, and houses a vast library, not, in the opinion of most scholars, the equal of that library that once graced the city's namesake in Egypt. Unlike the Egyptian Alexandria, the capital city of Iracuavia rises from the middle of a swamp, and is constantly plagued with mosquitoes.

Upon our arrival we were housed in the palatium of Pomponius Piso the Younger, the procurator of Iracuavia, with whom Papinian had never gotten along. Nevertheless, Pomponius treated us royally—even the two manumitted children, who were, you will recall, being repatriated out of my allowance. The oddest thing was, he kept apologizing for the meanness of his hospitality, when in fact everything "Roman" here seemed to be ten times grander than in Rome—not to mention ten times as tawdry, ten times as garish, and ten times as pretentious! The whole town seemed to be a grotesque parody of the Roman way of life. I suppose people get this way when they are far from what they consider civilization, and they will go to any lengths to try to convince themselves they haven't gone native.

No sooner we were shown to our quarters than we were summoned for one of those interminable diplomatic orgies; we lay on our couches, prostrate from the relentless onslaught of food, wine, and wrestlers, jugglers, dancing girls, gladiators, and animal acts. Pomponius announced that he had declared three days of games in our honor—three days of gore and spectacle in the huge arena he had named after himself, the Pomponian Amphitheater.

"Not the *real* thing, of course," he told us, as he munched languidly on a brochette consisting of the gizzards of rare fowls alternating with the procreative organs of rare reptiles, "but a paltry little Terra Novan *imitation* of true Roman spectacle. No more than a few hundred pairs of gladiators and things, what? It's the best I can do, I'm afraid, so far from home; I trust you will appreciate the spirit, and ignore some of the shortcomings, eh, Papinian, what?"

My stepfather nodded sagely and said, "I feel right at home already, old chap."

Meanwhile Lucius, who was reclining on the couch beside mine, resting his chin between the breasts of a serving wench, said to me, "What an ostentatious old fart. Why, a single one of those rare-beastie kebabs is probably worth a week's pay to your average centurion."

"You'll feel even *more* at home at the games," Pomponius said. "Oh, and, by the way, the next course will make you *homesick* for your old hunting grounds—it's raw aurochs' liver—" I perked up at this, but became

despondent once more as he continued "soaked overnight in a delicate marinade of cranberry juice and coe-
colacta, topped with a sauce of creamed feta cheese and
resinated wine, dotted here and there with clumps of
caviar..."

I was feeling very unhappy indeed. The wild splendor
of the Great Plains seemed as distant as it had been in
Rome. And whenever I thought of Lucius with my father, sailing through the time-lanes with the Dimensional
Patrol, I seethed with rage and envy. So far, Terra Nova
was nothing like what I remembered and expected. I
tried to console myself with the thought that this was,
after all, the east coast, which had been under the influence of Rome much longer than Lacotia; but in truth I
was beginning to despair of ever finding my dream, my
vision of the wilderness.

The next day, at the games in our honor, things
seemed even more bleak. There was a huge amphitheater, faced in marble, even vaster, I think, than the Flavian Amphitheater in Rome. As we were borne toward
the circus on our several palanquins, I could overhear
Pomponius Piso boasting to my stepfather about the im-
provements in the Terra Novans' way of life:

"Of course, old chap, we've been building, building,
building. This continent is practically limitless in its resources, so we haven't had to skimp the way we did
back home. Everything here is bigger, better, shinier,
more *glittering* than even Rome itself, eh? I mean, we
shouldn't forget Mother Rome and all that, but let's face
it...those monuments are pretty damn *ancient*. Why,
the Forum Romanum's hundreds of years old, by Jove!
And cramped, ungainly, and *filthy* besides. But here, Papinian, here in the New World..."

He waved his arms expansively about, and Lucius
and I looked around at the things Rome had done in this
virgin land. The streets were twice as wide as in Rome;

huge temples lined the road, both those of the main-stream gods and the latest fringe cults: Mithraism, Isis-ism, Cybelism, Christianity, and, of course, the local religions. By the time we reached the Pomponian Circus, I had just about had it with the New Rome.

At the entrance to the amphitheater there were the usual souvenir stands. Children hawked little alabaster busts of the emperor, some of them in his aspect of Peter Maximus Candidusque, Greatest and White Father of the Terra Novan people. In this guise, Trajan had on a warbonnet, which ill became his sharp, rodentlike fea-tures. They also sold such children's toys as wooden tomahauca, fake warbonnets made of chicken feathers dipped in brashly colored dyes, and phony scalps fash-ioned from cowhide.

"Look at all the warbonnets! Look at those scalps!" Lucius stared uncritically at everything, wide-eyed with enthusiasm. "How much for one of those scalps?"

"One denarius." An old woman held up a single finger and wagged it at us.

"It's fake, stupid," I said, punching Lucius in the arm. "How could you be taken in by this stuff?"

We were carried in through the procurator's archway, pausing only to step around one of the natives, who lay in a drunken stupor in our path.

"Remove him!" I heard Pomponius say, and forthwith came a brace of centurions to drag the drunkard off. "A couple of hundred lashes ought to keep him sober for a day or two." He turned to my stepfather. "Give them the benefits of civilization, and what do they do, eh, Papin-ian? These bloody savages can't get enough of the old aqua ignis, eh, what? Terra Novans simply can't hold their liquor, and they're always collapsing in the streets . . . spoiling the perfect *symmetry* of all the monu-ments . . . they don't appreciate us, that's what! Ah, the Roman's burden . . ."

Helplessly I watched as they carted off the wretch. I

was more and more enraged at what Rome had done to
the people of Iracuavia. The symmetry of the monuments indeed! In the shadow of the archway was a sight
I had seen countless times at the circus in Rome—the
young prostitutes of all conceivable genders, many of
them with their tunicae already hitched up above their
waists, standing in various languorous poses that did
nothing for me, although Lucius was nudging me and
making suggestive comments about shapely mammaries
and pert buttocks. "Why don't they clear *them* out of the
way," I said, "if they want to preserve the symmetry of
their bloody monuments?"

"What an idea!" Lucius said, genuinely shocked. "A
circus without prostitutes? Unconscionable! Why, that
would be like . . . larks' tongues without the aspic."

"Precisely," I said.

"Oh, don't be such a spoilsport," Lucius said. "Why,
old thing, we're in the New World! Oh, it's not wild and
untamed like your Lacotia, but at least we're on the
edges of it. This may be old hat to you, but I'm pretty
damn excited and I don't want you pissing all over it."

I gave up. For all that I had endeavored to teach
Lucius about the true ways of the Terra Novan, he'd
fallen for every romantic cliché about the western empire—every idiotic notion penned by the writers of those
endless, boring epic poems about the heroes of the
golden west.

The games themselves were pretty boring—second
rate, actually, compared with what you could see in
Rome, despite the blandishments of Pomponius about
Alexandria challenging Rome's cultural supremacy.
There were the usual Amazons versus pigmies, the usual
followers of strange cults being eaten by lions and, of
course, crocodiles. We watched from the procuratorial
box as the wild animals munched away at members of

assorted un-Roman sects. Aaye and the Sasquatius got into an argument about the crocodiles.

"Those jaws," the Sasquatius was saying, "are definitely gaping in the wrong direction!" He pointed a hairy finger at one particular crocodile, who was devouring a young woman with gusto as the audience cheered them on. "Those creatures can't really be crocodiles. I say it's a new species, and we should give it a new name. I rather fancy the epithet 'alligator,' to whit, 'that which binds,' because of the ferocious clamping of their jaws, from which no victim can escape."

"Nonsense!" the Egyptian responded huffily. "The works of Aristotle clearly state the direction in which a crocodile's jaw gapes; it follows that what we are seeing here is an optical illusion. I imagine it's accomplished by some fiendishly clever mechanical device inserted into the back of the jaw. My, the clever things these bestiarii can do now, with the aid of modern science! They can even make crocodiles bite backward."

"I have noticed," Pomponius Piso remarked ruefully, as he wiped the wine from his mouth with a fold of his gold-bordered purple robe, "that the crocodilia of the New World always gape in this *unnatural* fashion ... I've tried to get the trainers to make them behave like proper *African* crocodiles, so that our games will be closer to the ... ah ... *original* ... but they just won't."

"Ah," my stepfather said slyly, "a few remnants of savagery still cling to Alexandria, then, despite your best efforts to eradicate them!"

"You won't tell the emperor, will you?" Pomponius said, eyeing him nervously. "I mean, we *are* doing our best, you know. I'm always *crucifying* trainers over those damned crocodiles."

I burst out laughing. What a fool! Pomponius was even more preposterous than my stepfather. "Shut up!" Lucius said, kicking me. It just made me laugh harder, so he turned around to the procuratoria throne and said,

"Frightfully funny, eh, what? Look at that creature—it just tore off the old fellow's head!"

"Hilarious!" I said, although I must say that the circus was one Roman custom I could do without. But to have turned green would have branded me a sissy, so I watched manfully as the wild beasts finished their repast.

The afternoon dragged on, and the air grew sultrier and muggier, and the stench of death hung heavily in the thick air. Our two freed children were fanning Lucius and me with enormous feathers, while slave girls wiped the sweat from our faces with cloths dipped in snow that runners had brought in from the Montes Allegenii.

After a few rounds of gladiatorial combat, there was one of those grotesque chariot races—you know, ostriches yoked to zebras, that sort of thing. To add a special note of humor, all the participants were dwarfs, and the animals were particularly outlandish. Each charioteer was preceded by a flourish of tubae from the four corners of the arena, and was greeted by loud laughter.

"Splendid!" Papinian said, pointing at one odd combination, a dromedary yoked to a Terra Novan giant chicken, who was flapping furiously at its restraints while the driver vainly tried to control it with a flail. "Awfully funny, what! Quite the equal of Rome, Pomponius old chap."

Pomponius beamed, relieved, perhaps, that my step-father had said nothing more about his gaffe with the fake crocodiles.

At that point, another fanfare sounded and a final charioteer entered the arena. I gasped, and so did the rest of the audience. For the creature harnessed to the dwarf's car was one that was not supposed to exist at all. Not in our time. Not if the Dimensional Patrol had been doing its job properly, not if the evil, time-traveling

Green Pig had been correctly eradicated from our spatio-temporal continuum . . .

Only I, my stepfather, and the two academics had ever seen such a creature before. Admittedly, this one was clearly a baby, even though it was almost as big as a full-grown hippopotamus. But there was no mistaking it's identity.

"Good heavens!" my stepfather said. "A bronto-saurus!"

"Is *that* what the thing is called?" Pomponius asked with interest. "Oh, I say."

"Of course it is!" Aaye said. "I named it myself!"

As I sat there in the hot sun, the memory came back vividly to me. There they were—the general and the academics—trussed up and tied to crosses in the middle of an arena on a strange island in the middle of the Oceanus Pacificus—while the Green Pig, cackling hideously, released monster after monster from the portals of his infernal machine, the spatiotemporal bewilderizer. Only the coming of the flying saucers had saved us—and the entire universe—from the domination of his Porcine Majesty.

Lucius said to me, "What are you fellows all upset about? I think it's a splendid creature to be drawing a chariot at the games."

"You don't understand," I said. "That thing's only a baby, and where there's a baby there's usually a mother . . . and where there are brontosauruses, a Green Pig is usually not far behind."

"What are you talking about? Have you gone stark, staring bonkers, Equus old chap?"

"Didn't you read my stepfather's memoirs?" I asked.

"Oh! But that was just one of those *scientifictiones*, was it not? A romance, a rousing fable."

"Never mind," I said, leaning back on the couch and desperately trying to quell my agitation. Surely the Dimensional Patrol's dark nemesis could not have returned to our world. Perhaps this creature had merely been left over from the wreckage of the Green Pig's menagerie. After all, it must have been difficult to cleanse the universe of every single trace of the Evil One's tamperings. That's all the baby brontosaurus was. A loose end. You couldn't expect them to find every egg the mother might have laid. After reasoning it out to myself, I cheered up a little and sat up.

The race had begun. The brontosaurus was trampling some giant chickens whilst two of the ostriches buried their heads in the sand. Most of the dwarfs had been thrown from their cars and were shambling about the arena. The crowd was roaring with laughter. Pomponius was rolling around on the floor of the procuratorial box. Several handmaidens were ministering to him. The Egyptian and the sasquatch were now quareling over which of them had, in fact, been the first to coin the name *brontosaurus*.

Our friend didn't win the race. Instead, he stood in the middle of the arena, not budging, trying to pull the tail feathers from one of the stalled ostriches. Perhaps he thought it was some kind of exotic fern. In fact, there didn't seem to be a winner at all, so Pomponius declared one at random and awarded him a bag of gold and silver coins. The arena was cleared.

"Two more days of spectacle before you have to be off to the uncivilized border, eh, Papinian?" said Pomponius.

Two more days of this! I thought. I was almost ready to go back to Rome.

It was then that I heard the familiar pounding of a Lacotian drum, and heard the tremulous, throaty wailing of Lacotian voices from just beyond the arena. There came painted warriors on horseback, whooping as they circled, waving their lances and screeching the war cry of our people, *"Huka hey!"* Lucius sat straight up, an expression of unbearable excitement on his face. I was

profoundly moved. The warriors performed bravura
stunts, leaping from horse to horse, crawling beneath the
horses' bellies to shoot fire-arrows straight up into the
air. They gathered to one side, and, as the dust and
smoke settled, there came a long line of women carrying
between them a tall tree.

They planted the tree in the middle of the arena.

Suddenly I knew what was going to happen.

"A sundance!" Lucius whispered, awed. "Bloody
good show!" He clapped me on the shoulder. "I wouldn't
miss this for the world."

But I merely sat there and glowered. How could they
do such a thing? Had these braves lost all their honor,
that they would perform our most sacred ritual in front
of an audience?

It was just as I feared. One by one the warriors made
a slit on each breast through which a rawhide thong was
pushed. They were then attached to the top of the tree.
As the drums pounded, they began to dance, their bodies
thrashing wildly against the leather ropes that bound
them. According to tradition, they would dance until
they pulled themselves free, sacrificing their pain and
their strips of flesh for the sake of their people—*hecel
lena oyate kin nipi kte lo*, which is to say, "ut populus
vivat."

There is nothing more noble than the sundance, and
yet I knew there was something terribly wrong with this
one. For one thing, the dancers were all moving in perfect timing with each other, as if the whole thing had
been choreographed. For another, the women, who had
been chastely dancing in a slow circle around the men's
circle, began shedding their clothes and wiggling their
hips erotically at the audience, and soon some of those
ubiquitous dwarfs who had just been seen driving chariots came back on. This time they were wearing enormous leather phalli, and were dancing lewdly with the
women. My worst fears were justified when I observed a

man with a beard—a Greek, obviously, with his colorful clothes, holding a lyre under his arm—who was standing in a corner barking out orders to all the dancers.

"Jolly spectacular, isn't it?" Pomponius said. "That fellow Narcissos is just about the *best* choreographer in the world. He took one of those crude native ceremonies and *refined* it into something worthy of the circus itself..."

"Refined!" I barely stopped myself from choking.

"What's the matter, Equus Insanus?" Lucius said. "Isn't it authentic?"

"Authentic!"

"I say, is the lad all right?" Pomponius asked.

"Authentic! Refined!" What I was witnessing was such an obscenity that I just couldn't control myself anymore.

"Be civilized, now, Equus Insanus," my stepfather said. I could see in his eyes that he saw a little of my pain, but I knew he couldn't really understand. After all, he was still a Roman.

"Ad infernum with your civilization!" I screamed. "Our people had honor. We had pride. You took it all away, and what did you give us? Circuses. Aqueducts. Hummingbirds' brains." I got out of my seat and rushed at Papinian, ready to pummel him into the ground with my fists.

"Good heavens," Pomponius said. "What have you taken under your wing, Papinian old thing?"

My stepfather was flustered for a moment. "Well—as you know—culture isn't learnt overnight—"

"There's nothing wrong with the lad that a decent flogging won't cure!" Pomponius said. "Perhaps I could have one of my centurions oblige?"

"You can beat me all you want, but you're not going to civilize me," I said.

"That's the spirit! Bloody good show!" Lucius said, egging me on.

I could see that my stepfather would lose face if he tried to intervene. So I didn't struggle as I was led away for yet another heavy dose of civilizing.

It wasn't how I had imagined spending my first days in the New World, but it was better than being forced to watch that shocking travesty of everything I held sacred.

CHAPTER
XII

FERREQUUS

ONE THING I'LL SAY: THIS TIME THE FLAGELLATORS were real professionals. This, by Jupiter Vacantanca, was pain. About the third stroke of the lash, I thought it would be best to close my eyes and, as is the way of our people, use the pain to propel me into the spirit world. Although I had almost reached the age, in Roman terms, where a boy doffs the toga praetexta and becomes a man, I had passed through no Lacotian initiation. But I knew that pain of such intensity could give a man a vision. And so I drifted away from the agony.

And I was once again upon the westerly hills of Lacotia, running down toward the plains, which were black with thousands upon thousands of sacred aurochs. I was alone and running, running, the wind cold against my bare skin, exhilarating. In my heart I knew I was running toward a creature from the spirit world, a creature that would give me my true identity.

And then I saw a stallion rear up in the middle of the plain, his nostrils flaring. He was white and painted with designs that showed the lightning and the sun. I ran to him, my vision blurring from the tears and the hot sweat

100

that invaded my eyes. I ran with my arms outstretched, ready to embrace him. But when I stood beside him, flinging my arms around his neck, I encountered not fur, not flesh, but something hard and metallic. And instead of the horse's breath, I smelled steam and smoke. I remember crying out in shock and pain, for the iron was unyielding as I banged my head against it—

When I woke up, I was in a small rectangular chamber, lying on a pallet. It looked almost exactly like the room I had at the Papinian villa in Rome, and for a moment I thought that it had all been a dream—I mean, from the moment I fell asleep after quarreling with my stepfather about hummingbirds' brains. But there was a subtle difference between the two rooms. Not so subtle, I noticed suddenly, as the room clattered over a bump and I realized that the whole room was moving—and not gently. I rubbed my eyes and my sores. The welts seemed to be healing. How long had it been, I wondered, since I had passed out? I sat up. There were two small, high windows in the room, and, standing on tiptoe, I was able to peer out.

I blinked. A forest was rushing past the window at an astounding speed—perhaps as much as fifteen or twenty mille passuum per horam.

I was on some kind of monstrous vehicle. I must be a passenger on board the ferrequus! But I thought the thing hadn't been built yet! And where were the others? I looked around and saw another pallet made up at the other end of the chamber. I was sharing the room with Lucius then. But where was he? And how long had I been out?

There were doors on either end of the chamber. I selected one at random and opened it. At once, the wind blew in my face. The chamber was joined to the next by a precarious-looking system of chains and bolts, and the iron groaned and squeaked as the ferrequus lumbered ahead. The only walkway was a narrow plank that extended over the gap between the cars and was loosely attached to a peg at either end so that it could move freely. I crossed over and reached the other door.

It was a sort of triclinium on wheels. There were couches against the walls, a slave girl was doing a desultory striptease, and some Roman patricians were reclining and eating off silver platters on low tables in front of them. Because of the ferrequus' uneven motion, the floor was continually being spattered with bits of gravy, meat, and fruit. One portly gentleman was trying to stuff something into his mouth, but the ferrequus hit a bump and the food went flying across the corridor.

"Bloody railway food," he muttered, and the guests started talking all at once. "The meat's burnt, the vegetables are raw, and the aspic's all melted. And the wine list—by Dionysus, there isn't a single Greek vintage among them!—just Fallernian, Fallernian, and bleeding Fallernian."

Suddenly I spotted Lucius, who had been looking out the window. "Lucius, Lucius!" I said. "Where are we? Where is everyone?"

He turned. "Oh! You did give me a shock. You've been unconscious for days, old chap."

"Well, those henchmen of Pomponius Piso's did work me over pretty thoroughly," I said.

"It's more than that," he said, coming toward me with a tray of sweetmeats. "You went into one of those Lacotian trances, didn't you? One of those visionary things. That's why we haven't been able to bring you out."

"But are we on the ferrequus?" I asked. "I mean, wasn't my stepfather supposed to build the bloody thing? Surely they didn't do that while I was unconscious!"

"Oh, this! This is an experimental segment. It was put into operation months ago, before we left Rome—it's just a short little thing, from the edge of Iracuavia to the city of Omahopolis. From that point, the going gets considerably rougher. There's a map of the whole system in the engine room—but it's mostly wishful thinking, I understand. Fortunatus has already begun building from somewhere around the foothills of the Montes Saxosi. We are supposed to meet somewhere in the middle. It's sort of a race."

I swallowed the proffered food—I was starving, I realized—and asked Lucius where Papinian and the others had got to.

As if in reply, I heard a tremendous cracking noise, like a peal of thunder. It was followed by a high-pitched whistling, and then a thud.

"What on earth was that?"

"Target practice," Lucius said. "Come with me, you'll see."

"I could have sworn it was a catapulta."

"Swear away," he said, and led me out through the door to the next compartment of the ferrequus.

It was a sort of rectangular platform, open to the elements, with a low railing around it. Just as I had surmised, there were missile-throwing devices everywhere: scorpiones, catapultae, and ballistae. It wasn't that surprising; after all, we were supposed to be transporting military hardware to the western province. What *was* strange was that there were soldiers standing behind each of the weapons, and that they were loading them up for another round.

"Are we being attacked?" I asked.

"Equus Insanus! May Aesculepius be thanked, you've finally come to!" I saw my stepfather standing in the center of the aisle, directing the soldiers. "You're just in time for a bit of sport, what?"

"Sport? What sport?"

"Pull yourself together, dear boy!" One of the catapultae, having shot off its projectile, careened backward as a couple of centurions scurried out of the way.

I looked up as the stones flew up in an arc across the plain and—

"The sacred *pta!*" I cried out, almost beside myself. For the enemy at which the Romans were taking aim was none other than a vast herd of aurochs . . . of sacred buffalo. I had been gazing north, where the green stretched on and on to the far horizon. As I turned my gaze south, I could see them—thousands upon thousands of aurochs, maddened, stampeding—a sea of angry brown fur rushing upon us. My heart leapt with joy at the sight, for the aurochs are the life of the Lacotii. The ground rumbled. The ferrequus clattered, and there came from the west, where the locomotive strained to pull us, great puffs of wood smoke and hot steam.

"Capital sport, eh what?" Papinian shouted, and gave the command for a volley of stones to be fired.

I watched. Here and there, an aurochs fell and was trampled by the others. They didn't stop coming. "Give me a bow and arrows!" I cried, and they were handed to me by one of the legionaries. I crept up to the railing, alongside one of the ballistae, and took aim at a beautiful dark beast who was running straight at me, heedless of danger. Muttering my apology to the animal's spirit for taking its life, I let loose an arrow into its flesh. It tripped and fell. "Stop the ferrequus!" I cried. "I've felled one, and it is my right to cut out its liver and eat it raw!"

My stepfather looked at me as though I were crazy. "Stop the ferrequus?" he said. "Why, the very idea!"

"Wait a minute," I said, as the carcass of my prey receded slowly into the distance. "How are we going to collect all the meat? I mean, don't we need something to replenish all this hideous railway food that everyone's been complaining about?"

Lucius started to cackle hideously. I looked at him. He stopped, sensing something dark in my mood. I turned and saw that several of the Roman soldiers were laughing at me, although one, who was clearly of Lacotian ancestry, for a notched eagle feather dangled from his helmet, did not laugh.

Suddenly it occurred to me that they were just going to leave the dead aurochs lying in the plain. It seemed utterly insane, but quite, quite Roman . . .

"What a waste!" I said. Another carcass crashed against the side of the car. The ferrequus rocked. A cheer went up from the soldiers. "Do you realize how many people you could have fed with those dead animals? How many buffalo robes, tipi coverings, weapons, ornaments, and tools could have been fashioned from the leftovers? You make me sick."

"Come off it, my child," Papinian said, patting me on the head. I flinched. "You're a Roman now. You're one of the victors, not one of the savages over whom it is our destiny to rule. I know there are things about the old life that you miss—heaven knows, if I had been born a savage I could very well think savage ways superior to our own—but you've got to face the truth, my son. You're not just anybody. You're Titus Papinianus the Younger."

He spoke to me with affection and compassion. It wasn't his fault that he couldn't see. "What will you do if you kill them *all* off? For sport, I mean."

"Come, come, my boy. You can jolly well see that the number of aurochs is as limitless as the vastness of the Western Empire itself. What's the harm in a little bit of fun? Don't be such a prig!"

I shrugged. We were never going to understand one another. I knew that now. Perhaps he was right. Perhaps I just didn't understand Romans. I looked at my adoptive father for a few moments, knowing that he felt concern for me.

The ferrequus rumbled on. The tracks curved around a low hillock. The train was like a gigantic metal worm wrapped around the hill. In the front I could see the stately Ionian columns of the locomotive; behind was an area where slaves shoveled wood into great burners not unlike those used for heating the caldarium of a public bath; the chambers of state followed, including my small cabin and the refectory. Bones and breadcrusts were continually flying from the windows of the triclinium car, and now and then a bare-breasted female stuck her torso out for a moment before she was yanked back inside, so I knew that the orgy was still in progress in spite of the complaints about the railway food. Directly beyond the attack car on which we were standing was a temple on wheels, a sort of miniature parthenon with Doric columns and a marble roof. I could see an altar tended by priests and a few statues of various gods. The odor of incense wafted across to us. Behind the little temple were a number of barracks cars, flimsy things, two stories tall, designed to hold as many men as possible; beyond them, cars that held slaves and other merchandise, glorified oxcarts open to the elements. I could see bales of hay, some Imperial elephants, gangs of slaves chained to the railings, and stacks of chests, no doubt full of imports from the fatherland—cheap pots and pans and second-rate jewelry and iron goods: tomahauca and arrowheads, for with the coming of civilization, the weapons of stone had given way to weapons of metal.

I didn't want another argument with my stepfather, who was, in a way, as excited about coming here as I was. The herd of aurochs had disappeared from view. I was about to say something conciliatory when a tuba began to blare out an alarm.

"What's the matter?" Papinian asked.

"Dust storm, General, sir!" a centurion said. He pointed northward. There was a cloud of dust in the distance—and it was moving inexorably towards us.

"That's no dust storm," I said.

"Take cover!" said my stepfather.

"That's no dust storm!" For I had seen, poking from the dark cloud, the flash of an eagle feather war lance.

"You're right," Lucius Vinicius said, squinting.
"We're being attacked."

"Attacked? I say! Good heavens! What on earth for?"
Papinian cried.

I stared at the northern horizon. It was unmistakable.
Several hundred horsemen were charging at the ferrequus. I could hear their war cries now: I could not make
out the language. I hoped it was not Lacotian. Perhaps
we were being attacked by the Apsarochii, the traditional enemies of the Lacotii.

"Bloody rebels!" Papinian said. "The province has
certainly gone to seed since I was governor."

"Quam spectaculum est!" Lucius said, delighted
beyond all measure at the prospect of the coming fray.
"I'll help load up the catapultae, Uncle Papinian."

I could hear their wild ululations now, punctuated by
the pounding of hundreds of hooves.

Amid the pandemonium I thought I heard the war cry
"Huka hey!" My heart sank. Lacotii do not fight Lacotii.
I had come all this way, only to get involved in some silly
battle—on the wrong side!

CHAPTER
XIII

FERREQUUS UNDER SIEGE

MY STEPFATHER BUMBLED ABOUT THE PLATFORM, shouting orders to the centurions and bidding the trumpeters sound their alarums. Men were rushing about, loading up the catapultae. Lucius watched eagerly. I did not share his glee, and when Papinian finally noticed me and my dour face he said, "You two had best go inside. Wait in the dining car until the battle is done."

"Come on, Uncle Papinian!" Lucius said. "I can fight as well as anyone."

"Maybe so," he said, "but you're the emperor's nephew. Equus Insanus, guard your friend and make sure he doesn't leave that car!"

I dragged Lucius away. As we were about to cross into the next car, I heard Papinian cry, "Fire!" and the sky was thick with deadly stones.

We ducked into the triclinium as the ferrequus clattered on. Within, dignitaries and dancing girls were huddled beneath cushions, and the chef's piece de résistence, an enormous stuffed pig, stood so riddled with arrows that it looked more like a giant porcupine. "Come on," I said, "let's get under one of the couches.".

"But I want to fight! I came to Terra Nova for spectacle, by Jupiter, and we're missing precious secundae of it!" Lucius protested. I realized that he was at least halfway drunk. Those Roman vintages could be pretty deadly. I knocked him over and rolled him behind the nearest couch, then sat on his chest so that he wouldn't be able to wriggle free. "Let me go!" he said.

"This is for your own good," I said, as a flaming arrow whizzed into the chamber and set fire to the stuffed pig.

An old man—the same one who had earlier been complaining about the Fallernian wine—reached out from behind one of the couches, grabbed a huge amphora of it, crawled up to the burning pig and attempted to extinguish it. The fire spread to a silver platter piled high with figs. Smoke was billowing everywhere. The smell of roast pork and charred figs filled the chamber. Dancing girls screamed.

"This is insane," I said. "Why on earth are they attacking us?"

I couldn't figure it out. After all, the Pax Romana had ruled Lacotia for almost half a century. The summer warfare of the Lacotii tended to be waged against our traditional enemies such as the Apsarochii; many Lacotians were Roman citizens, and members of the Legions besides. I mean, everybody knew the Romans were all idiots, and that their much-vaunted "benefits of civilization" didn't mean much, but no one had made war with Rome since the treaty between the Emperor Nero and—

"Look out!" Lucius screamed, as another volley of arrows flew into the dining car. I peered from behind the couch and saw, through the window, a Lacota warrior on horseback, neck and neck with the ferrequus, magnificently painted, loosing arrow after arrow from his bow. One of the dancing girls, an arrow in her rump, was clambering around the dining car on her hands and knees. Another was attempting to hide within the entrails of the pig, who, having been well doused with bad wine, smoldered. Suddenly she emitted a piercing shriek—

The warrior had managed to leap from his horse and reach through the window! He was pulling himself through now, coup stick tucked under his arm. Soon there was another and another, their war paint glistening in garish designs, their plumage shuddering in the streaming wind. They ran about the room, smacking everyone with their coup sticks. Not gently.

"Thanks be to Jupiter Vacantanca," I said, "they're only going to count coup. They're not going to kill us." I dug my heels into the small of Lucius' back so that he wouldn't move. They hadn't spotted us yet. Indeed, they seemed more attracted to the dancing girls, some of whom, fearful that they might be killed, had begun to make eyes at the braves and to undulate their hips seductively, trying to direct their assailants toward the ramparts of love.

"Our women—they're going to rape our women!" Lucius cried. "I have to stop them!"

"Don't be silly," I said. "The women will distract them and we'll be able slip out the door. Besides, they're only practicing their profession."

"But honor dictates that I rescue them!" Lucius could be quite the stuffed-up prig at times.

"Shut up!"

Too late. Lucius had thrown me off and was climbing over the couch, brandishing a carving knife he had plucked off the platter with the smoldering pig.

"*Huka hey!*" Lucius shouted as he rushed at the nearest of the three braves. The brave pulled out a scalping knife and waited, laughing.

"Lucius!" I flew out from behind the couch, grabbed the hem of his tunica, and dragged him to the door. I pushed it open and we were outside. Ahead, the car of catapultae was in chaos, with scattered hand-to-hand combat and my stepfather bellowing out orders. We stood precariously on the coupler between the cars. A Lacotian emerged from the dining car, tomahaucum at the ready. I looked wildly around for a place to go. There was a ladder to the roof of the dining car—

"Quick! Up the ladder!" I said, trying to push Lucius along with me. We scrambled up to the top, which was tiled, like a Roman house. I had no weapon at all, and all Lucius had was his carving knife. "Keep low!" I whispered, as an arrow whistled past Lucius' head, almost removing his left ear.

"Phew!" he said. "That was close!" We crouched down. The Lacotian brave was climbing up the ladder. Already we could see a feather sticking up beyond the edge of the roof.

A hand was grabbing onto the tiles, then another—

I crept up to one hand and tried to pry it loose. The other held a tomahaucum and was now flailing wildly. Lucius made a desperate parry with his carving knife and broke the tomahaucum's handle . . . the axehead flew off, smashed into the roof, loosened a few tiles. I got up unsteadily and tried jumping up and down on the brave's free hand. He grunted but wouldn't let go. I slipped on a loose tile and sprawled back. The brave jumped up and started chasing us toward the front of the ferrequus. He didn't have his tomahaucum anymore, but there was a scalping knife between his teeth. "Wait a minute!" I said. "I'm not one of those Romans!" But he didn't seem in a mood for conversation. Besides, through force of habit, I had addressed him in Greek. Hardly the right way to convince someone that you know their language! Lucius and I retreated. At the edge of the roof we paused. The next car was a sleeping car—the very one where I had awoken but an hour before. There was a gap of perhaps half a passus in between the cars, and we were about to

round a curve. "Jump!" I screamed, and gave Lucius a
shove. He barely made it across. Then I closed my eyes
and took a flying leap and landed on my stomach with
my legs wriggling over the edge. I tried to inch forward,
but—

The Lacotian warrior had grabbed both my legs and
was trying to drag me back! "Lucius!" I gasped, and
reached for him. I held on to him as he tried to pull me
over. Meanwhile the ferrequus was lurching as it
rounded the curve. Dozens of Lacotii were keeping pace
with us and uttering bloodcurdling war cries as they attempted to board the ferrequus. I screamed as the tug-
of-war began in earnest.

Just as the pain became unbearable, Lucius' strength
gave out. My head dangled and I felt myself being
dragged back over to the dining car roof. Tiles scraped
my arms. "No, you don't!" Lucius screamed, and
jumped across. He landed on my stomach and stabbed at
the warrior, who was still holding onto both my legs. I
couldn't see much of what was going on—just Lucius'
backside and a few arms and legs furiously interlocked
—but evidently the Lacotian let go of me, because I felt
myself beginning to slip from between Lucius' legs—

I grasped the edge of the roof with both hands and
pushed myself into a sitting position. Too late! The Lacotian seized me by the hair—Lucius was pinned between us, his carving knife knocked out of his
hand—and prepared to lift my scalp. I looked into his
eyes. For a moment he seemed to waver. I blurted out,
"*Lamakota!*" which is to say, "Lacotius sum ego."

He looked at me dubiously. "By Vacantanca," I
shouted in the Lacotian tongue, "I am Equus Insanus,
the son of Aquila! Kill me, and the blood of a brother
Lacotius will be on your conscience."

He let go of me. "Oh, sorry," he said. "With those
funny clothes you were wearing, can you blame me?"

As the brave disengaged himself from me, Lucius wriggled free and made a mad rush for him and started to pummel him wildly with his fists. "Well," the brave said, "at least I shall kill this one!" He caught Lucius easily in a headlock and brandished the scalping knife yet again.

"No, you can't do that!" I said.

"Why not? He is obviously not one of us."

"He's my . . . he's my blood brother," I lied.

"Oh, all right," the brave said, shoving Lucius aside disdainfully.

"Would someone tell me what is going on?" Lucius asked, looking at our erstwhile assailant and me, who now seemed to be the best of friends.

"Are you not son of that Aquila who was summoned by the great chief in Rome, and raised to a member of the senatorial council, and who then was snatched up into the sky by the green men from the distant time?" the Lacotian warrior asked.

I nodded.

"Why, you are my sister's husband's second cousin's nephew!" he said, embracing me. "Allow me to introduce myself; my name is Ursus Erectus. Welcome home, brother! It is indeed a joy to see the hatchling once more returned to his nest," and other such expressions of extreme pleasure, though I must admit that I had never seen him before in my whole life. Oblivious to the arrows that rained on us from all sides, he spoke eloquently on the circle of being and the workings of the great mystery.

"Who is he, Equus? What does he want?" Lucius asked, keeping his distance as he bandaged a gash in his arm with a piece of linen from his tunica.

"I told him you're my blood brother," I said. "By the way, he's my cousin or something." To Ursus Erectus I said, "But why are you attacking us? Rome and Lakota Nation are not at war, are they?"

Ursus Erectus sat down. Behind us, the temple flamed, and there was a free-for-all going on in the war car. But Ursus Erectus was not to be hurried, and, amid the pandemonium that raged below, stopping now and then to dodge an arrow, he began to narrate the woeful tale of the coming of the ferrequus to the great plains . . .

CHAPTER
XIV

OMAHOPOLIS

"WHEN THE WORLD WAS YOUNG," URSUS ERectus began, speaking in a strange patois of Greek with Latin and Lacotian words thrown in, doubtless so that Lucius could understand as well, "the aurochs roamed, thousands upon thousands, and we hunted them. In the summers we made war, though few died; war was for sport, and to prove our manhood and cunning. Then came the explorers from across the Oceanus Atlanticus, bringing with them *shunkawakan*, that is to say, 'equus,' and giving our people the power to fly over the plains like the wind..."

"Oh, get on with it," I said, for I saw that Romans and Lacotians alike were clambering up to the roofs, and we would soon be in the midst of battle once more.

"Stop interrupting me!" Ursus Erectus said. "You should know better than to try to hurry up a narrative in traditional style, my cousin. In your years in Rome, you have forgotten much."

Behind us, on the roof of the next car down, there was some heavy hand-to-hand combat going on. Lucius, for all his boasting words of moments before, must have

115

suddenly realized that we really were in danger of our lives, because he was all huddled up and shivering. "Don't show any fear!" I said sharply. "Or he's liable to scalp you on the spot." That didn't help much. Luckily, Ursus Erectus was so absorbed in his narration that he didn't notice anything else.

"Hechitu welo!" he said. "When the *washichun*, the pallid-faced Romans from across the sea, came to our land, we greeted them as friends, for they had given us horses. But soon they began to take. But though we fought them bitterly, we were well matched, and though we were defeated, our people did not suffer too much, for the Romans interfered but little in our ways. They built cities and aqueducts and gave us *mniwakan*, the water that drives men mad. But on the whole, we went on hunting the aurochs as we had always done. Then, a few moons ago, they began to build this monstrous iron horse. The aurochs no longer roam freely in these areas, and those with vision fear that our way of life may end. Rebellion is our only recourse. For there have come hunters who kill for sport, racing up and down the iron rails with their catapultae, and leaving the animals to rot in the sun—killing far more than they will ever need. Moreover, these hunters do not apologize to the spirits of the animals they kill, but behave as though they were not living things at all, but metal and stone, like the hollow magnificence of their stone tipis. If the aurochs flee, what shall we eat? It is summer now, but soon will come winter—and in the Moon of Popping Trees there will be no meat for the villages remote from the cities—so that they will be forced to come begging for grain to those who have adopted the ways of the *washichun*."

"Are all the Lacotii in revolt?" I asked, fearful of my own position, for I had become half one and half the other.

"No. Most remain Roman, for they have flocked to the cities of Caesarea, Omahopolis, and Aricharopolis, and have fallen under the influence of *mniwakan*. Others have joined the legionaries, and now brother wars upon brother—something which will surely create a terrible rupture in the circle of existence."

I sat in contemplation for a while, dodging the odd arrow. Even though my stepfather was a doddering fool, there was no reason to go to war. Surely some compromise could be arranged. No one wanted the Lacotii to starve—not even the Romans, surely. They were not a malicious people as such, just, well, *different*. It was probably only from bureaucratic lack of foresight, and ignorance of the true state of affairs in the remote provinces, that they had failed to think things through.

"Can't you call this attack off until we...come up with some solution?" I asked.

"What solution?" Ursus Erectus responded.

"The emperor has commanded Papinian to build the railway, but maybe we could stop the indiscriminate aurochs hunting. Paperwork—that's it! We'll require that those of non-Lacotian ancestry must have a license from the governor to kill aurochs or something. The Romans love paperwork almost as much as they love flogging."

"I fail to understand how a scroll of papyrus can stop the sacred *pta* from going where they choose. This must be a very powerful magic," Ursus Erectus said, puzzled.

I crept up closer to Ursus and peered over the edge of the roof. The braves were clambering up the walls; behind us, they were already dancing on the roof of the temple-on-wheels. The carnage was ridiculous. Several priests were huddled up there, remonstrating with the warriors. One of them was wrestling with a sacrificial giant chicken. Several other giant chickens were running amuck over the roof, clucking and strutting and tripping up Romans and Lacotians alike. There was a sulphurous smell in the air, and I could see projectiles of brimstone hurtling down on the storming horsemen.

"Quam spectaculum est!" Lucius exclaimed, "this is

better than the arena!" Since Ursus Erectus was not harming us, my friend had recovered his wits, and was enjoying the battle immensely, like your typical Roman aristocrat brat.

"Listen," I said. I was getting desperate, and I knew that the slaughter was likely to go on and on for a while yet, for the Lacotian horses were easily keeping apace of the ferrequus. "Listen to me, Ursus Erectus. What can we possibly achieve by this fighting? Why can't we talk it out? Why can't we have a truce and figure out a way of—"

"Truces! Treaties!" Ursus Erectus laughed bitterly. "You have been too long with the Romans, my brother, else you would not speak of such things." In my heart I had to agree. "But since you are the son of Aquila, *and* the adopted son of Papinian, you are a man who faces in two directions. Perhaps you *can* talk both sides into a compromise."

"Me? But I'm just a—"

Ursus stood up, his hair and feathers streaming in the wind of the ferrequus' passage. He began shrieking at the top of his lungs, the cry of an angry wolf. "The son of Aquila has returned to his people!" he screamed. "Let us no longer fight, but greet our brother with joy!"

I got up, too, and looked around. I staggered over to the edge of the carriage and gazed down at the war car. The cry had been taken up, and those among our legionaries who spoke Lacotian had already put down their arms and were embracing their erstwhile enemies. Ursus Erectus pulled out a fresh scalp, still dripping, that he had stuck in his belt, and looked at it almost with regret. He shrugged. "Not such a good day to die," he said. "Lacota against Lacota. *Shiché lo!*" Which means, "Non est bonum."

My stepfather was still urging on his men. "What's the bloody matter with you lot?" he was saying. One of the braves laughed, and Papinian kicked him in the arse. "Did we win or lose?"

I shouted down at him, "It's all right, stepfather! Apparently I've saved the day by being the son of Aquila, and we're to make some kind of treaty now."

"What are you talking about?"

"Stop flailing away at the air, you bubblenosed old general!" I yelled. "The battle's over! I've managed to talk them out of fighting for the day."

Sure enough, the cries of *huka hey* had ceased, though the braves were still boarding the ferrequus in great numbers. The catapultae were no longer firing. A space had been cleared in the middle of the war car, and some chieftains were already squatting down as though for a peace council.

"Would somebody tell me what's going on?" my stepfather asked in consternation.

Lucius, Ursus Erectus, and I climbed down. "The son of Aquila has returned to make peace between our peoples," Ursus proclaimed, and the Lacotii chieftains looked at each other and nodded sagely as my stepfather stared.

"I say, old things," he said at last, "it's awfully good of you to stop attacking us, but I'm in charge around here, and you jolly well ought to deal with me."

"Silence!" Ursus Erectus said. "It is only with the son of Aquila that we will make peace. His father it was who defeated General Pomponius Piso at the battle of the Flumen Pulveris." At least this fellow knew his history! "He has promised us that you will desist from hunting aurochs from the ferrequus, and in exchange we will no longer attack the iron horse whenever it passes through our territory."

"Oh, I say, what," my stepfather said, and I realized they were all waiting for me to say something, looking to me for guidance. He fumbled around for a few more moments, then said, "Oh, jolly good, I suppose. Come on, men, let's pack up the ammunition." Which had been packed up long before. "No need to continue fighting, old chaps! Carry on!" He made a few more platitudinous remarks. Ignoring him, I seated myself on the floor, as did the other chieftains, forming a circle; and Ursus Erectus called for a peace pipe. Luckily, there was one on the ferrequus, for one of the senators who had been cowering under the couch in the dining car had purchased one in Alexandria as a souvenir. It was not made of pipestone, being a tourist version of the real thing, but was carved out of marble, the bowl being of solid gold.

He handed it to me.

And so it was that I, who had never, in my childhood among the Lacotii, been seated amongst the men in the council lodge, was now presiding over such a council— on the floor of a traveling tipi that was fairly winging its way through the countryside at a brisk twenty *mille passuum pro horam*! Lucius, squatting behind me in the circle, looked at me with new admiration.

My stepfather sidled up to us, trying to horn in on the council, but Ursus continued to disregard his presence. We smoked for a while—I did not do it right the first time, and so I was coughing and spluttering—and spoke of a treaty.

"In exchange for your concessions," Ursus said, "We promise to attack only the *other* ferrequus, the one that runs toward the rising sun."

"What other ferrequus?" I said.

Lucius poked me. "Don't you remember?" he whispered. "It's a race. These rails are going to join a second track that is being laid down from the western edge of the province . . . and being overseen by none other than Fortunatus."

"You will harass only them?" I said. My stepfather had crept up closer now, and was listening intently. "Done!"

"Wouldn't it be better," Papinian said, "if they didn't bother either of the groups?"

"Don't be silly, Uncle Papinian," said Lucius. "This way we'll win the race, regain the emperor's favor, and you won't get into trouble for kidnapping me."

"I didn't—"

At that moment, the Sasquatius and the Egyptian emerged from the temple behind us. To my astonishment, they seemed oblivious to all that had been going on, and were engaged in an esoteric discussion of the more recondite aspects of the theory of engineering. Things were fast returning to normal. I decided that it was time to end our discussion, to make and accept no more promises. "A banquet!" I said. "Clearly we must celebrate our new alliance with a banquet!"

"Jolly good idea," said my stepfather. "Now that I've successfully subdued these barbarian invaders . . . it is the way of Rome not to enslave the conquered—well, maybe *some* of the conquered—but to grant amnesty to those whom she once fought, eh, what? By all means— let food be brought to our new friends!"

"Then stop the ferrequus," I said, "and let's go back and get us some buffalo meat."

At last I was going to get a decent meal around here.

As the night progressed, the *mniwakan* flowed like water, and Ursus Erectus led a wild dance on the roof-tops of the ferrequus as we roasted great haunches of aurochs, converting the altar of Jupiter within the temple on wheels into a gigantic barbeque. Lucius and I sacri-ficed to Jupiter and then climbed aloft to join in the fren-zied dancing, and even my stepfather stripped to a loincloth and capered about, though the Sasquatius and the Egyptian considered themselves too elevated for dancing, squatting, instead, at the edge of the circle and scribbling notes on wax tablets.

Our Lacotian soldiers and their once-rebellious

brothers joined voices in a celebratory song:

Natanhiwan winyan wakaghe!

"What are they singing about?" Lucius asked.

" 'The enemy charged—but I turned him into a woman!' " I said. The stars had come out and the ferrequus was rushing through the night, through terrain that was growing more achingly familiar with each mille passus.

It was dawn when we pulled into the city of Omahopolis. It is a city of surpassing drabness, hardly more than a walled fortress surrounded by the tipis of the Omahae, who are related to the Lacotii but speak a dialect difficult to understand.

"Wake up!" Lucius was shaking me. I had fallen asleep on the roof, next to the smouldering bonfire of the previous night. There were empty wine jugs everywhere, and bodies—some dead, others dead drunk—scattered all over the place. "Look! There's some kind of spectacle in store."

The ferrequus belched great clouds of steam and foul-smelling vapors, and wheezed to a halt. As the screeching of the locomotive died down, we heard ceremonial music, and realized that a reception committee had been organized to greet us.

"Quick," I said, "we'd better put on some decent clothes. It looks like official business." I sprang up, stepped gingerly over drunken Romans and Lacotians, and climbed down into the carriage below. Lucius followed. There was a small wooden chest beside my pallet which contained our clothes: some rumpled tunicae, freshly cleaned togae, and calligae for our feet. I summoned our two Lacotian ex-slaves, and they obediently gave us a quick scrape with their strigils, wiped some of the blood, soot, and wine off our faces and arms, and dressed us in our best Roman finery. Then they brushed our hair with a device made from a porcupine's tail, and we each placed a single eaglefeather in our hair. We were perfect specimens of Terra Novan gentry by the time we were through.

When we joined my stepfather and our scientist friends, they were just climbing onto litters. Some makeshift steps led to the unpaved street from the side of the carriage. We stood in front of the gates of Omahopolis: huge, wooden fortifications lined with the tipis and lodges of Omaha tribesmen. There was an honor guard of braves on horseback.

Our own legionaries were rousing themselves from drunkenness, rubbing their heads and eyes. But when the bucina of our legion sounded, they leapt to their feet, for they were members of the most highly disciplined army on earth, and stood to attention. My stepfather surveyed his men as his litter was raised up on the shoulders of eight Nubians.

The gates of the city opened...

And a familiar-looking motorcar came puffing down the road. A familiar figure, robed in purple, was seated upon its dais, flanked by comely maidens with ostrich-feather fans. He gave some imperious commands, and the guard of honor executed various maneuvers with flawless precision.

Then Fortunatus turned to us. "You again, Papinian! We never seem to be able to escape one another, do we? I thought I'd come and greet you personally. After all, you're never going to finish the ferrequus... this project is going to kill you, old chap... you'll never see fair Rome again."

"What makes you so sure of that, by Jupiter?" Papinian asked. "My Sasquatius is a competent engineer, and as for the Egyptian—"

Aaye betrayed a particularly haughty expression as Papinian searched for something pleasant to say about him.

"Well," Fortunatus said, oozing unctuously, "I can at

least offer you the hospitality of a decent day's rest in Omahopolis before you begin. But I warn you, the daily attacks by rebel forces of Lacotii—"

"I can take care of myself," Papinian said smugly.

I looked at Lucius. "There's something wrong with Fortunatus. He's too...too coherent. He hasn't once forgotten where he is or where he's going, and he gave all those orders to the guard perfectly." For when I had first seen him, at the slave market, he had seemed little better than a village idiot, had actually mistaken the auction block for the public baths.

"Something else is wrong with him," Lucius said. "Have you taken a good look at his face?"

"Ugly as ever," I said.

"No, look again."

I did, as the motorcar approached closer. C. Lentulus Fortunatus did not squint as he had done every other time I had seen him; he seemed to have lost his near-sightedness completely. His porcine visage was, as always, hideous, but there was, indeed, something different about it...

"It's probably just the light," I said. "It's dawn, and the clarity of the air in this part of the world may render colors a little more vividly than we've grown accustomed to..."

"His face," Lucius said, "happens to be a most interesting shade of green."

"Dyspepsia," I said. "He's probably not used to eating aurochs all the time."

Lucius was frantic. "Don't you understand anything, you nincompoop?" he said. "There's only one reason for the spontaneous viridification of the human flesh tones."

"Oh, shut up," I said. "You're just imagining things." But my flesh was starting to crawl, for I knew what Lucius was going to say, and it jibed perfectly with the brontosaurus that we had seen a few days before in the circus at Alexandria.

"For his skin to turn that green," Lucius said, "he's got to have been traveling in space for at *least* a few years."

"But we just saw him a couple of months ago!"

"Relatively, Equus! I don't understand it either, but it's the word those little green men always use to explain things they can't be bothered to explain. What it amounts to is, he could have been gone for years and to us it'd only seem like a few months."

"This is nonsense," I said. "Why would Fortunatus be allowed to go into space? You know that the werejaguars from the future don't just go around picking up just anyone and lugging them around the dimensional lanes . . ."

"What if he hasn't been in space with the good guys?" Lucius said. "What if the Green Pig—"

"The Green Pig is no more," I said.

"But what if—what if—"

"You have been reading too much of those blasted *scientifictiones*," I said, trying to convince myself as well as him that nothing was the matter. But deep inside I knew that something dirty was afoot, and I was determined to find out what it was.

CHAPTER
XV

APUD FERREQUUM LABORAVI

I SHALL NOT DESCRIBE THE ENSUING ORGIES AND games; since you will by now have gathered that our arrival at each new destination entailed more banquets, games, gladiatorial combats, and dancing girls than the last, I am simply going to take such things as read from now on. One can only describe so many exotic dishes and bizarre entertainments. Suffice it to say that we were wined, dined, amused, and titillated to the point of making several visits to the garrison's communal vomitorium, and that the constant proximity of Fortunatus made it possible for me to ascertain that what we had seen that morning was not just a trick of the light. He was definitely green, and not with dyspepsia, for he ate as heartily as everyone else, and went to the vomitorium as frequently. There was only one possible conclusion.

Sometime since we had last seen him in Rome, C. Lentulus Fortunatus had been captured by a flying saucer!

My stepfather had been somewhat sobered by the fact that I, not he, had been the one to forge a peace treaty with the rebel Lacotii. The next day he was far harder on me than usual. Over breakfast, he not only forced me to eat an entire compôte of rattlesnakes' brains, but took me to task for misusing the optative voice of a particularly obscure Greek verb.

We bade Fortunatus farewell—he had to return to Caesarea for administrative duties—and thence journeyed onward to inspect the railway workers.

The conveyance on which we traveled was a most ingenious one. It was a sort of wooden platform on wheels; heavily-muscled slaves worked a gigantic lever back and forth, which set the wheels in motion along the very track itself, which extended westward for some thirty or forty more *mille passuum*. There was a drummer to keep the slaves' rhythm steady, and an overseer who paced back and forth, occasionally touching one of them up with a flagellum. Our party—Papinian, Abraham, Aaye, Lucius, and me—sat under an awning of dressed aurochs skins, on padded couches, watching the scenery go by. Ursus Erectus was with us, too, for, in celebration of our truce, he had been invited to inspect the project with us.

"This is tremendous!" Papinian was saying. "This is just the sort of thing that makes Rome great!" He waved his arms ecstatically as if to encompass all the great plains. "Soon, across this iron road, will come thousands upon thousands of settlers—there will be cities everywhere—arenas, baths, libraries, theaters, culture! It's splendid how we're dragging this primitive land right into the ninth century!"

"What a boor your stepfather is," Lucius whispered in my ear. "Measuring the centuries from the Foundation of Rome, instead of from the First Olympiad." Since the battle, Lucius Vinicius had become his cocky self again, and hadn't allowed a single Latin concept to sully his tongue.

Ursus said, "Arenas, baths, libraries. Have you consulted the Lacotian people about these things, O procurator? Perhaps they would rather have sweat lodges and sacred circles for the sundance."

"Well, of course you'll keep all your old traditions," Papinian said. "Didn't I always allow that when I was procurator? I mean, though, that you should have *better* sweat lodges and sundance circles. For example"—he closed his eyes, and an almost Homeric cadence informed his speech—"you could have a sweat lodge dozens of cubits long...combine it with a caldarium, frigidarium, and tepidarium, and you'd have a complete Roman bath...none of this sitting in a tiny tent and sweating it out! It would be a genuine social occasion. Social! That's it! You people could use a richer social life. As for the sundance...it's all very well out in the open, but imagine how much more solemn it could be ...in a gigantic marble temple, with a golden statue of Vacantanca looking on. Priests chanting in a stately, orderly way—none of this discordant yodeling that passes for Lacotian singing—we could adapt some of the Homeric hymns, perhaps, or the religious poetry of Sappho."

"These Romans are crazy," Ursus Erectus said to me.

Papinian continued to rhapsodize. "Perhaps the emperor himself could be persuaded to perform the sundance. After all, he *is* the pontifex maximus, and, presumably, the head of your religion, too. Of course, piercing the skin of the breast would have to be ruled out, but we could always have some surrogate—a condemned criminal, perhaps—suffer in the emperor's stead. That way, the Divinity would be safe from injury whilst scoring an important political coup..."

"But the whole point of the sundance—" Ursus Erectus began. I could tell that he didn't know whether to laugh or be insulted.

Perhaps it was time for me to step in with my newfound diplomatic skills. "Who's actually working on the railroad?" I asked. "I mean, where is the labor coming from?"

"That's another bone of contention," Ursus said grimly.

"Yes, it seems that our friend Fortunatus has imposed conscription upon the peoples of Lacotia," said Abraham bar-David, who, of all our company, was the only one who had been bothering to find out what was actually going on around us.

"Seems pretty reasonable," my stepfather said.

"Reasonable!" Ursus growled, and reached for his dagger. I was afraid we were going to have another battle scene then and there—and I didn't exactly know whose side I was going to take.

After traveling—and arguing—for half the day, we finally arrived at the end of the tracks. You could hear the hammers pounding and the scourges whistling long before the construction teams came into view. The site was a spectacle beyond belief. There were thousands of slaves, chained by the feet, laboring to implant the iron rails. The Lacotian conscripts were not, of course, shackled, for they were Roman citizens; many of them seemed to have been engaged as overseers, and were merrily whipping away. As we descended from our platform, I noticed a group of crucified people in the middle distance. "The poor things," Lucius said in a surprisingly un-Roman show of compassion. "I wonder what they did."

"Insurbordination, that's what!" a centurion said grimly.

One could see the facial expressions of the crucified quite easily, for these were not the tall display crosses one sometimes sees lining the Appian Way, but hastily assembled things barely tall enough to get the victim's feet off the ground.

The workers did not seem at all happy with their lot. At a signal from their foremen, they all stopped what they were doing and gave my stepfather a cheer, but it was a most desultory one.

"Bloody crucifixions," my stepfather said. "Bad for morale."

"Well, how else do you expect to keep slaves in line, O procurator?" said the centurion in charge, who was giving us a grand tour of the whole operation.

"Well, the least you could do is have them out of sight," Papinian said. "They smell disgusting."

"Of course they do, sir! Some of them are rotting corpses."

"Don't belabor the obvious, centurion. While I'm in charge, any disciplinary actions can be executed out of sight." My stepfather's attitude to crucifixion had become much less severe during our confrontation with the Green Pig, so bombastically narrated in Papinian's memoirs, when he himself hung from a cross for several hours.

I was bored. "It's about time we slipped away," I whispered to Lucius. "Surely no one needs us at the moment." The sight of thousands of slaves at work is not one to lift the spirits of anyone. Even Lucius, who was used to the idea, seemed uncomfortable. And the heat was almost unendurable. There was a clump of trees nearby, and a river, some tributary doubtless of the mighty Miserabilis; we headed in its direction.

We sat together at the river bank. We didn't speak for a while. The sound of clanking, pounding, and flagellating was fainter here, but we could still hardly hear ourselves think.

Lucius spoke first. "Lacotia at last! Adventure and spectacle!" But he sounded curiously unconvinced.

"You're sure you're having a good time?" I asked.

"Well . . . well . . ." He looked at me dubiously. "It's hard for me to say this, but . . . well, everything's so *weird* here. I mean, I know everything about your native customs and all, I've read a dozen scrolls about them.

But it's scary here. There aren't any people, and the landscape just goes on and on and on."

"What about all those construction workers?"

"Well, yes, but they're *slaves*, Equus. I wasn't counting them as people." The ability to make slaves appear wholly invisible was a peculiarly Roman trait. "But—I think you're disappointed, too, aren't you?"

"I suppose so." I kicked a few stones into the water. "You see, I had rather imagined there would be *fewer* people. And that we wouldn't be working on this stupid technological breakthrough that is going to end up destroying my people's way of life completely. I mean, you saw Alexandria, how it's turned into sort of a model Roman town, more Roman than the Romans. If we finish the ferrequus, the great plains are going to be crawling with tourists and immigrants and hunters and—"

"Listen!" We both pricked up our ears. Something was going on back at the tracks. All the noises had ceased abruptly. "What's going on?"

We raced back. Aaye was wringing his hands and the Sasquatius was scratching his head. Ursus Erectus had retreated to our moving platform and had begun to sing quietly to himself. Perhaps he was expecting death. "What happened?" I said, turning around and seeing that all the men had dropped their tools and were staring oddly at the sky.

"It's your stepfather," Aaye said. "He's been snatched up into the sky!"

Lucius and I glanced upward only to see a streak of brilliant light against the clouds...fading now, slowly fading.

"*Heyaha!*" Ursus Erectus cried, standing up and gesturing at the sky. "Grandfather, *tunkashila*, take me, too!"

"First Fortunatus, now Papinian," Lucius said. "Those flying saucers don't have much taste, do they?"

CHAPTER
XVI

REROUTING THE FERREQUUS

SINCE THE FLYING SAUCERS HAD INTERFERED, THERE was nothing for it but to carry on as usual. The Dimensional Patrol is not an organization whose inner workings are easily comprehensible to us primitive denizens of the past. When the little green were-jaguars tried explaining anything, it was liable to leave one as befogged as before. So I decided it would be best to act as if Titus Papinianus had just gone off on a stroll somewhere.

A supply train, laden with food, wine, dancing girls, and laboratory equipment, had just arrived, having departed from Omahopolis some time after we had. A group of slaves were unloading the train, and a second group were putting up tents. There was a large tent—the procurator's headquarters—where the evening's entertainments would doubtless be held. Another seemed to be some kind of laboratory, for our two learned men were hovering at the entrance. They were shouting instructions to their minions, who bore on their shoulders a strange selection of scientific instruments, dinosaur skulls, stuffed animals, fumigants, rocks, and statues of the gods. I went up to the sasquatch.

"Abraham bar-David," I said, "you must take command until my stepfather comes back." I'm not quite sure why I was giving the orders, but no one seemed to object.

Except, of course, for our cantankerous Egyptian. "What!" he said. "You'd let that hairy monster run the entire show—when it is the Egyptians who built the pyramids, the sphinx, and the temples of Karnak—when your ancestors were still running around in the skins of beasts!"

"Run along, Aaye," the Sasquatius said. "You can help unpack the experiments. After I'm through with instructing the foremen, I promise we'll go on to more intellectual pursuits together."

At the supply train, slaves were still unpacking. After all the chests were unloaded, there were still various creatures: white cows, bulls, rabbits, goats, several cages full of white doves, and an albino monkey. I wondered what they were for, but when I saw the last car of the train, one of those temples-on-wheels, I realized that they were probably due to be sacrificed. A bald priest in flowing robes stepped out and eyed the procession of sacrificial beasts; at length, he singled out one of the goats.

"No, no, not that goat, you imbecile!" Abraham seemed struck by a sudden panic. "Do you want to frighten off the entire work force?" He stalked up to the priest—Lucius and I following, for we did not want to miss any of this fascinating altercation—and kicked the goat out of the way.

"What's wrong with the goat?" I said.

Lucius kicked me in the shin. "Idiot! It's the device ...the uranium entrail analysis device..."

"He has it with him?"

"Obviously! You've seen how much laboratory equipment the Sasquatius has brought along."

I shrugged. "You Romans do set such store by these silly sacrifices."

A side door of the temple swung open, and we saw a statue of Jupiter Vacantanca within. Seated at his feet was a bronze image of Trajan himself, and in front of it was a brazier on which an old priest was throwing incense and mumbling in a funny language.

"What's he saying?" I asked, for although I spoke passable Latin and Greek I couldn't make out a word of this.

"It's Etruscan," Lucius said. "Who knows what it means? It's traditional stuff, you know, eight hundred years old."

The goat was being pushed up the steps. Several centurions gathered around. Lucius stood up straight and slicked back his hair. I just slouched against one of the marble columns of the carriage. After all, this was their religion, not mine. "Stand up straight!" Lucius whispered to me. "Show some respect."

"Why bother?" But I complied, though it occurred to me that Lucius hadn't shown much respect when we were pissing out of the eye of Jove back in Rome. I supposed it was that Lucius was simply concerned for his public image. Besides, being in a barbaric land and all, he wanted, I'm sure, to be a model of rectitude in front of the natives.

We stood stiffly through the chanting, the cutting of the poor thing's throat—it had been bleating piteously all through the ceremony—and the auguries, which were, of course, favorable—almost too good to be true. The Sasquatius endured the entire ritual with a supercilious smirk, but the members of the Roman army present were profoundly impressed by the omens. It is strange that a people so technologically advanced can stake their entire futures on a few livers and plucked-out hearts.

After the sacrifice, we watched the workmen for a while. It was very dull, and the sun rose higher and higher, and I longed to get out of the Roman clothes I had been wearing. So Lucius and I went back to the procurator's tent. It was cooler there.

The tent was empty. Some couches had been set out, and an enormous map of Lacotia hung on one wall, showing the path that the ferrequus was to take from Omahopolis all the way to the border of Siannia. Siannia, and the Montes Saxosi beyond, are not, strictly speaking, part of the Empire, but are client states. The region immediately west of Lacotia is known as Vaeomingum— a latinization of a word in one of the native tongues, not Lacotian. The ferrequus, as planned, ran in a more or less straight line from Omahopolis into the Vaeomingum territory. A deal had been struck with the tribes of Sianii and Siosionii, whereby Rome would annex a strip of land on either side of the railway, ten mille passuum wide.

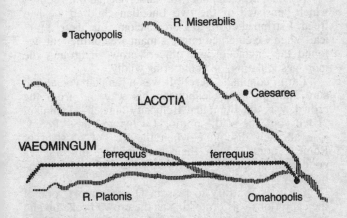

Presumably the journey from Caesarea to Omahopolis was to be made by riverboat—that outlandish conveyance that plied the River Miserabilis, using slaves on a treadmill, supplemented by steam, as its main source of power—for there was no spur of the ferrequus thither, even though Caesarea is the capital of Lacotia. I laughed when I saw that the map showed Tachyopolis, or Rapid City, for, as those who read my stepfather's silly memoirs might recall, that city was a fiction of a few tents and huts, hastily constructed for the purpose of tricking the emperor into thinking we had conquered the vast territory around it.

Lucius was fascinated by the map, and began going on about the splendor of the Empire.

"What a fool you are," I said, "if you think that just by drawing a few squiggly lines Rome can actually lay claim to huge chunks of the world..."

"But it says so right on the map."

"Come on, let's get out of these awful Roman clothes."

We had a little chamber for ourselves and our retinue, which consisted of the two Lacotian children we had freed. I stripped down to a breechclout, Lucius to a tunica. When we emerged into the main area of the tent, we found the engineers and officers crowded around the map, gesticulating, and chattering wildly.

"I'm in command here!" It was a familiar voice; and sure enough, madly ellbowing his way out from the crowd, was the Bumbling Bulbosity himself—Papinian! "I tell you!" he said, spotting Lucius and me. "People lose all their discipline when they're out of sight of Rome...arguing with their commanding officers...a good Roman should obey orders literally and unquestioningly..."

"But it is contrary to reason, O procurator!" one of the centurions was protesting as the crowd broke up and reconverged about my stepfather once more. "The straightest path the ferrequus can take is to follow the course of the southern fork of the River of Plato, all the way to the Vaeomingum Territory..."

Lucius and I looked at the map. To our amazement, the straight line that had represented the putative route of the ferrequus had been crudely scratched out. In its place, a new route had been sketched in:

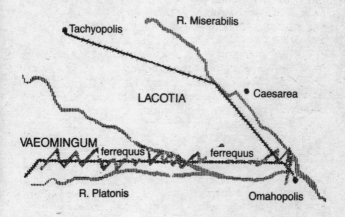

"Stepfather," I said, "are you quite all right? I mean, a trip in a flying saucer can be a pretty unsettling experience."

"I'm perfectly fine," he said. There was a strange savagery in his voice.

"But Tachyopolis is in the middle of nowhere...and the emperor—"

"*Caesar onze wahu!*" my stepfather swore in the Lacotian tongue, and it occurred to me that his accent had improved considerably in the hour or so that he had been away.

"Equus, Equus!" Lucius said, tugging my elbow and pulling me away from the crowd of agitated minions. "Don't you see? Look at the man's face!"

Indeed. It was unmistakable. Dread invaded my senses as I saw that my stepfather's face had acquired a distinctly greenish tinge. It was a color that could not have been imparted by a mere hour or two inside a flying saucer...

CHAPTER
XVII

MORE FUN WITH ENTRAILS

MY STEPFATHER SEEMED TO BE POSSESSED OF A fantastical new energy. Of course, if he had been traveling through time and space for many days—perhaps centuries—he could have picked up a great deal of superior learning. Perhaps he *did* know what he was doing, although there seemed to be no logic at all in the idea of making the ferrequus veer all the way north to Tachyopolis.

Was there a way to find out what had happened?

I followed Papinian around for the rest of the day. His knowledge of engineering was astounding; the Sasquatius, appropriately astounded, could only trail behind him, scribbling frantically on a wax tablet. Standing upon a knoll and surveying the slaves as they labored, my stepfather discoursed darkly on scientific matters: "Torque...angle of declination...ratio of fuel to distance..."

"That settles it," I said to Lucius. "They've done something to his mind. Pumped it full of superior intelligence somehow."

"About time someone did," Lucius said, and I had to agree.

My stepfather paced frantically about the hillock, and suddenly began pointing. "Look! They're slacking off, the little buggers! Apply the lash a little harder, will you?"

A group of sorry-looking fellows was banging away at the ground with picks and shovels. Their overseers moved in with their iron-tipped rods, but these creatures were too tired to go on.

"I won't have it!" my stepfather said. There was a kind of madness in his eyes. He summoned a tribune and said, "Pick a couple of them and have them crucified at once. On the double."

"With the others, sir?" the tribune said, saluting.

"No! I want to make an example of them . . . I want every miserable slave on this work force to see that I will brook no insubordination from now on, do you hear? Right in front of my tent—where everyone can smell the stench."

I blanched. "Now I *know* something's wrong," I said to my friend as we slipped into the background to avoid my stepfather's wrath. "Papinian may be a fool, and he *does* believe in Roman discipline, but he's never crucified anyone capriciously before."

"Let's get out of the way before he has us flogged or something," Lucius said.

"Yes. Come on. We can go and torment the sacrificial animals."

"Sounds like fun."

Lucius and I raced down the hill. From below, I could see my stepfather having an apoplectic fit. His face was quite, quite green; I couldn't see why everyone else hadn't noticed it, unless it was simply that they were frightened of being chastised for criticizing his appearance.

In front of the temple car, the sacred animals were all

penned up in makeshift corrals. Lucius and I climbed
into the enclave of the sacred bulls. There was one huge
creature, an albino, who snorted mightily when he saw
us and charged. But we were fast, and we got up on top
of the wall and made faces at the dumb thing as he ran
full tilt into the fence. A priest entered the pen and
waved angrily at us. "Stop bothering the sacred beasts!"
he shouted. "They've enough troubles as it is, what with
bearing the fate of the world on their shoulders!"

"How long can *you* stay on its back?" Lucius said to
me, nudging me.

"A bloody sight longer than you!" I said. "Why, when
I was ten years old, we used to leap from aurochs to
aurochs when the grownups were hunting."

"Quam tauri merda!" Lucius scoffed. "Watch this,
you silly savage, you!" The bull was circling suspiciously. As it approached our side of the fence, Lucius
did a reckless flying leap and landed, arse-backward, his
arms wrapped precariously around the creature's rump.
Angered, the bull bucked. I was sure Lucius would be
thrown, but he managed to stay on.

I didn't want to be outdone, so the next time the bull
came within reach, I jumped, too. I landed right behind
the neck, jabbing my crotch so hard that I screamed.
Lucius laughed. "So much for your superior savage abili-
ties!" he said, clinging for dear life.

"It's the soft Roman living," I shouted, "it's made a
woman of me, I'm afraid!"

At the moment, a whistle sounded, and the bull came
to a sudden stop, so abruptly that we both fell off.

I ached all over. I sat up, rubbing the dust from my
eyes, and saw Lucius slumped beside me. "Come on!" I
said, shaking him. "Something bizarre is about to happen."

For the high priest, playing a set of panpipes, was
proceeding, with an appropriately stately gait, toward

the white bull, who seemed utterly transfixed by the sound of the music.

"Magic!" I said.

"Rubbish!" said a familiar voice, and I saw that it was the cantankerous Egyptian, who, robed in ceremonial garments, had followed the priest into the corral, holding a basket of grain in his arms. "Science, not magic. The creature has merely been trained to know that the sound of the pipes signifies that dinner is on its way."

"That grain looks rather strange," I said, for it was bright blue.

"Of course it's strange!" Aaye said. "It contains a concoction of substances sensitive to the transcendental radiation of the uranogoraph . . ."

"Uranograph?" Lucius asked.

At once, we both remembered the laboratory back in Rome, the chamber of the farting cow, and the metal plate which Abraham bar-David claimed to be able to read. "When is the creature . . . ah, due to . . ." I said.

"Return to its father in the sky?" the priest said, finishing for me. "Around lunchtime tomorrow, I'd say. Two eagles were sighted going east this morning, which normally portends disaster, so we've decided to accelerate the sacrificial regimen."

"I see," I said. I had the germ of a plan. Lucius was looking at me very oddly.

"Are you thinking what I'm thinking?" he said. "You look as though an oil lamp just lit up on top of your head."

"The uranograph . . ." I said.

"Your stepfather!" Lucius said. The bull, in a remarkable display of docility, was allowing itself to be fed out of the basket, while the priest continued on his panpipes.

"Yes . . . my stepfather. Oh, Aaye, where is it that they keep the sacred blue grain for the sacrificial animals?"

"In the laboratory tent. But don't you go stealing any—"

We were over the fence before he had a chance to finish.

Dinner was a particularly unpleasant experience. It was intended as a farewell banquet for Ursus Erectus, who was returning to his people that evening, and so there was, perforce, entertainment. A half dozen or so slaves had been crucified just outside the entrance to the tent, and their wails quite overpowered the recitation of Sappho's poetry that my stepfather had selected as the evening's edifying entertainment. Sappho's poems are hard to understand at the best of times, being six hundred years old and in a funny dialect of Greek, especially when they are being brayed by a half-drunk bard who, whenever he forgets the words, breaks into long passages of virtuoso yodeling in the Aeolian mode; it was rendered even worse by the screams of the dying. Halfway through one of the odes, this dissonant duet was further embellished by the howling of a distant pack of quoiotuli, which are a wolflike creature native to Terra Nova. Everyone was busy holding their ears—too busy, indeed, to notice the food.

It was perhaps fortunate that all this distraction was going on, for Papinian paid no heed whatsoever to the fact that the bread he was stuffing into his mouth was bright blue. We had bribed one of the cooks to make up a special loaf of it for my stepfather from the transcendental grain we'd stolen from the laboratory.

"Delightful music, eh, what?" he bellowed to us, although we were only two couches away, in between mouthfuls. He appeared to be the only one enjoying the show at all. Then, turning to one of his officers, he said, "Double the paces to twenty or thirty mille passuum a day . . . get more slaves if necessary . . . go across the border and capture some Comanxae . . . I want to reach Tachyopolis by next month, do you hear?"

* * *

As soon as everyone retired, we slipped off to the laboratory tent. It was humid, and the groans of the crucified had not entirely ceased. I held my nose as we tiptoed past the sentries and across the grass, for at least one of the victims had already succumbed, and was stinking up the night. We each carried a torch. As we crept up on the tent, Lucius said, "O merda! There's a light on inside."

"I hope it's not the Egyptian," I said.

We entered the tent and saw Aaye fast asleep on the ground, his head resting on one of those Egyptian pillows—a bracket for the head, sculpted from ivory, and surely most uncomfortable. In another corner, the sasquatch was hunched over some scrolls, reading by the light of an oil lamp, muttering to himself in Hebrew. He was so absorbed that we were actually breathing down his neck before he noticed us.

"Ah! An audience!" he said. "You have come to learn at my feet, doubtless . . . what will it be tonight? A discourse on the Ptolemaic model of the universe? Arguments pro and con the atomic theory of Demokritos?"

"No, no, Abraham," I said. "We need to borrow the uranograph."

"I see," the Sasquatius said, nodding. "You have the same suspicions as I do. I noticed the blue loaf of bread, even if everyone else was too . . . ah, transported . . . by the music to see what you fellows had been up to! Indeed . . . you did for me what I had been planning to do all along. And now . . . if you will come with me, we'll investigate." He took a device from the table and tucked it under one hairy arm.

"Don't you need one of those metal plates? For the image, I mean," I asked him.

"Already taken care of, young man." He groped around the table a little more until he located a flask of some liquid, which he placed under his other arm.

I was a little miffed that my brilliant plan had been

thought of by someone else, but followed the Sasquatius back to the big tent. The sentry gave us only a casual glance as we entered; my stepfather's private cubicle was unguarded. I put my torch in a bracket and we gazed at the snoring, green-faced visage of the special procurator of the railways.

"How silly he looks," Lucius said. I could see that he was desperately resisting the impulse to poke, tickle, or otherwise torment my stepfather.

"Step aside!" the Sasquatius said, and he advanced toward the pallet of my stepfather. Waving the device once or twice over the body to irradiate it with the transcendental humors, he mumbled a few more incantations, in particular a reference to the Tetragrammaton, which is the symbol of the unutterable name of the Jewish deity. Then, placing the device on the floor, he bent down and yanked, from beneath the pallet, a metal sheet which he had undoubtedly planted there sometime during the banquet.

"Now—if the blue loaf has done its work—the entrails of the procurator should be clearly visible upon this plate," he said, "and we will know for certain whether the thing we have been dreading is true . . ."

"Whether he's really my stepfather or—"

"Someone—some*thing* else!" said Lucius, trembling.

It was at that moment that my stepfather woke up—not lazily, as was his wont, but snapping abruptly into wakefulness, as a lamp does when it is lit. "Help, ho!" he screamed. "Guards! Intruders in my tent!"

Torches were being lit. My stepfather sprang out of bed, and several sentries swarmed into the chamber, swords waving, boots clanking.

We stared at Papinian, his face a brighter shade of green than ever.

"Arrest these traitors!" he screamed at the guards. They moved threateningly towards us. "These vermin—posing as my loyal son and his stalwart friend and a man of learning—have tried to assassinate me!"

We were surrounded. Abraham cast the metal plate down on the floor and smashed the flask down onto it.

"Behold!" he screamed, pointing at the raging Papinian. "It is him, not us, whom you should arrest!"

Fumes rose into the air. In the flickering torchlight we saw the image that was forming on the sheet—

What kind of internal organs were these? Stomachs, livers, bones, were all twisted and angular. Peculiar shapes, spiked, coiled, and spiral, swam amongst the organs.

"Proof!" Abraham cried. "This is not General Papinian but an impostor. As chief engineer, I am taking over command of this entire operation until the real General Papinian can be found..."

"It's bloody mutiny!" cried the pseudo-Papinianus, as the guards stared stupidly at all of us and the metal plate seethed and bubbled.

CHAPTER
XVIII

PAPINIAN EXPLODES

"WELL, DON'T JUST STAND THERE," I SHOUTED to the guards, "do something. We've got to capture him—chain him up—prevent him from escaping."

"Capture who, Young Papinian?" one of the centurions asked. "The hairy scientist, or the general?"

"Don't be ridiculous!" I said. "The general, of course. He's a phony, as this metal sheet clearly demonstrates."

The sentries stood scratching their heads.

"Perhaps we'd better arrest everyone and file a report with the Procurator Fortunatus," the centurion said. "After all, he *is* the chief magistrate of Lacotia . . ."

"Yes," said the green-faced simulacrum of my stepfather, "but I am the Special Procurator of the Railways, and it so happens that the strip of land for several mille passuum in either direction of the railway is under my jurisdiction, for it constitutes a separate territorial entity from the surrounding province—"

"An interesting legal point, O procurator!" the centurion said.

"Oh, what's the use?" Lucius said. "Fortunatus is one

of them, too. Who knows where the real ones are! They might as well be on Mars—probably are, as a matter of fact—dullest place in the universe. They don't even have gladiatorial combat there."

"What nonsense, Lucius," I said, "you've never been to Mars, and you're just confusing the issue." Actually I was just jealous of him; I was sure that he had done everything he had claimed to have done on his flying saucer trip from Rome to our ship.

At that moment, the pseudo-Papinian began to shake violently as if in the throes of epilepsy. He frothed at the mouth—the froth was green—and uttered inhuman cries. The soldiers quickly backed away, and several made the sign of aversion, for Roman soldiers are a superstitious lot. My simulacrous stepfather fell to the floor of the tent and rolled around wildly for several moments. "Catch him!" Abraham bar-David cried. "At least hold him down before he does some injury to himself!" When the sentries hesitated, Lucius and I jumped forward and each grabbed one of the creature's arms while he thrashed about. We pinned him down, and at last the guards moved in to help us.

"What are you?" I cried. His eyes seemed to glow. "Whose side are you on? Why have you come here?"

"You idiot!" pseudo-Papinian cried, glaring at the Sasquatius. "This is what you get for fooling around with scientific discoveries before your time ... we future beings are more sensitive to radiation ... you've gone and upset the delicate balance of my cyborg parts ... discombobulated the interlacing of the positronic ROM module ... and now I ... I ... I ..."

"What's he talking about?" I said.

The megapus had whipped out a wax tablet and was hastily jotting down everything with a stylus. "I haven't the foggiest notion," he said, "but it must be of great scientific value. I'll analyze it all later. I didn't realize that the transcendental humors could have such a dramatic effect upon their subjects, but of course, those who have experienced extraterrestrial travel must by their very nature be more sensitive to such humors—"

At that moment, the pseudo-Papinian came apart! Lucius and I staggered back, each holding on to a flailing arm—for each of the creature's body parts seemed to have its own life. One of the legs was jumping up and down and kicking a centurion in the rump. The other leg was twitching and oozing a greenish fluid onto the pallet. Cracks appeared in the torso, and little metal wires sprouted forth, with tongues of blue lightning darting back and forth between them.

"This is tremendous!" the sasquatch said, amending his notes forthwith.

The head of the false procurator detached itself from the body and elevated itself from the ground on metal stalks. It began to scuttle about the chamber, wheezing and regaling us with the futuristic jargon common to all green creatures from flying saucers: ". . . transdimensional vector askew . . . must inform primary unit of inoperative module . . . bombardment of gamma radiation has addled simu-brain functions . . ."

"Remarkable!" the sasquatch said.

"Have you figured out what he's talking about?" I asked.

"Well, not exactly. But he's obviously very uncomfortable with the situation that has developed," Abraham bar-David said. "However, I'm pretty sure that he's not really alive at all. You know, Homer mentions that the god Hephaestus, master craftsman of Olympos, had a number of young women, made entirely of gold, who obeyed his every whim. They were womanlike, you see, but not truly human. I would call them *gynaecoid*, I suppose. Which means, by the same linguistic token, that this creature here, which imitates a man, would be called an *android*."

I shuddered at this newly coined word, and at the

daring of the Sasquatius' concept. "You mean...
someone, somewhere, is controlling him from afar?"

At that moment, the head exploded. We were sprayed
with fragments of bone, brain tissue, and funny little
metal things, and a wet, gooey substance not unlike pea
soup.

"This is horrible," said Lucius as he tried to scrape
the foul matter from his tunica. The legs, trunk, and
arms of my false stepfather erupted all at once, spewing
all sorts of disgusting fluids over everybody. Abraham's
fur was matted, and his wax tablet was bubbling, but he
continued with his notes.

"Well!" the head centurion said, surveying the remnants of the pseudo-Papinianus, whose remains were
now smeared over the walls and furnishings of the tent.
"I think this puts this issue of the general's authenticity
in quite a different light, doesn't it? I mean, you don't
see people coming apart like this everyday—not by
themselves, I mean."

"Spontaneous dismemberment," the Sasquatius said,
"upon exposure to the transcendental humors...
absolutely fascinating."

"I take it you're not going to arrest us?" I asked the
centurion.

"I think that the explosion of the general has proved
your point," the centurion said. "He's a fake all right."

Lucius said, "Of course, that leads us to an even more
important question... where's the real Papinian? And
the real Fortunatus, for that matter?"

"And who," the centurion said, "is to be in charge?"

"Well, the sasquatch is the most knowledgable of the
engineers," I said. "You'd better leave the building of the
railway to him."

"Well, that's all very well, Titus the Younger," the
centurion said, "but he doesn't have any military rank. I
don't think the men would... besides, he's not even a
Roman citizen." The hairy scientist hulked over us all,

glowering; the soldiers all took a step back. One of them slipped on the frothy mess that had once pretended to be my stepfather. The resultant pratfall set off another commotion, as soldiers tripped over each other and slid around on the fragmentary innards of the late simulacrum. They looked so stupid that Lucius and I could not refrain from laughing.

Lucius said, "Well, if it's military rank you need, I might as well remind you that I *am* a tribune. Not to mention the emperor's nephew, and therefore quite possibly the ranking officer. So I command you to obey the orders of the megapus as though they were my own."

"Oh," the chief centurion said, scratching his head once more.

"And while you're at it," Lucius said, "uncrucify those poor bastards out there, will you? Their howling is keeping the whole encampment awake."

It was at that point that the Egyptian came charging into the tent. He barely glanced at the mess. "Enough of this horseplay!" he said, scarcely able to control his agitation. "Something serious is afoot...come outside, come quickly!"

At once, we heard an ethereal music from somewhere far away, far above our heads. It was everything that the drunken bard's yodeling over dinner had failed to be—a symphonia of heavenly voices and trilling flutes, punctuated by a solemn, sensuous drumbeat. The words were in the Lacotian tongue, but were so faint I could not make them out.

We ran outside. The night was bright, much too bright. The illumination came not from the moon; it seemed that the whole sky glowed from within. Those crucified prisoners who had managed to survive thus far looked up and seemed to take comfort.

And there it was...spinning amongst the clouds to the sound of this divine music...a flying saucer!...I hardly dared hope.

The saucer came to rest upon the hillock that over-
looked the railway tracks. We all rushed up to greet it,
centurions, slaves, scientists, Lucius, I, our Lacotian
children who had been wakened by the tumult, priests,
even a sacred bull or two who had managed to break free
from his pen... for the music that emanated from the
celestial vehicle was utterly mesmerizing, its magic irresistable.

The portals of the saucer opened!

And there he was at last: the greatest hero of the Lacotian people, the traveler through space and time, the
conqueror of the Parthians, blazer of trails, darling of
Roman high society—my father, Aquila.

He was magnificent. He rode out of the flying saucer
on a stallion whose flanks had been painted with lightning bolts. Yes, Aquila, too, was green, as was his horse.
But I knew that he had become viridified through his
long travels, and not through some fiendish trick. For
when he saw me he gave a mighty shout and urged his
horse onward, and I saw that there were tears in his
eyes. His face was as withered as the bark of winter
trees, and his long, pale green hair streamed behind him.
He wore a bonnet of eaglefeathers and held aloft a war
lance. He also wore the senatorial toga praetexta, for in
his days on earth he had been made a senator by the
Emperor Domitian. When he came to where I was
standing, he leapt from his horse and embraced me, crying "*Chinkshi, chinkshi*... how tall you have grown, how
handsome... have so many years passed? Ah, my heart
soars to see you again, *chinkshi*."

I don't quite know what happened next. I suppose the
correct, and very Roman, thing to do would have been to
stand, stiff and proud, betraying no emotion at all; or at
the very least to show my father how pleased I was to
see him. I'm not sure why, but instead I began to weep
bitterly and to accuse him of deserting me. "I was sure
you had come for me that night on the ship—and all you

did was deposit that rat Lucius on board! Oh, *até*, why did you never visit me? Why did you let me be taken to Rome and be subjected to so much civilizing that my buttocks are a permanent maze of welts?"

"Oh, Equus, don't be so maudlin!" Lucius said, kicking me. "Uncle Aquila's really gone out of his way to visit us...and he really hasn't got any time for petty domestic squabbles. I mean, the fate of the universe is at stake and all that, isn't it, O Uncle Aquila?"

I turned on Lucius in a fury. "How dare you call him Uncle Aquila?" I screamed. "You're just a bloody *washichun*—a paleface!—and no kin of mine!"

"That's where you're wrong, my son," Aquila said mildly. "Lucius Vinicius happens to be your brother."

"That's not funny," Lucius and I said at the same time.

"Don't worry. I don't expect you to fall into each other's arms or anything. But facts are facts, my son. You know, don't you, that your mother was a Roman patrician?"

"Well, it's a rumor that I always deny whenever someone dares mention it to my face," I said.

"Does the name of the Lady Vinicia mean anything to you? Daughter of a senator, cousin to the emperor himself, she used to visit me frequently when I sojourned in Rome...when she wasn't trysting with gladiators," he said, wrinkling his nose.

"No!" I said. "You can't be serious!"

"Well, fancy that!" Lucius said. "I know my mother likes to fool around, but I didn't realize that she would stoop to mating with, ah..."

"Say it!" I hissed. "Say it, you supercilious, condescending, racist, colonializing son of a—"

"Leave your mother out of it," Lucius said, "and I'll do the same with mine."

The idea that I could actually be related to him made

me almost physically ill. "You double-crossed me to the emperor!" I said.

"I took your side at the schola, didn't I? Nobody's perfect."

I was about to sock him in the jaw when my father put up his hand and restrained us both. "Do not turn on each other, my children!" he said. "Only the direst circumstances have forced me to return to this universe, and I am flouting the most stringent strictures of the Dimensional Patrol. You notice that I'm alone here—usually the Dimensional Patrol sends hundreds of units on any official mission. This isn't official. I'll be in severe trouble if I'm caught. Although, of course, if I am successful in my mission, I'll be given the highest honors. It's sort of like stealing horses—there is much honor in success, and none at all in failure. But you probably have no idea what I'm talking about."

"Your words are dark, father," I said.

"Is there anywhere we can sit down and talk?" Aquila asked. "It would be good to be alone with my son and his half brother for a little while . . . considering they are about to embark on the most perilous adventure in their lives, and that their chances of survival are virtually nonexistent."

"Father!" I exclaimed.

"Uncle Aquila!" Lucius cried, profoundly horrified.

"Do not worry, my children! I am sure you will both exhibit the greatest bravery. Even you, Lucius, braggart and coward though you are at the moment. I have absolute faith in you. If you do succeed in saving the universe, you will achieve great honor. If not—ah, it will have been a good day to die."

TERTIA PARS:

TACHYOPOLIS

CHAPTER
XIX

VISION QUEST

LUCIUS, MY FATHER, AND I LEFT THE MOB, WHO WERE all clustered, gaping, around the flying saucer. We reached Papinian's tent. The crosses had all been cleared; at least one or two of the crucified men had been able to cling on to life long enough to be rescued, for they hobbled forward and fell on their knees before Aquila as though he were some kind of god. Aquila took it in good stride, pausing to wave a benediction over them.

"Thank you, divine one, who has plucked us from the cross!" one of the wretches croaked.

"Bless you," Aquila said.

"Aren't you laying on the godhood a bit thick?" Lucius asked him.

"Don't be impertinent," I said. I was trying to tell myself that it was only a mother we shared, and that at least Lucius' father was not the incomparable Aquila.

"No, no, Lucius is right, in a way," my father said. "It *is* presumptuous of me, but it's a lot easier to try to fit in with these simple people's worldview than to explain about transdimensional warping. That's how your

Roman emperors became gods, you know. Old Julius Caesar realized it was simpler to let the savage Goths and Gauls worship him than to try to explain the mysteries of aqueducts and catapults..."

"But the emperor *is* a god," Lucius protested. "I should know, I mean, he's my uncle. You make it all sound like some fraud perpetrated on an ignorant populace—"

"Ah, but it only took a hundred years for you Romans to start believing your own advertising, you see!"

"He's got you there," I said, singularly pleased that Aquila was putting Lucius down.

We entered the tent. Lucius started to sit down on the couch; but when he saw Aquila and me getting ready to squat down on the floor, he clambered down and got between us, eager for his share of the attention. Aquila pulled an enormous pipe out of his toga. It was not made of pipestone, but some translucent substance. He looked around for something to light it with. I started up to fetch a taper from the brazier, but he motioned me to sit down again. Then he pulled a metallic rod from a fold of the toga. He pointed it at the pipe and sang a few phrases from a song; a bolt of blue lightning shot out and hit the bowl. "Now that's a powerful song," I said.

"Oh, that's my firestarting song," Aquila said. "The rod is equipped with a programmable voice-recognition device, so I simply taught it to remember the song that I learned from an eagle one evening while I was having a vision." I began to see that my father had become strange to me. On the one hand he spoke like a true *wichasha wakan*, that is to say, a homo medicinae, when he recalled learning a song from a beast during a vision; that is the most proper way to acquire a new song. On the other, he would sprinkle his remarks with the jargon of the were-jaguars from the future, and Lucius and I would stare blankly at him until he reverted to normal talk.

"Well, father," I said, trying to steer him back to subjects I might be able to understand, "how have you been keeping these past few years?"

"Years?" he said. "It is impossible to understand years anymore. They don't have seasons, you know. And some of those alternate universes are pretty crazy. There's even one where the Lacotian Empire rules the earth and the Romans are running around in loincloths. And you know what? You start to feel for the Romans, though they are not fortunate enough to be born Lacotian. Then there are other planets, of course—though most of these are about as dull as Omahopolis. *Na.*" He handed me the pipe.

"*Ku.*" I said, taking a puff. "I hope you were joking when you were talking about, you know, Lucius and me going off and dying and all that stuff."

"Ah, you must see it all in perspective. If you are so scared of death, you must have forgotten much, my son. The Romans fear death greatly—that's why they're always building their eternal monuments. They think they'll live through their statues and aqueducts— through stone and metal. Crazy people!"

"What *is* the mission?" Lucius asked.

"I can't exactly tell you. You see, what I'm doing now isn't exactly cricket." He stopped himself. "I mean kosher. I mean . . . oh, it's so hard to limit oneself to the native worldview! . . . there are lots of things you're not supposed to know yet. But this world has already deviated so much from its true path, owing to the interference of the Green Pig, that it is becoming a rogue universe. I suppose I'll have to explain."

He had already lost me, but I didn't want to interrupt him. "There are trillions of parallel universes," he went on, "each deviating from the one next to it only in some trifling detail. The universes are as ears of corn in a field . . . when the wind blows, they all bend as one. But if one cornstalk should grow crooked, and refuse to bend with the others, then . . . snap! Well, our friend the Green Pig caused havoc in this universe. Motorcars were invented before their time; steamships came into being; dinosaurs and bicycles were introduced."

"But," I said in bewilderment, "we defeated the Green Pig, didn't we?"

"Perhaps so. When the Dimensional Patrol straightens up a universe gone wrong, it usually reverts to its true path after a few years. But the anomalies have continued here, and the Council for the Protection of Transdimensional Continuity has ruled this world a rogue universe. That means it can't be fixed anymore. Unfortunately, there are some things about universes on the edge of extinction—things regarding the nature of matter itself, and the stability of certain substances—that render them peculiarly attractive to certain . . . *criminal* elements . . ."

"The Green Pig!" I said.

Aquila said, "I didn't tell you that. Remember, I'm not one to interfere. As for the universe . . . it's been abandoned, the flying saucers have all been ordered out, and the entire universe is due to self-destruct shortly— no one quite knows when. When that happens, why, we will all perish."

"You mean *we'll* perish," Lucius said with some bitterness, "because *you* can just get back in that machine of yours and go back to the future."

"Not at all, my son. My election to come here is defiance of the Dimensional Patrol's regulations. I cannot return. Unless, of course, you succeed in your mission."

"Unless *we* succeed!" I said.

"Yes; I'm afraid I'm going to have to send the two of you off save the universe. I can't. You see, the more I interfere, the quicker this universe is propelled toward extinction. I'm one of the very anomalies that's causing the rogue universe phenomenon; and if I do too much, why then—splat!—valete, O amici!" The old man seemed to be staring at something infinitely far away. "And I do not intend to die among strangers, in an alien time and space. *Hechitu welo!* I will die in a place sacred to the Lacotii; in the Montes Negri will I lie down to depart this existence. I, Aquila, have spoken."

This was not the message I had expected my father to bring me. Even Lucius was sobered by Aquila's revelations, although he was usually the first to perk up at the thought of adventure. This much adventure, all at once, was a bit much for either of us to contemplate. We sat there in an appalling silence, while the fumes of Aquila's pipe rose up from the sacred circle to fill the corners of the universe. The doomed universe, that is.

At last, my father said, in the same tone with which he had projected the extinction of the cosmos, "And now, my children, I want to eat. Have them make me some food—and try to make sure it isn't green. I don't really mind the taste of green pemmican or green buffalo livers, but I've never really gotten used to the thought."

Lucius clapped his hands, and our two ex-slaves emerged from the back. "Bring Aquila some food," he said. They just stood there, gawking at the man who was, after all, one of the greatest figures of Lacotian history. Eventually they ran off and returned with a tray laden with leftovers from the banquet we had held for the departed Ursus Erectus.

"Great stuff, Aquila!" Lucius said. "The cooks really outdid themselves . . . since it was all in honor of Ursus Erectus, the entire repast was on an ursine theme: bears' paws stuffed with honey and baked in a puff pastry . . . bears' hams roasted in their own juices . . . bears' cheeks in aspic . . ."

Was I imagining things, or was Aquila's face turning an even brighter shade of green? Nevertheless, he accepted the food gracefully, and ate greedily. Lucius and I too ate, for politeness' sake. But no bards yowled and no criminals screamed, so there was nothing to distract me from the taste.

"What about this mission of ours?" Lucius asked. The

food appeared to have restored his sense of adventure. "Where must we go, and what must we overcome?"

"Well, I can't tell you that," Aquila said. "That would be interfering, wouldn't it?"

"But, *até*," I said, "if we aren't to know what to do, how can we do it?"

"My son, it is time for you to become a man. It is time for you to embark on your vision quest. That's why I've come back, you see. If the universe should end, I would not have you die without entering fully into the community of our people."

"Father, that's ridiculous! We haven't got time for that now. Aren't you interested in saving the universe at all?"

"Not particularly," said Aquila.

"But a vision quest . . . a journey into the wilderness to seek a message from a spirit . . . how can that help?"

"You've become rather Roman, haven't you?" my father said. "Being a Roman is infectious. There's something about the Roman's obsessive materialism that really—"

"*Até!*" I cried, stung by his rebuke. For during my time in Rome, suffering from the flagellum of Androcles and the dyspepsia of the cuisine, I had clung steadfastly to the notion that I was not as these people. I saw now that it was time for me to be tested, and that it was quite possible that I would fail. When was the last time I'd put on my own clothes or hunted my own food? For years I had waited to see my father again, and now his coming made me miserable and ashamed.

"You'd better take Lucius with you," Aquila added. "He'll probably die, but at least he'll have experienced a real adventure for once in his life."

"But, father—" It seemed like adding insult to injury.

"Not another word!" he said. "I have to be off now. I'm sure the sasquatch will manage the building campaign very nicely until you get back. You might want to drop off those two brats you rescued, too; I think their native village is on the way."

"On the way to where?" I said.

"To Tachyopolis!" Aquila said. Then, covering his mouth, he added, "Uh oh. I've said too much again, haven't I?"

"Tachyopolis!" Suddenly an inspiration hit me. "That's where they've taken Fortunatus and Papinian, isn't it? That must be where the Green Pig is hiding out ...isn't it?"

"Shh! I didn't tell you that!" my father said.

He stared up at the ceiling of the tent for some moments, and then broke into a wheezing chant. As he sang, clouds of green smoke erupted about his person, and he began to float upward. Lucius and I stood up, as if trying to hold onto him. But it was too late. His head had hit the ceiling, and, in a moment, he was blurring into a fine mist and filtering into the outside air.

CHAPTER
XX

INTO THE WILDERNESS

THE FIRST FEW DAYS OF OUR JOURNEY WERE EASY going. The farther away we got from the Roman encampment, the more I began to feel at one with nature, and the more truly I felt myself a Lacotian. The terrain was flat. We rode all day, swiftly, with the wind in our faces, Lucius and I and the two children. Though Lucius left the camp in the uniform of a tribune, and I wearing the toga praetexta, we shed our Roman clothes piece by piece. I tore up my toga to make breechclouts. We hunted and ate well.

We carried only a few clothes now, and our weapons; we also took with us one of those uranograph machines and a supply of the metal plates. I hadn't wanted to do that, but Lucius, for some reason, insisted. "Maybe we'll need to sacrifice some animal on the way," he said, "and we'll need to make sure it's the right animal."

In the summers, the Lacotii are gregarious; small camps from all over Lacotia often join together to form huge metropolises of tipis. One such city of poles and skins was rumored to be found on the north fork of the Flumen Platonis, or River of Plato; it was thither that we

164

journeyed first. This was so that we could deliver the children to their relatives, if such there still were, and so continue toward Tachyopolis by ourselves, perhaps to seek our visions on the way.

Hours before we arrived at the temporary city, I could smell roasting aurochs and see thin lines of smoke against the horizon. The children and I could scarcely contain our excitement. We stopped at a stream to water ourselves and our horses, and Lucius said, "Why, Equus, you're shaking all over. What's the matter?"

I said, pointing at the distant smoke-trails, "Look! Don't you see?"

He squinted. "Well—"

"We're about to see how real human beings live," I said. "The tables are turned. You're the one who's going to have to be civilized now—Lacotian style."

"Oh, that's wonderful!" Lucius said, going all starry-eyed. "I can't wait to steal horses, go into battle, count coup, and all those other thrilling things you people do."

"You'll see," I said.

Though we had been traveling several days, neither of us had mentioned Aquila's great revelation—that we were brothers—to the other. I don't think either of us liked the idea much. Even though Lucius had these romantic ideas about the Lacotii, he still *knew* we were inferior savages. And *I* knew that Lucius, although he could talk up a storm, wasn't ever going to be much good in a real fight. I hardly knew why my father had made me bring him with me.

We reached the outer ring of tipis and found the city curiously deserted. We stood at the edge of the urbs, not quite daring to go on. The children seemed subdued, and stood behind us, staring at the lines and lines of tipis—thousands in number, it seemed.

Lucius said, "By Jupiter, this place stinks. How can you people live like this?"

That was just the sort of thing that made me want to knife him in the gut right then and there, but when I stopped to sniff the air, I had to admit that it did smell rather strange . . . a pungent meld of aromas: of piss, buffalo meat, excrement, human sweat . . . familiar childhood smells, but much more overpowering because I had been without them too long. I had to agree with Lucius that they were not as pleasant as I had remembered . . . but I dared not tell him how I felt.

"You'll learn to enjoy the smell," I said, taunting him, "or you'll never become one of us!"

Certainly, the two children did not seem adversely affected by the odor of the camp. They were starting to cheer up now. Was it just me? Had I become so tainted by my stay in Rome that my own culture was making me uncomfortable?

"Let's see if we can find someone," I said at last.

We tethered our horses to a tree and entered the encampment with our few belongings on our shoulders. Why did I feel as though I were entering enemy territory? I could see the others tensing, too, and they did as I did: darting from the shadow of one tipi to another, moving swiftly and silently, like stalking animals.

We rested for a moment. There was still no sign of human activity. A few dogs scuffled about; one had an enormous piece of roast aurochs in its jaws. We had reached the inner circle. There were the remains of a fire, and the ground was littered with bones and refuse, as though a feast had been hastily interrupted.

"Do you think they've been raided by an enemy?" Lucius asked.

"Unlikely. The Pax Romana holds sway in Lacotia. This is the heart of the province . . . any raiding would be around the borders. Besides, I don't see any scalped corpses lying around." I could tell that Lucius was getting more and more uneasy. So was I, but I had to look as if I knew what I was doing, or I'd look like a fool.

"Maybe," I said, "they've all gone to—" I never finished my sentence, which was just as well, since I had no idea how I was going to finish it. I saw something moving. A tent flap on one of the tipis on the other side of the circle. A face emerged . . . a familiar face . . . Ursus Erectus! "Quickly!" he said. "Before they come back!"

"Before who come back?" I shouted.

He gestured for me to be silent, and beckoned us to cross over to him, all the while staring from side to side as though we were in imminent danger from enemy braves.

We ran into the tipi. "What's going on?" Lucius asked, unable to follow our Lacotian. "Who are we running away from?"

"I don't know!" I said.

Ursus motioned me to be quiet once more. I looked around.

It was dark in the tent; the only light came from some glowing logs. The tipi was crammed with people; frightened women clinging to their children, old men huddled under buffalo robes, and a few braves who attempted to hide their nervousness by preening their hair and adjusting their war paint.

"Would someone please tell us what is going on?" Lucius said.

Ursus said, "O my friends, I must now renew unspeakable grief—"

"Virgil—the *Aeneid*—Book II," Lucius said. "So much for your famous native rhetorical brilliance."

"Leave him alone," I said. "He's trying to tell us something."

"Your classical rhetorical devices, young man, are some of the few useful things we've taken from you Romans," Ursus Erectus said in Latin. He then continued in the usual pidgin Greek with Lacotian phrases thrown in. "When the world was young . . ."

It was twenty minutes before he got to the tale of how

a great treaty had been forged between the Lacotii rebels and the procurator of the railways through the mediation of yours truly; and another ten while he described our Ulysses-like epic journey to return the two Lacotian children to their mothers. "Our people, all camped together along the north fork of the Flumen Platonis, rejoice at the return of our brother Equus Insanus and his friend the *washichun* who is his blood brother. *Hechitu welo!*"

Lucius wasn't at all used to this leisurely pace; even I was about ready to fall asleep when Ursus Erectus finally got to the part of the tale that we hadn't heard yet. "But alas, there is grief mixed in with our rejoicing. In the past days, ever since we made the treaty with the Romans, a flying saucer has been menacing our encampment, and green men have been descending to abduct our people into the sky. One such attack occurred shortly before your arrival, which is why there was no one to greet you or even to tend to the cooking of the aurochs meat."

"Those green men..." Lucius said, voicing my thoughts. "Do they resemble anyone you know?"

"They do appear to look much like certain Roman officials, but it is hard for us to tell, for all you people look alike," Ursus said, knitting his brow.

"Didn't you fight back?" I asked.

"The green men—nothing will stop them! Our braves, forsaking honor in the wake of this terrible danger to all the Lacotii, forswore the counting of coup and went straight for the kill. But you can stick them with arrows and beat in their heads with clubs and stab them with knives, and they just keep on coming. I do not think they are really alive at all."

I said, "Well, we have something that'll work against them. If, that is, they are what we think they are . . . the artificial creatures that the Sasquatius calls *androids*."

"My hunch!" Lucius said. "About bringing the uranograph, I mean. I thought we might have to sacrifice an animal," he explained to Ursus Erectus, who scratched his head, mystified.

Hadn't the pseudo-Papinian exploded when exposed to the transcendental humors of the uranograph? I did not know what kind of range the device would have, and I was not quite sure how it could be tested. "Well, we can take a stab at it," I said.

"It's strange," Lucius said, "what uses a technological breakthrough can be put to, isn't it? This is just the sort of thing that excites the writers of *scientifictiones*. First there was a device for improving the positive results of the college of augurs, and influencing the future ... and now we're using the same thing to ward off attacks of green men from the future. Who knows what other wonders will result from the discovery of these transcendental humors?"

His eyes lit up with the romantic fervor that he always displayed whenever we talked about Lacotian tribal customs. He really was a very silly boy, my friend Lucius, but there were times when I envied him his flights of fancy.

We proceeded to introduce the two children to the group. By comparing genealogies and anecdotes, they managed to figure out who were most likely to be their relatives; and the sister of Ursus Erectus' wife, who would have been married to Ursus as well if the tragedy had not struck the encampment, offered to look after them. So that at least seemed a happy arrangement.

"The flying saucer rarely attacks more than once a day," Ursus said, "so I think we should return to our feasting. After all, it may be a long time before our bellies are full again."

That evening we ate well. It was the first decent food I'd had in many moons, although it gave Lucius a terrible flux of the bowels, which he was forced to alleviate all night long. There was no *mniwakan*. No one was drunk; there was a dark solemnity in our rejoicing.

The men danced in their finery, preparing for war. Painted from head to toe in green, and wearing a tattered Roman toga and an old captured war helmet from Nero's time, one man mimed a green *android*. He ran around the fire in pretended fear as the young braves leaped about him and struck him with their coup sticks. The women sang songs of encouragement as they danced, separate from the men, in a great circle, stamping their feet and swaying their hips sensuously and slowly in time to the drumbeat.

Lucius sat at the circle's edge, watching, when he wasn't off discharging his diarrhea. The dance was nothing like what we had seen in the streets of Rome. There were no hucksters hawking souvenirs, no prostitutes walking up and down the street, no senatorial partygoers in gaudy litters stopping by for a view of the dark side of life in the capital of the known world. I danced for a long time, flinging myself into it with joy and desperation.

When I was too exhausted to go on, I went and sat beside Lucius. He was gnawing on an aurochs bone and drinking some berry juice. "I wish I had some wine," he said.

We watched the dancing. I was bursting with the kind of joy that Rome had never been able to give me. Lucius said, "How can these people act so happy, be so oblivious of the fate that may await them tomorrow? Personally, I'm shitting myself, and it's not just because of the awful food either."

For all their love of superfluous violence, the Romans are really quite frightened of death. I suppose that's why they laugh their heads off at some poor wretch being eaten by lions in the arena. I tried to be afraid the way Lucius was afraid, but I was becoming more and more calm within myself, not more and more terrified. I was sorry for Lucius . . . much the way, I suppose, that he had been sorry for me when I was an alien amongst Romans, unable to appreciate their ways.

"Come on," I said at last, "I'll teach you this war dance."

"I couldn't. I mean . . . this is the real thing, isn't it?"

I finally pulled him off his haunches and dragged him back to the circle. He struggled, at first, against the power of the drumbeat. But at last he could no longer hold himself in, and he gave himself up to the pounding rhythm, leaping up and down and stamping his feet like any other brave.

CHAPTER
XXI

ATTACK OF THE GREEN MEN

WE COULDN'T GET TO SLEEP FOR A LONG TIME, BUT kept whispering back and forth across the chorus of snoring. Lucius and I were jammed together under a single buffalo robe, and there were at least three other people in there with us, people of indeterminate gender.

"Why don't they just run away?" he asked. "I mean, they're just a sitting target here for the depredations of the green men."

"The people feel defeated...haunted by a dark spirit," I said. "Perhaps if one of them could have a vision...and lead the people in a mighty sundance...it would put the fire back into their hearts."

"Sundance? I'm not sticking any sharp objects through *my* tit, let me tell you!"

"*You* don't have to," I said. "You're only a Roman."

"You people are just as bigoted as we are, aren't you? If not worse. I still say it's barbaric to pierce one's breasts and thread them with leather thongs and string yourself up to poles and try to rip yourself free. Bloody disgusting, if you ask me, old chap."

"You enjoyed watching it in the arena, didn't you?" I said angrily.

"Well, of course. But that was entertainment. People will do anything in show business."

I clenched back my anger, remembering the time we'd seen wolves raping women to death in the Circus Maximus back in Rome. They were being punished for insulting the emperor. Their remarks had been overheard and reported to the secret police, and the Praetorians had come for them. Show business, indeed.

We slept at last, crowded by dozens beneath the buffalo robes. Just before dawn, Lucius shook me awake. I started. It was dark, and the air was thick with the smell of sweat and the sound of snoring. "Come on!" he said. "We've got to figure out a plan. Come outside where we can talk."

He and I made our way stealthily over the sleeping bodies until we reached the door-flaps. "For one thing," he said, "we've only got one of those uranograph devices. And who knows how many of the enemy there are."

He was right, of course. Even though we did have a weapon capable of making pseudo-Papinians explode, we didn't even know if it would work every time, or *how* it worked, or how many times it could be used before it ran out of transcendental humor.

We slipped outside, crossed the camp to where our horses were tethered, and got out the uranograph. In the twilight we peered at it closely, trying to find some extra clues as to how to use it. Unfortunately, what instructions there were—if such they were—were inscribed upon it in the Hebrew tongue, with here and there an Egyptian hieroglyphic thrown in. All it was, really, was a wooden box. Five of its sides were lined with metal—lead, it seemed to be—and the sixth had a circular opening covered with a round, fat piece of crystal or glass, with a kind of hood over it. "I imagine we take the hood off to fire," I said.

"But what about all those magic formulae he was reciting as he waved the device over Papinian?" Lucius asked.

"Probably just nonsense words he uses to impress us suckers," I said. "All scientists do that. Long words sound more scientific. If they didn't have them, people like us just wouldn't believe it was real science. Or real sorcery, for that matter. It's all the same thing."

"All the same, I don't feel right just pointing the damn thing at anything green that rushes at me."

"Say anything," I said.

"I suppose," he said dubiously.

I shrugged. "All right. What you need is a personal song, one that's taught to you by some spirit animal in a dream. The sort of thing you'd learn when you go on a vision quest."

"We *are* on a vision quest, aren't we?"

"What temerity!" I said. "*We*, indeed! You're not even a Lacotian! You heard what Aquila said—you're just along for the ride, *and* you're probably going to die before we reach Tachyopolis anyway..."

"Shut up! Listen!"

From far above our heads came a high-pitched whine. We looked up. Dawn was breaking over the plains, and a flying saucer was hovering ahead, glittering with fiery light.

"In the name of Jove, how are we going to fight that thing?" Lucius said.

"I don't know. Let's keep out of sight for a moment."

"Maybe it'll miss us altogether."

"Miss us?" I scoffed. "We're going to battle it with this infernal machine... we're going to go down fighting ... it is a good day to die!" I had to screw my courage up. It would be shameful to run away in front of all my people ... and even more embarrassing to flee in front of

Lucius Vinicius, my ever-so-aristocratic half brother.

The flying saucer was getting closer now. Somehow it seemed to know just which part of the camp was inhabited, for it flew right past the empty tipis, and paused only momentarily where Lucius and I were standing next to our horses. Then it swept over to the cluster of tipis where what remained of our people were hiding.

"After it!" I cried.

"After it? With our bare hands?"

"You hold onto the uranograph," I said, with considerably more bravado than I actually felt. "I'll use my bare hands."

Lucius clutched the device in both arms. We ran toward the inhabited sector as the flying saucer descended lower and lower until it hung motionless directly over the tent where we had slept. No sounds at all came from within the tipi, but I knew that they were all inside, holding their breath. Even a Lacotian infant does not cry, for by the time it is a few weeks old, it has learned that it dare not so. It might alert an enemy and betray the entire village. Our people are good at keeping silent, and so it must have been with some technological device of the far future that the flying saucer was able to detect their presence within the tipi. The silence was so complete that Lucius was completely unnerved, and we stopped dead by a tree across the clearing from the tipi. Even I felt chilled by the unnatural stillness.

For a few heartbeats the saucer just hung there.

Then, without warning, the whining crescendoed to a roar. A vast portal opened up in its belly, and dozens of hot-air balloons came bursting forth!

"What on earth—" Lucius began.

"Those are hot-air balloons!" I said. "No time to explain—you weren't with us on our last adventures—but they're what the Olmechii use for transport!"

"Olmechii—"

"You know, down south . . . they have their own

empire . . . by the maidenhead of Venus, didn't you read my idiot stepfather's memoirs?"

"You mean . . . the pyramid-building, sun-worshipping southerners who are ruled by the were-jaguars and build enormous stone heads . . . *those* fellows? Good heavens! I thought Papinian had made the whole thing up."

"Of course not! Come on!"

The hot-air balloons dangled over the camp for a moment. Each balloon was painted to resemble a huge face —one of those flat-nosed stone faces that my father had once described to me, faces of the people of the Olmec Empire. A basket hung from each, and people were moving around in them. From below I couldn't tell if they were green, but some of them certainly looked like Papinian and Fortunatus.

One of them held up some kind of futuristic device, and suddenly we were in the midst of a tornado! The tipis were flying apart. Aurochs skins and lodgepoles were scattering, being sucked into the sky. Our people were abruptly revealed, squatting, huddling, squeezed together in too few tipis. As soon as they became visible the panic began. Women, cradling their babies, ran in every direction. Warriors stood shaking their weapons impotently. "We're going to get blown away!" I said as the wind buffeted us against the tree.

"Up we go!" Lucius shouted, springing up, grasping the swaying branches. I followed suit. Pieces of wood pelted my face and the leaves got into my mouth and nostrils, but I went on climbing. We wedged ourselves into adjacent forks and held on for dear life.

Green men were leaping down from the hot-air balloons, and hundreds of ropes were being thrown down, so that each balloon appeared to be the center of a gigantic spider web. Although the fall would have killed a normal man, these *androids* appeared to feel nothing at all. As they approached the ground, little flames burst out from cylinders they wore on their shoulders and on the heels of their sandals. They were maneuvering about in the air by means of those flames, chasing after the Lacotians. Every time they grabbed one, they would tie a rope around the victim and he would be hoisted up until he dangled, kicking and screaming, from the basket of the hot-air balloon. "What a spectacle!" Lucius cried out. "If only we could have such a thing in the arena!"

I rolled my eyes. People were flying around in the air—some of them being jerked up and down on the ends of cords, others being sucked up by the whirlwind-making device, others still, the green reproductions of our favorite Roman high officials, darting about on their flame-propelled sandals, occasionally swooping down to tie up another hapless Lacotian. Screams filled the air as Lacotians flailed helplessly at their captors. The pseudo-procurators seemed invulnerable as braves hammered at them with tomahauca and knives and even Roman swords.

"What are we going to do?" Lucius wailed.

I couldn't think of anything. Although I had been well trained in the hunt, and in the art of sneaking up on an enemy encampment to count coup, and had a reasonable theoretical grasp of other aspects of the Lacotian art of war, this was one contingency that my father had never mentioned to me when he taught me how to fight. Improvising, I said, "We wait here until there's an opening. Then we make our move."

"You have no idea how reassuring that is," Lucius screamed.

"Shut up!" I said as the two children we had once rescued sailed past my face and up toward a waiting hot-air balloon. The little boy screamed out my name. I reached out toward him. For the tiniest instant his fingers brushed against mine, and then he was swept up. I heard his cry upon the wind, *"Chiyé! Chiyé!"* that is to say, "O frater!" and watched them both become like little dolls, swinging back and forth, back and forth, while the raging wind blasted my face . . .

There was still no sign of the Green Pig, only his diabolical lackeys, who, as they flew by, urged each other on in voices that sounded precisely like those of Papinian and Fortunatus. "Bloody good show! Caught another one, eh, what? Jolly decent!"

"I can't stand this any longer!" I said. "I've got to do something! *Huka hey!* It is a good day to—"

"Not so fast!" Lucius said. "I've got the uranograph, and I'm staying right here. You're not going to get me to go charging into this mess." He hugged the device to his chest. I tried to pry it loose, but he only clutched it harder.

"Give it to me!" But he wouldn't budge. I started pummeling him with my fists, and when that didn't work, I resorted to tickling him under the armpits. He started to screech with laughter and he was bawling at the same time. "What a crybaby," I said. He butted me away. I punched him in the face. I was furious. It was just like Lucius Vinicius to back out every time I really needed someone responsible beside me. I punched him over and over until he howled with fear and rage.

Suddenly I heard a familiar voice behind my shoulder. "I say, Titus Papinianus Junior! Rather a silly time to be roughhousing in the treetops, isn't it? I've half a mind to have you flogged on the spot!"

I let go of Lucius and turned my head. Just as I feared, one of the pseudo-Papiniani was hovering beside my branch, knotting a rope and getting ready to haul me in. "Oh, no, you don't!" I said. "Give me the confounded uranograph!" Lucius was so mortified at the proximity of the *android* that he lost his grip. The device flew from his arms and lodged itself in another fork, just far enough away so I couldn't reach it.

Pseudo-Papinianus laughed. He flew in closer, his green hands clutching the rope. "Sorry, old thing, but I have to take you in. You happen to be on the priority list. Can't be helped."

"Get off me, you—you—"

I swung out with my fists. All I did was knock myself off balance. I was hanging upside down, holding on by my crossed legs.

"Are you all right, old chap?" It was Lucius, coming out of his state of shock. "Uncle Papinian, what are you doing to him?"

"Grab my legs, stupid!" I screamed. Just as I was about to lose my grip completely, he managed to seize them. My head collided with a swinging branch, and I saw the uranograph bounce farther down the branch. Several more Papiniani and Fortunati had closed in on us. They were standing on the bough I was on and jumping up and down to try to dislodge us.

I managed to grab onto the next branch, yelled to Lucius to let go of my feet, then swung myself across like a monkey. The green men saw that I wasn't on the same tree limb anymore, so they began swarming across. "Shake the branches, Lucius!" I cried out, and he did so, sending about half a dozen of them sprawling. They were hanging on as best they could—by their arms, by their legs, one even by his chin. I kicked him off.

"Playing hard to get, are you?" he said as he dropped down. The flames on his sandals cut in, and he was aloft again. He pulled a metal box out of his toga and started to talk into it. "Time to turn on the suction again, boss," he said. As soon as he spoke, the entire tree began to shudder. I saw that a hot-air balloon was directly overhead, and that the whirlwind-creating device had been aimed directly at us. The pseudo-Fortunatus burst into a fit of supercilious cackling. The tree was being pulled into the air by the roots! In consternation I held on tight, my hands only a handspan away from the uranograph, inching my way toward the device.

At last my fingers closed around it. I dragged myself

along the branch, the bark cutting my arms and legs. The whole tree was spinning madly as we rose into the air. We were drawn upward by an irresistable force, and soon we were flying high above the encampment, the treetop firmly stuck to the side of the balloon, and humans swinging from strings all around us, screaming, cursing, and puking into the morning air.

I pulled myself together. The flying green men were gone. I saw them flitting about beneath us, roping in more hapless Lacotii. Lucius' elbow was in my face. I moved it and he yelped in terror. "It's only me," I said. I looked around us. Several balloons floated around us, each with its own strings of captives streaming below it. We were all moving toward the belly of the flying saucer, which seemed to fill half the sky.

We were a couple of cubits below the basket itself. "Come on," I said. "Let's start climbing."

"What for?" Lucius said.

"I've got this now." I brandished the uranograph.

"Oh, good," he said, much heartened. I suppose he must have realized by now that if we didn't do something we'd just die in vain. We clambered up until our faces were peering over the edge of the basket . . .

And beheld six or seven Papiniani and Fortunati, all green, sitting around on couches, drinking wine from silver goblets and having a smashing time. "We'll soon have the entire area cleaned up," said one of them, "and the entire population moved to the mines." He tended the flames in the center of the platform, which, by an elaborate system of pipes and vents, sent hot air into the balloon itself.

"I don't understand," said another. "Why doesn't Viridiporcus Rex just swoop down in a spacecraft and scoop all of them up at once? These hot-air balloons do seem a trifle clumsy, what."

"His Viridiporcine Majesty thinks that the introduction of too much futuristic technology would destabilize the universe and only hasten its collapse, and we might not be able to get all the stuff out in time. I say, old thing, got any more of that Lesbian wine, what?"

Viridiporcus Rex—had the Green Pig set himself up as some kind of emperor over a kingdom of funny green duplicates of my stepfather? What stuff were they trying to get out, and why? I hung on to the side of the basket, trying to puzzle it all out.

"I do believe we're all being summoned now," said one of the green men, putting a metal box to his ear. "I'd better activate the homing device."

Glancing to one side, I noticed that the flying saucer had opened up wide the portal on its underside, and that several balloons, with their attached captives, were already being pulled inside, again by one of those invisible, irresistable forces that these creatures were so fond of using. There wasn't any time to lose. Pulling myself up with what remained of my strength, I managed to haul myself over the side and onto the platform itself. "*Huka hey!* Alea jacta est!" I shouted, and pointed the uranograph at one who had most recently spoken, who was fiddling with the knobs of yet another of their devices. I yanked the hood off the crystal opening and rammed it into the green man's face. He exploded, spattering me with green slime. I charged, spraying the green men with the transcendental humors. I slipped in slime and dropped the uranograph, but Lucius was right behind me, picked it up, and threw himself into the attack. It was over in seconds.

The couches were running with green ooze, and various body parts lay jerking spasmodically. A decapitated green head hit me in the stomach and sent me reeling.

"You idiot!" the head said. "The homing device hasn't been set. Now we won't be able to get back inside the flying sau—"

I kicked the head overboard.

Whatever it was that had plucked up the tree must

have been turned off, because the tree dropped away. In fact, the entire whirlwind effect seemed to be over. All the balloons, except our own, had been absorbed into the belly of the saucer.

"Look—it's another saucer!" Lucius said, pointing at a second vehicle that was approaching. "It seems to be attacking the first one."

It was true. The second saucer flew in circles around the first, and blasts of brilliant blue light were hurled from it like the thunderbolts of Jove. The first responded in kind.

"It's my father," I said. I knew that Aquila had come, risking a further deterioration of the universe's reality, to rescue the Lacotii. But was he too late? I could not tell. For the two flying saucers chased each other far into the distance, until they were two tiny disks against the mid-morning sun, shooting delicate filaments of light at each other.

We had been left behind. Lucius and I looked at each other, and then over the basket's edge, from which about twenty or thirty hysterical people were suspended. The countryside drifted by; the encampment was already about a mille passus to the east. We threw the remains of the green Papiniani over the side, wiped off one of the couches as best we could, and sat down for a much deserved rest.

"What now?" I asked.

"Well, there's still a lot of wine lying around," Lucius said, picking an amphora off the floor and sniffing it. "Not a bad vintage, either—Chian, I think—bottled as far back as the reign of Claudius. After a stiff drink, we'll have to figure out how to land this thing."

CHAPTER
XXII

THE MONTES NEGRI

A HUNDRED OR SO MILLE PASSUUM AND ABOUT three jugs of wine later, we weren't in much of a position to figure anything out at all. The wind was carrying us steadily toward the northwest; and since our mission was supposed to carry us toward Tachyopolis, I saw no harm in just drifting. We lay back on our couches, wallowing in wine and green slime, as the sun rose higher and higher in the sky. Now and then we went to look over the edge at our human pendants, most of whom seemed to have fainted, though one or two were actually enjoying the ride. There were a couple of children, in particular, who were whooping it up at the top of their lungs. Our two children, as a matter of fact. We hadn't succeeded in returning them to their next of kin after all.

"Bloody good show, wasn't it?" Lucius said, burping. "By Priapus, I feel like puking." He staggered over to the edge and stood beside me.

"Not on the people," I said, laughing.

"I need to take a piss, too."

"Not on the people! They'll just take it as another

example of imperialist arrogance." I reached for the wine amphora. We had exhausted the fine Claudian vintage, and were now downing a sour, vinegary liquid that burned our throats. But we were past caring. Truly, *mniwakan* is a miraculous substance.

As for trying to land the hot-air balloon: we played with the various pipes and levers in an attempt to steer the balloon, or to raise or lower it; nothing seemed to work. We were in the hands of Jupiter Vacantanca, and in the power of the wind and the wine. An ecstacy seized us as we caroused. The wind was so strong that we were often pinned to the couches we sat on, or against the side of the platform as we gazed at our hapless passengers.

"How does this bloody apparatus work, anyway?" Lucius said.

"Hot air, I think."

"Well, how about cooling down the air?"

The center of the platform contained an enormous brazierlike device, from which the hot air, pushed through tubes in a manner similar to the operation of the caldarium of a public bath, issued forth. We could see red-hot logs; piles of neatly bound faggots lay to one side. Presumably there were normally slaves to stoke the flames, but we had none, for all the denizens of the basket had been reduced to green slime. "Eventually," I said, "this thing will presumably cool down anyway, if we just leave well enough alone; the fire will go out, and then, I suppose, we'll start to drift back down to earth."

"Well, it better hurry up," he said, "or we're liable to smash into yonder mountains..."

I looked to the west. There were, indeed, mountains: mountains covered with pines, black against the horizon. "The Montes Negri...the black hills sacred to the Lacotii," I said. "We have almost reached the edge of Rome's dominions!" What a thrilling thought, to know that Rome had boundaries—to see those boundaries so close. For, although Rome laid claim to lands westward of here, the kingdoms of the Siosionii and the Quaquiutii, and indeed all the way west to the Oceanus Pacificus, we all knew that this was a fiction, and that Papinian's so-called western conquests were nothing but propaganda.

The sight of the hills, and the sunlight making the treetops glisten like the thousand shields of a distant army . . . for the first time, I felt that I was coming home. For these hills had been the sacred burial grounds of the Lacotii for many generations. My grandfathers and their grandfathers lay here, laid out on simple scaffolds in the trees, open to the sun, wind, and sky. Romans had seen the Montes Negri, and named them in the Latin language, but they had never built settlements here, unless you counted the bogus Tachyopolis, which was surely abandoned by now. I whooped for joy. So did Lucius, catching my mood. We drank more wine and tossed the used jugs overboard, much to the chagrin of our hangers on. At length I was so full of the heady liquid that my bladder felt like bursting.

"I really have to go," I said. "And so do you."

"Not off the edge!" Lucius said. "Or the people down there'll think it's the gods or something."

"Lacotians are not credulous like you Romans are."

"Remember when we pissed on the priests? Jove, that was funny."

"I wish we could live that day all over again."

"Let's have a pissing contest—"

"The fire! That's it! We'll douse the fire and that'll cool down the hot-air balloon until it lands."

"Why didn't you think of that before?"

"I was drunk, stupid."

"You're still drunk."

"I know I'm drunk! Wahoo!"

I pulled out my *sluka* and staggered over to the central heating unit. My aim was poor, but there were at least three or four amphorae of wine in me. I drenched the whole apparatus. It started to steam up. Lucius presently began to urinate himself.

"By Jupiter, the smell!" Lucius said.

It was true. We were choking so hard on the stench of burning piss, and there was so much smoke, that we didn't notice we were falling for quite a long time.

Until we heard the screaming...

We ran to the edge. One of the hills reared up, horribly close. We were going to crash. The balloon made a noise like the flatus of a whale, and we were careening through the sky. Down below us, our passengers were all quite, quite awake now, and none of them was pleased. They were screaming; some were thrashing against the wind. We're going to die, I thought, without ever finding out what's really happening to this universe of ours.

"Grab something—anything!" Lucius said. "Or we're liable to fall out of this thing!"

We were both hugging couches. They were sliding up and down as the balloon swerved. I tried to grasp Lucius' hand as my couch veered past his. We both crashed into the edge. I slipped. My legs smashed holes in the thatching. My crotch slammed into one of the supports and prevented me from falling to my death. I yelped from the sharp pain. I looked back and saw Lucius rolling around on the floor.

"This is where your artistic pissing patterns get us, you ignorant, ignoble savage!" Lucius yelled. Or something like that. The wind was roaring so loudly that he could barely be made out. He crashed into my back and crushed my procreative parts even more firmly against the wooden support. I wanted to kill him right then and there. But I was thoroughly pinned down, the wind was buffeting us, and we were falling now—not just casually drifting landward, but dropping precipitously onto the side of a mountain. Thousands upon thousands of lodgepole pines jutted straight up at us.

In that moment, knowing that death was near, I

searched my mind for a deathsong that I had once overheard from a solitary warrior who had decided to seek
the ultimate honor by allowing himself to be tethered to a
pole so that he could not turn his back upon our enemies, the Apsaroke. I closed my eyes and began to mur-
mur the words as best I could remember them. The wind
seemed to burn me. I tried to make myself calm, and to
send my spirit away from myself, for already I must be
at the edge of the Land of Many Tipis, from which we
can appear to our earthbound friends only in dreams and
visions. As I sang softly to myself, my fear lifted. My
heart was light, as though I had already become an eagle.

"What are you singing for?" Lucius shouted. He
wasn't in the least bit calm.

"Just like a Roman," I said loftily, "to be so excited
about death . . . even though the sight of gladiators killing
themselves affords nothing but amusement." And went
back to the song.

"Yes, but when it's one's own death one is contemplating—"

"Come, Lucius, I laugh at death." For the words of
the song were "Come and fight me! Or are you a
woman? Fight me, fight me!" I tried to make him sing
them with me. But my spirit was already detaching itself
from these events, and as I looked up I could see,
beyond the excruciating sunlight and the vistas of tree
and mountain, a creature that could only be part of the
vision I had been seeking . . .

I was walking through the clouds. The sun was in my
face. The brightness hurt my eyes, but I could not avert
my gaze, for I knew that if I looked down I would see the
world spinning dizzily below and I would fall. Mists
parted to let me pass. I stared at the circle of fire, letting
hot tears stream down my cheeks. Dancing, I stared at
the sun. And the creature danced, too. It was a bird,
perhaps; at first I thought it must be an eagle, for my

father might easily come to me in an eagle's shape.

"Are you my father?" I called to it. But then I saw that its wingspan far exceeded an eagle's and that its wings were vast and leathern, like a bat's. It screeched, and its cry was curiously plaintive, like that of a new-born baby. And there was something about it that was like a lizard as much as a bird . . .

The creature spoke to me.

"The world is a circle and you have stepped out of the circle. But within the circle is renewal. Enclose it in such a circle, and the world will have life again. You will lead the people in a dance, for all the universe exists by virtue of its dancing. I, the Great Mystery, say this to you. *Hechitu welo!*"

And I cried out, "Grandfather, how?"

But the lizard-bird did not answer me. It flapped its wings once, twice, three times, and then swooped down upon me, talons wide, with its wings outstretched, falling against the burning sun disk—

And I found myself singing a new song, not the one I had overheard the long-dead warrior sing, but a secret one whose words shall be known only to me.

"What the—" Lucius was shaking me. Abruptly I snapped out of my vision. "The lizard-bird," I said. "The lizard-bird that spoke to me—"

"Of course there's a lizard-bird," he said. "And it thinks dinner's being served!"

I looked up. Yes, the creature from my vision was there in the flesh, gripping the hot-air balloon with its claws. There were, in fact, dozens of them. They held us aloft in their beaks and talons, and they looked, indeed, remarkably hungry. Although they had undoubtedly saved us from crashing into the mountainside, it seemed as though a worse fate might be in store for us.

"But I had a vision!" I said. "And in the vision—"

"This is reality, Equus. You Lacotians and your visions! You sit there, all glassy-eyed, contemplating the ineffable, while I'm being scared out of my wits."

The creatures were worrying at the balloon, and while they did so we were no longer falling, just rocking precariously back and forth. I managed to squeeze myself free and to stand unsteadily, holding on to the side with both hands.

"It was an important vision," I said, "and I think it shows us a way out of this dilemma." In truth, I wasn't sure what the vision meant at all, but it was my vision and mine alone and I had to show some sort of solidarity with it.

"What *are* those monstrous birds, anyway?"

"I would say, judging from my previous experiences in the stronghold of the Green Pig, that they are beasts from the world's distant past, of the kind that my stepfather's learned friends call *dinosauria*," I said. I remembered the baby brontosaurus in the arena in Alexandria... the nasty tyrannosaur that tried to eat Papinian during his crucifixion... and how the Green Pig had brought the creatures through a time portal for his own entertainment. What was it the Time Criminal had said? "I've always loved Romans, Indians, and dinosaurs. I wanted to have them all in the same place." The Green Pig persisted in calling the inhabitants of Terra Nova *Indians* because, in an alternate universe he was more used to, Lacotia had been conquered by warriors who crossed the Oceanus Pacificus from India.

The sight of these animals disturbed me. I knew that the Green Pig, who would stop at nothing in his relentless attempt to muddy the river of history, must be nearby. The fact that one such creature had actually invaded my transcendent vision confused me even more. But I know now that all creatures—no matter how bizarre—spring from the Great Mystery, and that one's spirit grandfathers are nothing if not inveterate pranksters.

In any case, all the above thoughts raced through my mind for only the tiniest moment, for we were, after all, hurtling headlong from the sky. The winged dinosaurs had stopped pecking at the balloon, and they were actually flapping about beside, around and beneath us. Eventually they would probably realize they could start plucking a few plump morsels off the balloon.

"We'd better jump," Lucius said.

I looked down at the treetops as they rushed past. The pines looked deadly—not much to buffer one's fall. But ahead there was a thicket of much leafier trees with spreading branches and fluffy foliage. It wasn't much, but it might be a softer landing.

"Now or never!" shrieked Lucius.

"What about them?" I said, pointing at the dozens that still dangled beneath us.

"It's every man for himself," he said, preparing to leap.

We were right above the spot now. Lucius couldn't wait. I said, "I'm going to cut these people free so they'll at least have a chance." For the vision had told me that I was part of the circle of life, and that to step outside the circle would unsettle the balance of the universe.

"I'll leave the heroics to you," Lucius said, and jumped off the edge.

I pulled a sword from the paraphernalia still scattered about the platform and began sawing at the ropes that bound our passengers.

"What are you doing?" one of them screamed. "Trying to get us killed?"

"At least you'll have a chance this way!"

I ran around, hacking at the ropes as fast as I could. One dinosaur was tangled in the ropes that attached the balloon to the basket; several were squawking at me and trying to get at me with their beaks; one or two gripped pieces of the balloon and were trying to fly in opposite directions.

I cut off the last of the ropes. I looked back and saw people swarming all over the canopy of foliage. But it was too late for me. I was back among pines. "I'm going to be killed," I thought. At least I had saved the lives of my people. Even Lucius. I saw him now, clinging to a treetop. Should I jump? Wildly I stared at the terrain below, hoping for another clump of soft trees. Nothing of the kind. I was about to jump anyway, praying to Jupiter Vacantanca that I would only break a few bones and not my neck, when one of the flying saurians seized me by my breechclout and dragged me from the basket!

Helplessly I watched as balloon, basket, and all crashed into the trees. We were climbing higher and higher, and the creature's claws dug into my sides . . . and my breechclout was coming loose. Had I not expended my bladder on the dousing of the brazier's flames, I do not doubt that I would have emptied it now. I was so frightened that I could not even remember the words of the warrior's deathsong. The dinosaur circled, and then separated from the flock and soared even higher. I was dizzy and lightheaded, and I couldn't breathe.

At last I divined the dinosaur's objective. A ledge of naked rock jutted from the surrounding green. A ledge piled high with enormous, mottled, spherical white things. I wondered when they were going to hatch . . .

I was going to be dinner all right . . . dinner for a gaggle of baby lizards from the past.

My only hope was that I'd be too exotic . . . the dinosaurian equivalent of larks' tongues in aspic or braised hummingbirds' brains. Although if the father dinosaur was anything like a Roman paterfamilias, they'd be eating me whether they liked me or not.

CHAPTER
XXIII

THE CITIES OF GOLD

I WAS UNCEREMONIOUSLY DUMPED ONTO THE LEDGE. I rubbed my arse and looked around. It all seemed very precarious. I tried not to look over the edge. There was probably some hideous abyss yawning away below. Trying to figure out how far I would fall before breaking my neck seemed the sort of futile academic exercise that sasquatches and Egyptians are prone to.

It was late afternoon and the sun glared down on me. I was tired and hungry and still a bit drunk. There were about half a dozen of the dinosauria eggs scattered about. They were enormous—about the size of the head of the Emperor Trajan. These flying lizards seemed to be a lot more careless than real birds would have been, for there was no nest as such, and there were fragments of dozens more eggshells lying around. The eggs were obviously an easy target for predators. I thought of what those predators must be like. I shuddered.

Then I got to thinking about how hungry I was . . .

I approached the nearest egg—with some trepidation —and knocked to see if anyone was home. There didn't seem to be any answer, so I took out my knife and painstakingly bored a tiny hole in the small end. Then I leaned back against the rock and started sucking. It felt wonderful to be eating a decent raw egg and not an egg custard simmered with brains and honey.

The yolk was warm and made my stomach positively hum with well-being. Indeed, I was so comfortably replete that I wanted to curl up and go to sleep, and it was some moments before I noticed the rat-tat-tat of cracking eggshells...

I nearly jumped out of my skin when I turned around and saw a couple of baby lizard-birds squawking and craning their necks and padding back and forth over the debris. They were scrawny, ugly creatures. I watched in a sort of hideous fascination as they started to hop about. At length they espied me. I'd better get out of here fast, I told myself. But there didn't see to be a way to leave the ledge. Unless...

At last I forced myself to look at what I had envisioned as the great yawning abyss. In fact, it was only about ten cubits wide, and there was another ledge across and a little lower down. It was just too far to jump across. Or was it? I stood right at the brink of the precipice. Jumping was the only way across. I looked down. I screamed. It just seemed to go down and down and down, and it was rock all the way. It was making me dizzy. Everything was swirling: the rocks, the distant trees, the brilliant sky.

I turned to see the baby dinosaurs making halting attempts at flight. They were spreading their wings and trying to catch the wind as they ran along the ledge. I was still screaming and I guess I attracted their attention. One of them became airborne and made straight for my eyes.

I was too startled to be scared. I just leapt the entire distance across the gulf. I landed flat on my face with my legs dangling over the edge. Everything ached. I pulled myself all the way onto the shelf. The baby dinosaurs didn't seem confident enough to fly at me, so I giddily taunted them, turned my back, and climbed higher.

The face of rock wasn't that steep here. I found a few hand- and toeholds and was soon straddling the very summit. To the east, the vistas of hill and forest seemed to stretch endlessly. But what I beheld when I turned my eyes to the west was a spectacle of such magnitude that I blinked and rubbed my eyes several times before I could even believe what I saw.

Carved into the rock was a narrow stairway that wound its way, it seemed, all the way down to the valley below. The steps were faced with mosaic stones that depicted mythological scenes, just like those in a Roman house. It was like a thin white worm wiggling through the forest . . .

And in the valley itself stood buildings: archways, polygons, great curving roads that hung in the air without supports, pylons, towers, ziggurats, temples, coliseums, palaces . . . complexes within complexes. The entire city appeared to have been dipped in gold, and in the bright sun it glittered and brought tears to my eyes. Sailing between the structures were fleets of hot-air balloons; many of them were transporting the huge, flat-nosed heads of which my father had once told me . . . the artifacts of the southern empire, the land of the Olmechii.

There were other cities, too, smears of gold against the hills. And more astonishing yet, the cities were linked by a network of railway tracks upon which dozens of ferrequi puffed. I couldn't see them all that well, but I had the uncanny suspicion that the insignium upon the side of each of the railway cars consisted of the letters "VPR"—rather than the "SPQR" that was blazoned upon all Roman vehicles. So I knew for certain that this was the domain of Viridiporcus Rex . . . that the Green Pig had carved for himself a small empire in the midst of the most sacred territory of the Lacotian people!

Angrily I began to climb down the steps. There must have been thousands of them, and the pathway was tortuous and steep. But I was so full of fury at the sacrilege that I didn't get tired. I fairly bounded down that serpentine stairway, three or four steps at a clip. When I was about three-quarters of the way down, however, my energy ran out and I slumped down beside a tree trunk, panting and mopping off the sweat with a bundle of leaves.

When I'd recovered my senses a bit, I became aware of a clanking sort of sound somewhere behind me. It was not dissimilar to the sound of the slaves working on the railroad as they pounded in the metal spikes that held the rails in place. There was a distant drumbeat, too, somewhat like that of the drummer on a trireme whose job is to keep all the galleyslaves rowing in rhythm.

The noises seemed to be coming from behind a wall of boulders that prevented me from seeing what was making them. I crept up closer, found a chink between two rocks, and peered through. There were dozens of Papiniani, Fortunati, and several Lacotians—all green as crab apples—laboring away at the entrance to a cave. Some were grinding down rocks with enormous metal tomahuaca. Others squatted by the edge of a creek and appeared to be sifting through the water with miniature fishnets. Yet others were operating a small ferrequus as it plied its way in and out of the cave. This ferrequus was remarkable in having no steam locomotive; instead, a gang of chained Papiniani pulled it back and forth. The cars were piled high with mud and loose rocks, but here and there was the glint of gold.

Gold. Was that what this was all about? When I was a child among the Lacotii, it had never occurred to me that men would place so high a value on the shiny metal. But in Rome I saw people kill for gold. I saw children prostitute themselves for it and men go mad at the sight of it. I saw the rich adorn themselves with it; I saw human lives being exchanged for it; I saw people's achievements being measured in terms of it. So the idea that men would move mountains to obtain gold did not surprise me.

But why would the Green Pig want gold? And gold from the rapidly disintegrating universe—disintegrating, that is, from the impact of His Porcine Majesty's own ceaseless meddling? Looking back down into the valley, I could see the futuristic cities, glistening and glittering; but stunning as it was, I couldn't imagine that the Green Pig would be destroying the universe just as an exercise in urban planning. There had to be something more to this. But I couldn't put my finger on it.

I decided to investigate a little further.

I inched my way along the rocky outcropping until I found an opening wide enough to squeeze through. I darted from bush to bush until I came up right behind a group of the *androids*. They were being exhorted by an overseer—*not* a green man, for his complexion was definitely olive, and he had the flat nose typical of inhabitants of Terra Nova—who wore a jaguar skin as a cape, a gold-embroidered loincloth, and a feathery headdress. I had had such men described to me by my father, and knew at once that he was a member of the Olmechian Empire. He was addressing his underlings in Lacotian, however, and so, eavesdropping, I managed to hear a conversation something like this:

"Your quota for the day! You have fallen short by ten milligrams!"—whatever *they* were—"Back to the factory with you, you bubbleheaded clone scum!"—whatever *that* meant.

"But master—" The speaker was a viridian copy of Fortunatus, and aped his smarmy manner with alarming accuracy. "Can't you just give me a few more hours?"

"Absolutely not! There's a million more of you where

you came from, and the protoplasmic pool awaits those who are incapable of showing the proper efficiency."

Cringing, the miscreant *android* fell to his knees. But the Olmec merely waved a hand, and, as though he had been struck by one of Jove's thunderbolts, the green man vanished in a puff of smoke. The others, who had been milling about, quickly returned to work.

Presently, a second Olmec joined the first. This one wore a cloak made entirely of the brilliant plumage of exotic birds. Doubtless the brains of those birds had been exported to Alexandria or Caesarea, there to grace many a patrician's banquet table. The fellow also had enormous ivory pendants in his earlobes. The first Olmec deferred to the second. They spoke to each other in a bizarre language for a while; but then, when a third Olmec approached, switched to Greek, perhaps to avoid being listened to on.

"A couple of dozen new cloning templates came in earlier," said the first, "when we raided that village. But a bunch of them got away. We'll have to go back."

"What a pity. You know how His Porcine Majesty hates to leave loose ends. There's the small matter of the renegade Dimensional Patrol officer to deal with, too . . ."

That, I realized, had to be my father they were talking about. My pulse quickened and I crept even closer.

"Frankly, I don't entirely trust the Green Pig," the first one was saying. The second gaped at what seemed tantamount to sacrilege. "Now, don't go repeating my words, but don't you think he's a little different from the divine were-jaguars that have, in the past been guiding the destinies of our empire?"

A little different! Were these Olmechii so stupid as not to realize that they had latched onto the wrong side . . . that the Green Pig was not one of the beneficent green creatures like V'Denni-Kenni and K'Tooni-Mooni, the two were-jaguars I had met in my previous adventures?

"Yes," the first Olmec continued, "it's true that we've been promised dominion over the entire earth...the Roman Empire included...in exchange for a few paltry duties, like overseeing the clone vats and plugging the templates into the *android* processing system...taking care of the gold mines for him...there's got to be a catch, I'm sure of it!"

"I don't see why," the other said. "After all, we ought by right to be ruling over those Romans. They're such ...unrefined people. Imagine not having human sacrifice! What boors! I wonder what they do for amusement."

"Well, of course it's our right to rule over them...but this all seems too good to be true." The Olmec waved his arms. Several paces away, a hapless Papinianus dissipated into thin air. "Whoops! I didn't mean to do that. I'll have to send for a replacement." He clapped his hands and another Papinian popped into existence. "Get to work, you lazy sod!" the Olmec told him.

"Well," the other said, "I suppose I'd better go and see to the *androids*. If the templates ever got loose, the entire *android* work force would be deactivated, you know. It's a very responsible job the master has entrusted me with. The factory is in the very heart of the city—right beneath His Majesty's throneroom, as a matter of fact...have I said too much? Oh, we've just been given a new password and I'd better test it out."

"Password?"

"Yes...it's 'spectacle.'"

As soon as he uttered the word, he vanished.

"Spectacle?" I whispered to myself. "But if *I* say it aloud—"

Too late.

* * *

I was standing in a dank tunnel of some kind. There was a fork ahead, and the Olmec was purposefully making his way toward it. I followed, hiding in the shadows. The tunnel branched and branched again, and presently widened into a cavern, where I saw. . .

Rows upon rows of Romans and Lacotians, all standing on pedestals, each attached to the wall by a strange assemblage of wires. Each was green; each wore Roman or Lacotian costume—but none had any features. The faces were perfectly oval. And yet the creatures seemed to breathe.

I followed the Olmec further into the recesses of the cave, where I came upon an even more staggering sight. For, floating in what seemed to be an enormous glass amphora, with dozens of metal cords and tubes attached to the base of his skull, was my stepfather!

Other amphoras lined the cavern. I saw Fortunatus bobbing up and down in one of them. I saw also many prominent Lacotians. Each amphora had a kind of control panel in front of it, full of dials, knobs, and levers, over which radiated a pale blue aura, almost like a halo.

The Olmec looked around. I dodged back in the direction of the green men on pedestals. The Olmec began fiddling with one of the control panels, and—lo and behold—the nearest green man's face began to shift, wrinkle, transform—into the very visage of Titus Papinianus!

"What a spectacle!" I said, impressed in spite of myself.

I shouldn't have said that word, for in an instant I was transported back to the side of the mountan once more —to the exact spot from which I had departed moments before.

It took an entire day and night of vigorous mountain climbing to get back to my friends, who had, for the most part, landed without serious injury, and who had set up camp in a clearing on the other face of the mountain.

Sitting in the men's lodge, exulting in my newfound manhood—for had I not had a vision, unconventional though my spirit guide might have been?—I smoked and recited my adventures, from the encounter with the flying dinosaur to the descent into the gold mines to my encounter with the Olmecs and my visit to the *android* factory.

"Somehow I've got to get back," I said, "and rescue our people—even Fortunatus and Papinian—or the Olmecs and the Green Pig are somehow going to join in an unholy alliance to destroy civilization as we know it . . ."

"That's wonderful!" Lucius said. "We were made for this adventure, you and I. Equus Insanus and Lucius Vinicius, brothers, saviors of universes . . . I can hardly wait." He seemed to have completely forgotten his cowardice of two days before.

"Who said anything about you coming along?" I asked. "After all the times you've pulled out at the last minute and abandoned me to some hideous fate . . ."

"Well, naturally I'm coming," Lucius said. "You might need me to talk our way out of being impaled alive or something."

I sighed and took a long drag from the ceremonial pipe.

CHAPTER
XXIV

THE CIRCLE OF THE UNIVERSE

THE NEXT MORNING, I AWOKE LONG BEFORE DAWN.
Lucius and I had been sleeping close to the camp-
fire. We had no tipis, of course; there was not even a
kettle to cook in, and even though it was the eve of a
great confrontation, we had gone to bed hungry, dispirited, and without any dancing.

I went by myself, weaponless, deep into the forest. I
sat down by the edge of a brook, watching the water,
now and then bending down for a sip. I let the darkness
and the quiet seep into me. This was a sacred place, and
it salved my troubled heart. It was a while before I noticed an unearthly green shimmer on the water, and saw
a familiar face reflected on its mirrorstill surface . . .

"*Até!*" I cried out.

He looked at me with a solemnity I'd rarely seen in
him before. As always seemed to happen when my father
appeared to me, I started talking too much, too fast,
unthinking. "Are you angry at me because I didn't greet
you with the proper reverence last time you came, father? But I was only jealous because you'd given Lucius
a ride in your flying saucer and not me, and it wasn't

that I don't love you, father . . . I do. And now I've seen the Green Pig's gold mines and I know I have to somehow go down there and launch an attack but I'm too confused . . ."

"What can I do to help?" Aquila asked. His eyes twinkled, and I was sure that he had some ready-made answer for our problems. After all, he'd always managed to get silly old Titus Papinianus out of trouble, hadn't he?

"Don't tell me," I said. "Last time I saw you, you were fighting it out in your flying saucers, you and the Green Pig. You've already defeated him, haven't you? And you've come to tell me all is well . . ."

"Alas . . . far from it," my father said. "My saucer was disabled by a laser blast, and I narrowly avoided a crash."

"You're not going to rescue us at all?" But I must admit that I had suspected the answer to that question all along.

My father shrugged. "Why do you not follow the advice of the spirit animal that visited you in your vision, *chinkshi*? By the way, what sort of an animal was it? An eagle, perhaps? It is because an eagle spoke to me during my childhood that I am called Aquila."

"I guess I'm a little confused. I mean, yes, I had a vision . . . but the animal who spoke to me wasn't one of the usual animals. It wasn't a bear or a wolf or a white aurochs or an eagle . . . it was, well, a sort of flying dinosaur."

Aquila shrugged. "Oh, a pterodactyl?"

"Ptero-what?"

"That's what they're called. You know your Greek. *Pterodactylos* . . . winged fingers. Well, I don't see any reason why a pterodactyl can't appear in a vision and tell someone the meaning of life. After all, even the bizarre beasts that have so plagued the world in recent years must have their place in the great circle of existence. The

Great Mystery wouldn't be worth much if it wasn't, well, *mysterious*, my son."

"The great circle . . . that's just what the vision talked about, father. A great circle and a great dance that will free the world."

"Well, there it is, *chinkshi*. You cannot rush impetuously into an attack on the citadel of the Green Pig and just expect to hack and slash your way to victory. That is the Roman way, but it's not our way. You must do what is right for the heart."

Aquila's long white hair streamed behind him in the wind of morning. Though his face was green, I knew that this was no android but my true father. Because I could feel his love for me, and his concern. "Why are you so melancholy?" I asked him at last.

He said, "There are things in these universes, my son, that I would give anything never to have seen."

"Can things be so bad, father?"

He sighed. The wind shook the treetops and he pulled his cloak tighter around his toga. I was dying for him to tell me exciting tales of his exploits in the Dimensional Patrol, but I had the feeling he was weary of such tales. Instead I said, "Why does he want the gold? I mean, aren't there a million other universes he can plunder? Why does he have to do it here?"

I knew before he even opened his mouth that this was going to be one of those explanations that would go right over the head of us primitives from the past, as usual. "Well, it's to do with what isotope of gold we're talking about, my son. The destabilization of this universe has caused a certain isotope to have a far longer half life than it should, and the anomaly between the laws of physics here and in the rest of the universes is what enables the gold to be used as an energy-focusing device . . ."

I didn't even bother to ask him what he was talking about. My father wasn't as bad as the were-jaguars from the future themselves, whose jargon always sounded like the academic discourse of drunken Egyptian philosophers. Here at least I could understand about one word in three! Sensing my unease, Aquila said, "What it boils down to is this: All those devices of his—the dreaded spatiotemporal bewilderizer, the flying saucers, the *android* driver that controls all the imitation people he's been making—they're all powered by gold. This particular gold, not just any gold. Gold from rogue universes that have somehow wandered away from their correct spatiotemporal path. The supply of rogue universe gold is very carefully guarded by the Dimensional Patrol, and the Green Pig isn't allowed to have any."

It still didn't make any sense to me. "And there's something else," I said. "Why does he bother to create these *androids* and import the Olmecs to oversee them, and to promise the Olmecs the Roman Empire, when he knows the whole universe is going to disintegrate anyway... why doesn't he just build some huge device that'll dig up the entire Montes Negri and get him all the funny gold he wants?"

"It's to do with the spatiotemporal dislocation quotient," my father said, sounding impressive, even a little smug. "As I've tried to explain before, every introduction of some new element from the wrong dimensional coordinates accelerates the breakdown of this present reality. By making lots of copies of real people instead of simply building robots, Viridiporcus hopes to somehow trick the universe into thinking nothing new has arrived here—you may wonder how the universe would give a damn, but the fact is that most subatomic particles carry a certain primitive level of consciousness—as for importing the Olmecs, it's the same thing. Spatial displacement, in the case of the Olmecs, and numerological displacement, in the case of the proliferating Papinians, are not nearly as disruptive as spatiotemporal interference—not by some degrees of magnitude. If only I had a

Riemannian chart available! As for promising the Olmecs . . . I've no need to mention his love of intrigue for its own sake," he added, rubbing his chin.

"That," I said, "has got to be the most incomprehensible speech that anyone has uttered since the beginning of time."

"I know, my son, that it sounds a little weird," my father said, patting me on the head, "but I got it from an extra-intelligent super-being, so I'm just taking his word for it."

"Not even the most persuasive writer of *scientifictiones* could get away with such gobbledygook," I said. "It's just a bunch of long words strung together."

"Veritas mirabilior qua fabula," Aquila said.

"Maybe it *is* stranger than fiction," I reflected. "But I still think—"

"Ah, thinking," my father said. "Just as long as you don't do it too much. After all, look at what a surfeit of thinking did to our Egyptian friend . . ."

I laughed, a bit nervously I suppose. My father went on, "Well, just what was it that the pterodactyl said to you?"

I thought back to the time of my vision . . . in my mind I saw once more the great winged lizard flying against the circle of brilliant sun. Circles . . . circles . . . I knew then that I was the only one left who could lead the assault on the citadel of the Green Pig . . . I, Equus Insanus, child of two worlds.

When I returned to our meager encampment, I didn't talk to Lucius at all. I asked Ursus Erectus to help me build a sweat lodge. It was not like a Roman bath, which is designed only for people to sit around chatting about the latest scandals, but a stark place, full of mystery. Immersed in the sacred steam, I sat alone. I felt Rome itself oozing from my pores and melting into the air. I do not know how long I sat. From outside came the contin-

ual pounding of a sacred drum. Sometimes it was so loud
it seemed to be my own heartbeat. At other times my
spirit seemed to leave my body and go far away, and the
drumming was as distant as the valley below.

I felt feverish and I dreamed of monsters. I was in a
dense forest of steam and gigantic plants, with exotic
insects the size of hummingbirds darting to and fro...
the trees so tall you could not see the sky. The forest
merged into swampland, foul-smelling, and herds of
brontosauruses basked in the mud, their necks bending
and craning to pluck ferns from the trees. This was no
forest of Lacotia...there were no familiar creatures, no
wolves, no birds, no small furry creatures at all...and I
was lost in it...lost...I trudged through mud and
breathed in the thick steam and sweated and bled as the
plants tore at my feet and ankles almost as though they
were mouths with tiny teeth.

A long time passed. I grew wearier and wearier. I
knew that I was climbing, for the ground was angling
smoothly upward and each step was a struggle against
the pull of the ground. At length I reached a plateau, or
so it seemed in my fever dream, and there were patches
of sky here and there. The sun, red and glowering, completely filled one of them and a pterodactyl was flying
back and forth, its call plangent and curiously heart-
breaking.

"What do you want of me?" I asked the lizard-bird.

And there came a plaintive voice inside my skull, "I
have strayed from my country and been plucked into a
strange time and place. But the Great Mystery has linked
us together across the dimensions. This world you see is
my true world, but you see it in a vision. It is the vision I
long for. Only you can bring it about. If you reenter your
world you will open the way for me to reenter mine."

"Was I, too, plucked from my world?" I said wonder-
ingly. But I knew it was true.

And when I looked down at myself I saw that I was

clothed in tunica and toga praetexta. My sandals were gilded and a gold wreath covered my head. The clothes were damp with the steam from the swamp.

As I made my way across the plateau, the forest began to give way. Again and again the pterodactyl wheeled overhead, calling my name.

I came to a sacred circle. The skull of an aurochs lay in front of it. I heard the keening of sacred flutes. My Roman clothes stuck to my skin, oppressive and confining. I began to tear them off.

The lizard-bird flew around and around the mysterious circle. A figure stood at its center . . . green-faced, wearing a toga, bulbous-nosed, sporting a supercilious grin . . .

"Stepfather!" I screamed at him. "You don't belong in there—the circle is the circle of my people!"

I rushed into the circle and as I did so the apparition transformed itself into a vision of my father. He no longer wore Roman dress, but appeared as he must have at the Battle of the Flumen Pulveris: black-maned, his face unlined and slick with war paint, shaking his war-lance at the sun.

I stared upward into the sun's face. I spread my arms wide and cried out the words of the song the pterodactyl had taught me. I danced in the circle, in the light.

The mists moved in.

I stirred and awoke from my trance.

Ursus Erectus was beside me, ladling more water onto the hot stones, and outside the drums were pounding and the rhythm was the rhythm of my heart and blood.

"I'm ready to lead the people," I said. "I will dance, and we will bind the fabric of the universe together once more."

CHAPTER
XXV

THE PASSWORD IS SPECTACLE

W HEN I EMERGED FROM THE SWEAT LODGE, young maidens had already gone into the forest to fell the sacred tree that would be the center of the circle of the sundance. They were erecting the tree. Lucius was waiting for me at the entrance to the lodge.

"I say! You're really going to go through with this whole tit-piercing deal, aren't you?" he said.

I didn't answer.

"Well, if you expect *me* to do anything of the kind, you can forget it," he said. "I draw the line at pain."

At first I felt like socking him in the jaw, but then I realized I had my new dignity to consider. So I merely said, "You're a Roman and I'm a Lacotian and we're in Lacotia now and we'll do things our way." And tried to leave it at that.

Lucius said, "Wait a minute! Lacotia happens to be *in* Rome now! Or had you forgotten?"

"Go and eat some hummingbirds' brains, you imperialist puppy," I said. Then I walked away from him. I was already sorry for insulting him. After all, I reflected, I ought to pity him for not knowing any better...

* * *

The pain was excruciating. I lay on the ground. A very holy man, a *winkte*, that is to say, a transvestitus, carved two slits above each of my nipples and slipped in two narrow stakes to which were attached the rawhide cords that linked me to the sacred tree. Tears welled up in my eyes. I gritted my teeth and thought of the beatings in Androcles' school in Rome. Surely if I could withstand those floggings . . .

Slowly I stood up. I wore a deerskin apron and a wreath. The homo medicinae put a flute between my lips that was decorated with the quills of porcupines. I blinked and then looked skyward into the face of the sun . . . and then, stretching the thongs taut, I danced. The pounding music heightened the pain. My wounds throbbed with every drumbeat, with every stamp of my bare feet on the hard earth. I blew on the flute and danced. The sunlight seared my eyes but still I stared at it.

As I danced I became aware that others were dancing beside me. They, too, were pledging their flesh, suffering for our people—not dancing for the amusement of the Roman mob. We danced. My eyes were burning, my flesh was burning. But there was joy in this pain. As I danced I strained hard against the sacred tree, struggling to tear the flesh from my piercing and break free. The piping of flutes filled the air, shrilling against the drumbeats and the wheezing litany of the old men's singing. We danced, bunches of dried sage in our fists, the leather cords crossing and crisscrossing as we circled. The ground thudded. We danced with great solemnity and gladness.

I saw the pterodactyl once again, flying across the disk of the sun. Perhaps it was a recurrence of my vision. The pterodactyl cried my name.

I, too, gave a great cry as the flute flew from my lips and my flesh tore and I fell . . .

And falling I saw—was it my imagination?—something so outlandish that I thought I must be dreaming. I saw a Roman youth dancing beside our warriors, staring at the sun as well as one of us, bravely bearing the pain like a Lacotian. The wounds in his chest were deep and uneven. Perhaps he had pierced himself. He was not wearing the ceremonial garments, but something hastily assembled from a ripped-up tunica. He danced awkwardly, often missing the beat and colliding with one of the other dancers. But there was a new seriousness in him, and though his dancing was ungainly it didn't make me laugh. Obviously all this was making a man of him after all.

"Lucius," I whispered as I passed out . . .

"Imperialist puppy, my arse," he was saying as I came to in the early evening, under the shade of an immense lodgepole pine. "Jove, that's got to be the most agonizing pain I've ever suffered in my entire life."

I was still feeling groggy. In the firelight, I saw that Lucius' chest scars were beginning to form. "You did well," I said. "For a Roman," I couldn't help adding.

"For a Roman?" He smiled a surprisingly sheepish smile, and then groaned from the pain. "Roman, you insufferable barbarian?"

"No, you just did well." I couldn't begrudge him that. "You did well, brother." For the first time I didn't really mind thinking of him as that.

Ursus Erectus knelt down beside us and tried to feed us some thin gruel. Someone had managed to hunt up some meat amid all this confusion. I was glad of that.

Lucius said, "Listen, Equus old chap. I think I've endured enough savage rites for the time being. When we go into battle, I think I'd rather go as a Roman tribune. I mean, those loincloths and feathers are all very well, but they're not much protection against the super-weapons of the future."

"We are what we are," I murmured. But I knew that Lucius had done a great thing for my sake, and in spite of everything he was my friend. "Where are the other braves?"

Ursus said, "They are waiting for you, Equus Insanus. Some of them are already putting on their war paint."

"Well, what are we waiting for?" Lucius said. "Alea jacta est! Let the battle begin!" He started to leap to his feet; a spasm sent him reeling back to the ground. "By Priapus, what pain."

"Time for a war council," I said.

Within a few hours my little band were gathered. There were only about a dozen of us, but we had all drawn strength from our vows to the sun. We had erected a makeshift tipi by using the fabric from the hot-air balloon and by tearing strips of wood from the platform. It was held together by some of the cords from which my people had lately been dangling. These were not made of rawhide but of a bizarre, shiny material, completely flexible, with no visible imperfections.

We sat and smoked and took counsel.

"We should get reinforcements," Ursus Erectus said. "It's only a few days' ride back to the Flumen Platonis. We could even get Roman legions to back us up. I could go down to the ferrequine building site and talk to the Sasquatius . . ."

"We haven't got any horses," I said. "What are we going to do—lasso a pterodactyl and try to break it in?"

"We should just attack! It is a good day to die," Lucius said, really getting into the spirit of this thing.

"I suppose you're right," Ursus said. "Although we might be able to hijack one of the hot-air balloons down there in the Green Pig's city."

"Better hijack someone to steer the thing while we're at it," Lucius said.

"You're right," I said. "Just counting coup on the Green Pig isn't going to save the universe. We have to defeat him utterly." I wondered where my father had disappeared to, and whether he would turn up at the last minute to rescue us. I had my doubts—Aquila knew that each time he made one of his appearances, he was hastening the universe's end—and I knew my father didn't have all that much hope for this madcap mission of ours in any case; he had come back to our world to die in a place sacred to our people.

"Since it was my idea," Ursus said, "let me attempt to steal a hot-air balloon. Only show me where they are tethered. It can't be much different from stealing horses. If I have your box-that-causes-green-men-to-explode, it will probably make it fairly easy to accomplish."

Some of our group volunteered to go with him, leaving about six or seven of us for the assault on the citadel itself. Though the odds were unbelievable, I felt a surging elation. It wasn't at all the same as when I'd led the group of Roman schoolboys on a rampage through the house of C. Lentulus Fortunatus ... even though, just like last time, Fortunatus was in there somewhere. It seemed odd to be rescuing the man instead of beating him on the head with a tomahaucum, but that was only the least of the ironies of this whole situation.

"Enough small chat," I said. Clearly I had been chosen as war chief for this expedition, and the others accepted my authority without qualm—a sure indication that my vision and my dance had truly made a man of me. "Let's go and put our faces on. It wouldn't be proper to die without decent makeup."

It took us the remainder of the night and one more day to climb up to the vantage point from which I had first seen the cities of gold. When we emerged at the rocky ledge atop the hill, I saw that all the pterodactyl eggs had hatched and that the baby dinosaurs were nowhere to be seen. That at least was a relief. It was early evening; the golden spires caught fire from the sunset. My braves gaped in astonishment. We could see that all the hot-air balloons were gathered together at the outskirts of the city, like a cluster of grapes in the sky.

Ursus said, "It will be a simple matter to cause any green men in the vicinity to explode, and then catch one of the balloons." He was trembling with anticipation. He probably hadn't gone on a good horse-stealing expedition in years. "Perhaps," he said, "I can even purchase a decent wife with a couple of the balloons. For a change. I wonder what the exchange rate would be, how many horses for one balloon, how many balloons for a good woman."

The other warriors in his group laughed and nudged each other. Doubtless they were all thinking much the same thing. It was a splendid notion. I could just imagine myself, one fine day many moons from now, strutting over to some chief's tent in all my finery to offer him hot-air balloons for his daughter. Of course, we'd have to adapt the balloons to fit our way of life: paint them with colorful designs, hang scalps from them, or what have you. It wouldn't be the first time we've managed to absorb something useful from another culture. It could be the most exciting innovation since the coming of the horse to our great plains.

"You'll do down there," I said, "steal the balloons . . . maybe cause a minor ruckus, enough for us to slip down to the mining area unnoticed, use the secret password, and materialize right beneath the Green Pig's throne-room. If what I overheard is correct, releasing the captives from those *android*-making machines will automatically deactivate all the *androids*, thus leaving the city's defenses weakened . . ." The others listened eagerly, but I couldn't help thinking how tenuous my plan was, preposterous even . . . though no more so than the scientific casuistry with which Aquila had "explained" the universe to me earlier. I hadn't even figured the Olmecs into the plan. I didn't know how many of them there were. But we'd take care of them somehow. A few Olmechian scalps would look good on my toga of manhood . . .

It was with some regret that I handed over the uranograph to Ursus Erectus. But I realized that his mission would involve creating pandemonium, whereas ours had to be carried out in perfect stealth.

Hardly able to contain his excitement, Ursus decided to lead his men down the hill immediately. I watched them as they climbed over the edge and began the descent down those endless stairs to the bottom of the hill.

Which left Lucius, four or five other intrepid braves, and me. I looked at my small band. We were a pretty impressive bunch of saviors of the universe, no doubt about it.

Lucius had managed to scrape together a sort of tribune's uniform from bits and pieces of the few belongings that had been plucked into the air along with our people. His helmet was a little big and his cuirass had a spot of green on it here and there. He wore a buffalo robe instead of a cape. At the last minute, he hadn't been able to resist the war paint. His face was a dark ocher with streaks of bright blue across each cheek. Terrifying! And the others, too, were decked in all the finery they could muster, as was I, who had covered my face with black and white. I was wearing a deerskin shirt sewn with hanks of human hair and decorated with images of slain enemies, and in my hair I wore an eaglefeather that commemorated the night I had counted coup on the hapless Fortunatus.

Although I had planned that one of us would stand watch while the others slept, none of us could quite get to sleep that night. We all sat on the ledge and watched the stars come out. Even in the starlight the city glowed. At last, a few hours before dawn, one of us noticed something and attracted my attention.

I looked.

Far below us, the cluster of balloons had spawned a baby cluster which was slowly rising. Lights were being turned on in the city as though by magic. The balloons glowed eerily from within as their flames heated the air.

"*Huka hey!*" I cried. "Follow me closely, and don't let yourselves be seen until I give the signal! And remember, the password is 'spectacle'!"

We readied our weapons: simple knives, bows and arrows, and, in Lucius' case, a gaudy gladius that looked as if it had been stolen from the arena. Single file, blending in with the foliage and the night, we started to work our way down the hill toward the gold mines.

CHAPTER
XXVI

THE LABYRINTH

T HE ENTRANCE TO THE MINES WAS PRACTICALLY DE-
serted. A cold light shone from lamps that appeared to contain no flame, but burned with a chilling
steadiness. Ferrequus tracks led into the tunnel. A couple of guards were easily disposed of and scalped. We
looked around, our footsteps silent as the night itself.
There was nobody else. Why should there be? I thought.
The Green Pig probably feels quite secure here in his
secret domain.

Making sure my group was gathered together, I said,
"Let's say the password now, all together."

"Spectacle," we said.

In a trice we had been transported to the bowels of
the citadel. The tunnel we found ourselves in was lit with
the same eerie flickerless light that illumined the entrance to the mines.

"Remarkable," Lucius said, "how these lamps glow
without giving off heat and without flames. More superscience, I suppose."

"They've probably managed to harness whatever
power it is that makes fireflies work," I said.

216

I tried to get my bearings. Which way had it been to the *android* factory? Straight down, wasn't it? I motioned to my men to follow. We had our bows and arrows at the ready; if an enemy showed up, it would be best to strike him down from a distance and keep running. There were no shadows to hide in. But we moved noiselessly. Except for Lucius, who had not quite mastered the art, and now and then tripped over himself or couldn't resist talking.

I remembered the way to the *android* factory pretty much perfectly. It wasn't long before we reached the corridors lined with faceless green men, ready at a moment's notice to assume the identity of my stepfather or some other familiar figure. We inched along the wall, using the unfinished *androids* themselves as camouflage. I ran through the repertory of animal noises to make sure all our signals were covered. Proudly, I added a new one based on my vision: the plaintive squawk of a pterodactyl was to signify *attack*!

"There's a chamber with these gigantic glass amphoras," I told the others, "each of which contains an imprisoned member of our group. The last time I tried to disable one of these futuristic mechanisms, I discovered that they're pretty delicate; a few buttons pushed, a little something smashed, and they're useless. We should be able to get our people out easily enough."

"I suggest a direct approach," Lucius said. "We'll just bash the amphoras open."

"Sounds good," I said. "Now, if you'll just follow me . . ."

We crept along. So far, we appeared to have eluded notice. A brace of guards walked by, Olmecs in bizarre headdresses. I darted behind a green man and so did the others. As soon as they left we dashed across to the next green man. That was how we traversed the corridor—in little quantum bursts of dashing, each burst the distance between one motionless *android*-to-be and the next.

At last the cavern widened and I saw the hall of amphoras and strange devices. There they were! The hallway sloped downward from where we stood, and there were exits all the way down, from some of which emerged the tracks of a ferrequus. Clearly there was some mining activity going on even here. There was Fortunatus, bobbing up and down in a jar of purple fluid ...there were several famed Lacotian braves...and, yes, there was my stepfather, bound by tubes and pipes, his face locked in a supercilious smirk, his mouth opening now and then to discharge a stream of bubbles. Each of the captives had metal wires at the base of his skull, extending out of the top of the amphora into a master device at the center of the hall. Colored lights blinked and flashed, and other machines emitted buzzings, beepings, and flatulent thunderclaps.

My comrades looked at the devices and each other, and lapsed into subdued mutterings, with a lot of *Hechitu welo*-ing and *han-han-han*-ing. Someone was bound to show up if we didn't get a move on.

"No time for amazement," I whispered. "The chamber appears unattended. *Huka hey!*"

I squawked like a pterodactyl. The others lifted their voices in wild ululation. Tomahauca and war clubs upraised, we charged at the nearest row of glass jugs. I was face to face with a grinning fat Roman I didn't recognize; the glass distorted his face and distended his belly. His eyes were closed in an expression of profound smugness. For a moment I didn't really feel like saving any Romans. Then I thought, We're all in this together. I brought my war club crashing down on the glass. It made sort of a *boing-oing-oing* sound and bounced back, slamming me between the eyes and sending me sprawling. "It's not glass!" I said.

"If I see one more piece of this bloody superscience I'll scream," Lucius said.

"Come on! We'll tip 'em over."

I and my comrades shoved our shoulders hard against the amphora. It started wobbling. The Roman's eyes popped open and he seemed to be trying to say something. "Harder!" I said, trying not to shout.

"It's moving—"

"I think it's—"

"Whoa!" I said as the jar tipped over on its side and began to roll. It collided with the next amphora. The machine in the middle of the chamber began to emit a rather obnoxious *poot-poot* sort of sound. I ran over to it and gave it a kick. The alarm ceased. "Catch the jar and pull the top," I said. "Get that Roman out of there."

The amphora knocked over several others. Wires snapped. Tubes became snagged on other tubes. Sparks flew. "By Jupiter Optimus Maximus," I said, "help me hold down one of these devices!"

I turned around and saw a glass jar containing my stepfather rolling toward me. I ran blindly and collided with a wall. The jug slammed into me and pinned me to the wall. I stood there, staring at Papinianus, whose face was frozen in that selfsame supercilious smirk he had been wearing all along.

"Curse you!' I said. "You and your hummingbirds' brains and your superior airs . . . you got us into this . . . if I succeed in saving your life, I'll kill you myself!" I started pummeling the amphora with my fists.

At that moment, a force of angry green men marched into the chamber. There were samples of my stepfather, of Fortunatus, of many Lacotian warriors. They walked in complete step with each other. They raised their arms in unison. They grunted in unison. It was though none was a complete person—merely a puppet of the Green Pig's will . . .

"We'd best get out of here and regroup," I yelled. "And then pop back down here to finish off our business. Everyone, repeat after me . . . SPECTACLE!"

"SPECTACLE!"

Nothing happened... except that the green *androids* kept advancing...

A huge voice echoed through the chamber. "Foolish primitive creatures from the past!" it said.

"Uh oh... it's His Porcine Majesty at last," said Lucius, who was trying to pry the amphora loose so I could breathe.

"Don't you realize," said the reverberating voice, "that the password changes upon my whim? My sensors knew that an alien presence had entered the bowels of my palace... and I immediately switched to another password so that you'll never escape... you're all doomed... and mechanical copies of you are going to serve me in the gold mines, and you'll spend eternity sitting in a glass bottle acting as a somatic template for my *android* manufacturing device... nyah, nyah, nyah!"

My tiny group gathered around me. We pulled out our bows and arrows and we fired. Green men went sprawling everywhere. I was still pinned to the wall, but I could shoot. One of the androids, stuck full of arrows like a porcupine, kept advancing toward us. I could see that these fellows couldn't be stopped by the usual tactics. It was useless. Frustrated, I slammed my fists down on my stepfather's amphora again and again... until I noticed that there was a small panel near the top, with color coded buttons flashing merrily away... was that the secret of opening them?

No time to think. I jabbed the nearest button, which was blinking a bright green...

I heard a hideous clanking sound from just beyond the chamber... an ominous wheezing... I banged on the button several more times... until I realized what I must have done.

"You idiot!" Lucius said. "You've just activated a dozen more of those Papinian things!"

Sure enough, they were tramping down toward us, uttering, in unison, drearily familiar words. "I say, Papinian Junior! Wait till I get my hands on you! You'll get such a flogging you'll never question the value of Roman discipline again!"

"I'd better try another button," I said "No one's going to capture *me* and make millions of *android* copies to use as slaves."

I picked the next one. It was blue. My stepfather seemed to come alive. He was squirming now, and banging at the side of the amphora and mouthing something that looked suspiciously like "Let me out! Let me out!"

I shrugged. He looked very irate. I hit another button —a sort of chartreuse-colored one with magenta zebra stripes and yellow dots—and suddenly the entire amphora vanished into thin air, and Papinian, wriggling like an enormous dolphin, was in my arms. "It's about bloody time," he said. "Hurry up! I need to finish laying down at least one more mille passus of track before dinnertime!"

"Uh, stepfather, we're not at the railway site."

"Well, where the bloody infernum am I? Give me some answers, my lad, or you'll taste a bit of Roman discipline, what!" he spluttered.

"I've just saved your miserable hide, you...you stuck up, bulbous-nosed, ignorant imperialist buggerer of elephants!" I said.

Around us, pseudo-Papiniani everywhere were exploding, spattering us with assorted cogs, wheels, spokes, and green slime. But those *androids* that were in the shape of others had not slowed their advance. Indeed, they were right upon us. But I wasn't pinned down anymore, and I let Papinian slip from my arms. He landed, rubbed his arse, and continued to complain. I rushed one of the green men with my scalping knife, seized him by the hair, and started sawing away. The hair came off easily, but there was no scalp. Instead, a viscous green rheum started spilling from his head and dripping down his face. He flailed jerkily around, but he didn't seem to know where he was or what he was hitting.

"Scalping disables them!" I shouted to the others. "And hitting the funny colored button will turn off all the green men that look like whoever's in the jug."

We began to fight with a will now, running from amphora to amphora, hitting buttons left, right, and center. The *androids* were easy targets once you got hold of them by the hair. But there didn't seem to be any end to them, and we were slipping and sliding in mushy green remnants of those that had already exploded. The amphoras were still rolling around and knocking things over. We were still heavily outnumbered. At last the chamber was so full of *androids*, some in the process of exploding, others shambling aimlessly with their heads dripping, and yet others advancing upon us with menacing mien and demonlike precision, that there wasn't any room to maneuver at all. Add to that the fact that our newly resuscitated friends had absolutely no idea what was going on, and several of them seemed to assume that *they* were in command and were barking at us to obey them . . .

"This is preposterous," I said to Lucius, who stood shoulder to shoulder with me as we fended off a horde of green Fortunati—for we had yet to disengage the amphora that contained that worthy. "We've got to get to the center of all this—to the heart of this crazy· domain —to the Green Pig himself!"

"And where might that be, know-it-all?"

"Up there—somewhere." I pointed at the ceiling. For I recalled the conversation between the Olmecs that I'd overheard on my last visit to this labyrinth . . . they'd said something about the Green Pig's throne being directly above the *android* factory.

"Let's go, then!" Lucius said. "One of these tunnels has got to lead upward—"

Somewhere out there, Papinian was shouting, "All of

you stop this nonsense and listen to me—we've a quota
to fulfill—can't have any of this wrangling amongst the
slaves—"

"Ready—set . . . " I said.

"Go!"

We kicked our nearest opponents sharply in the groin,
cleared off just enough space to dash out, and made for
the nearest exit.

"This is absurd," I said. We were in a cramped pas-
sageway and there were three openings in the rock,
doubtless leading in various directions. I examined them.
One seemed to lead upward, though it was hard to tell,
for they were not well lit.

"Well," Lucius said, "there's only one possible solution."

He threw off his cuirass and pulled off his tunica,
leaving himself only in a loincloth. He worried at a
thread of the woollen fabric until it came loose, and then
he tied it firmly to a bracket from which depended one of
those futuristic flicker-free lamps.

"What on earth are you doing?" I said.

"It's like Theseus and the labyrinth and the ball of
yarn," Lucius said offhandedly.

"Who and what?"

"Listen to me. I've done everything your way so far.
I've even stuck little wooden barbs in my chest and par-
ticipated in your exotic mutilation rites. I've put on war
paint. I admit that your ways are effective and even have
a certain glamour. But right now, my barbarian brother,
it's about time I demonstrated some of the advantages of
a classical education."

CHAPTER
XXVII

THE LACOTIAN MINOTAUR

S O SAYING, LUCIUS PUT THE TUNICA BACK ON, THREW
his buffalo robe cape back over it, and entered the
tunnel and bade me follow. I saw the wool of his tunica
unwinding and I suddenly realized how we were going to
find our way back out again. But I didn't quite see how a
classical education had led him to this brilliant solution.

"I can't believe that this sort of eventuality is covered
in such military authorities as Xenophon," I said.

"All knowledge," Lucius said smugly, "is contained
somewhere in the body of ancient and modern Greek
literature."

Perhaps there was something to the flagellatory
school system of Rome after all.

The way led sharply upward for a while, then seemed
to level out and veer off. The walls were dank and there
was a distinct odor of aurochs excrement, though I could
not imagine how a herd of buffalo could possibly be
wandering around inside these passageways. There was
a bit of light; the walls themselves shed a faint, cold
glow, unearthly green.

224

"Use some of those Lacotian skills of yours," Lucius said, "and try to figure out where we are."

I put my ear to the wall.

"Strange."

"What?" said Lucius.

"I could had sworn I heard hoofbeats."

"We're near the surface then."

"Aurochs' hoofbeats. But not on grass. Somewhere in the cave, I think."

"What's a buffalo doing in the basement of the Green Pig's palace?"

"It sounds pretty annoyed."

"Well, where is it?" The cave was broadening now and once again seemed to be ascending, and as I continued to listen I began to hear other things, too, including a familiar cackling I remembered from my previous adventures.

I said, "We've got to be near that throneroom. I can hear the Green Pig chortling hideously."

"Merda!" Lucius cried out. "Look ahead!"

We were standing against an Ionian column carved out of living rock. More columns lined the walls. The hall we had come upon was so vast I could hardly see to the other end; but there was indeed a throne there, and on that throne, wearing a cloak of royal purple and a gold wreath, was the enemy whom I had been dreading for the entirety of these operations . . . Viridiporcus Rex.

He seemed to be quite alone at the moment, and he had not yet seen us. He was completely engrossed in an enormous papyrus scroll. He chuckled as he read, and burst now and then into a wheezing guffaw, his jowls quivering, his beady eyes seeming to shine of their own accord. In front of the throne was one of those control panels that these futuristic types always seemed to be unable to live without, with the usual flashing lights, levers, buttons, jags of lightning, and clouds of purple smoke.

"That's got to be what he uses to control everything that's going on around here," I said. "If I can get my hands on that thing, I can probably generate enough random sabotage to bring the whole operation to its knees."

"So what are we going to do? Charge in and scalp him?"

"Why not?"

"Hold on a second! Let's get the lay of the land a little better," Lucius said, worrying at his tunica, which had dwindled to a short little thing that most immodestly displayed his nether garments. "He hasn't seen us yet."

We crept closer, keeping in the shadow of the Ionian columns. In the very back of the hall was a wide staircase, the sort of thing you'd expect to find in front of a Roman temple. It was lined with statues of the Green Pig in every conceivable classic pose, wearing elaborate costumes. The top of the staircase was awash with ruddy light. The sun was up, and the steps must lead outside—perhaps to a veranda or rooftop of the Porcine Palace.

Directly behind the Green Pig was a row of framed pictures. That's what they seemed to be at first, just representations of various parts of the palace; but when I squinted I could see that they were full of moving figures.

"Oh, those are just magic glasses," Lucius explained. "Every sorcerer worth his salt has those. They show what's going on in other times and places."

"Strange." Advanced though they might be, these people from the future did have a few noticeable shortcomings. After all, I didn't need any devices to see other times and places. All I had to do was endure a brief regimen of extreme starvation and pain, and my spirit would soon be off to look at anything I needed to see. And there were dreams besides. You can travel anywhere you want to in dreams. Maybe in the future that would be another one of those lost arts. Like the ability to remember long stretches of oral history—we Lacotii had no trouble with it, but the Romans always had to refer to those endless scrolls and wax tablets, and they always had to have a name for everything.

I was so engrossed in musing on these profound syllogisms that my Lacotian senses failed me for a moment. The familiar odor of a bull aurochs on the prairie, heavy, pungent, and a bit flatulent, had constantly been in the background since we had started climbing up to this level. Suddenly, in mid-reverie, I became aware that the stench had become overpowering.

"We'd best take cover," I said abstractedly, "I think that angry buffalo is around somewhere, I don't quite know why—"

"Bit late for that, isn't it?" Lucius said in a strangled sort of voice. I whipped around to see that he was against the wall, desperately trying to find a handhold, and that he was being menaced by the most enormous aurochs I had ever seen...

Well, not exactly an aurochs. It had a buffalo's head all right, but its body was as well-muscled as a gladiator's, and most definitely human—except that it had hooves for feet and hands, and couldn't quite make up its mind whether to stand on its hind legs or paw at the ground like an animal. The creature had been oiled and scraped all over, and his musculature rippled impressively as he snarled.

"What in the world—" I said, only to be poked in the back by a pudgy finger—

Which belonged to none other than the Viridiporcine One himself!

"Get off me," I said defiantly. "Get out of our universe!" I backed away... right into the flanks of the human buffalo itself! It lowered its horns. I panicked and ran, smack into Lucius, who was still trying to clamber up the wall.

"Not yet, my lovely abomination," the Green Pig said to his pet chimaera. "They can't possibly die before I've had a chance to deliver oration of my—hee hee—unspeakably evil plans for controlling the universe."

The Pig contemplated us for a moment. He was still seated on his throne, reading his scroll and surrounded by the flashing console. Apparently the entire apparatus was capable of flying around the room.

"What have we here?" said the Green Pig. "Two sniveling, snotty-nosed little boys . . . is this the best that the Might and Majesty of Rome can do? Pshaw!"

"At least someone has the guts to hunt you down," I said. If these were going to be my final moments on earth, I'd better do it in style. "It is a good day to die, and I might as well take you with me if I can." I spoke with a great deal of desperation. The buffalo man snorted at us, his nostrils flaring. Was it as intelligent as a man? I could not tell.

"You'll never get away," Lucius said. "By now reinforcements will be on their way—and we've crippled your army of *android* facsimiles . . ."

"What do you think of my genetic experiment?" the Green Pig said. "An interesting conceit, no? Ancient Greek mythology recreated right here in the laboratories of the Montes Negri."

The Green Pig cackled and made his throne fly around the chamber a few times. "Have you read this?" he said, waving the scroll. "It's a copy of your stepfather's memoirs. What a self-satisfied nincompoop he is! I nearly died laughing."

"Why are you still here to torment us?" I said. "Didn't the Dimensional Patrol capture you and erase your brain waves or something? Wasn't the memory of the Green Pig wiped out in every one of the known universes?"

"Little do you know," he said.

"Let him rave," I whispered to Lucius. "He never kills people before he's had a chance to explain every nauseating detail of dastardly plans to them. Evil people are like that. If we let him go on for a bit, an opening may present itself."

"Indeed!" cried the Green Pig, becoming increasingly enamored of his own voice. "When V'Denni-Kenni and K'Tooni-Mooni of the Dimensional Patrol hauled me up before the Court of Dimensional Transgressions, I and all the copies of myself from various continua were indeed sentenced to have our brains erased. But there was a catch. After all, I do not believe I flatter myself if I boast that I am one of the more wanted criminals in all the universes. When little Equus Insanus banged on my Spatiotemporal Bewilderizer and sucked millions of versions of my humble self into your universe, to be arrested and arraigned by the patrol, a principle known as the First Law of Conservation of Multiplex Realities came into effect. Because each universe is only different from its neighboring parallel universe by some tiny detail, it was intolerable to the reality balance that your universe should contain all the versions of myself and that none of the next-door universes should contain me at all. Reality bounced back upon itself, and—in a sort of ripple effect as the anomalous reality began to reproduce itself across neighboring universes—the same events were instantly repeated in all the universes from which my presence had been sucked, thus causing millions more copies of myself to be created in each universe to reflect events here. Get it?"

I had already begun to have the sinking feeling that always seems to accompany these elaborate scientific exegeses. The fact that the buffalo-man showed no signs of abating his ire wasn't particularly thrilling either. The Green Pig seemed to want me to respond before he would deign to continue his discourse, so I mumbled something and he continued loftily, "Upon our arrest, we Green Pigs were all taken to a bulk brain erasure facility on Sirius XI. We were all placed in a huge tank, and our heads bombarded with a constant stream of antineurons, designed to completely blank out all our memories and, most importantly, our evil thoughts."

"Then why are you still running around messing up the dimensions?" asked Lucius, whose attempts to climb up the wall had so unwound the remaining threads in his tunica that it now came down only to his navel.

"Little did the Dimensional Patrol know," the Green Pig said, puffing himself up, "that, upon a mind of *my* advanced capacities, the antineurons had the effect, not of nullifying, but of amplifying! Moreover, the Second Law of Conservation of Multiplex Realities, which states that anomalous realities must rebound elastically back into less anomalous realities, took effect at that very moment. All this, combined with the antineuron ray, produced a unique effect never hitherto observed: All the million versions of myself contained within the erasure tank slingshotted back into a single soma: me!

"Imagine, then, the shock of the Dimensional Patrol. Instead of a million zombie Green Pigs, there was something quite different waiting for my captors when their treatment was done: a super-gestalt Green Pig, containing within a single corporeal form all the concentrated viciousness, capriciousness, and vindictiveness of all the Green Pigs rolled into one!

"It was a simple matter to feign the childlike idiocy that is the usual state of criminals after the erasure procedure. So arrogant was the Dimensional Patrol, so confident of the success of their rehabilitative technique, that they applied only the most cursory of tests to my person . . . and delivered me to my home planet, my body and brain and—last but not least—my bank accounts—intact!"

I was beginning to understand why *scientifictiones* are such a popular form of literature. These fantastical romances provide a much-needed escape from the true complexities of life in the modern Roman age . . .

By now, the Green Pig was so carried away by his

rhetoric that he was hardly looking at us. His throne was hovering way up in the air, and he was gesticulating wildly.

"Here's our chance!" I whispered to Lucius.

"What are we going to do? I mean, this minotaur's staring us in the eye here."

"You remember our little bull-riding escapade back at the camp? With the sacred bull, I mean? Well, I bet I can stay on longer than you can. Come on, help me distract his attention."

"How?"

"Give me your tunica."

"But we need it to find our way out—you know, the classical parallels and all that—"

"Ad infernum with your musty old classics!" I said.

I fairly ripped the tunica off his back and began waving it at the bull. "What are you doing?" Lucius screamed.

"Distracting him! They go for movement."

The bull charged.

I wrapped the cloth around its horns. Lucius and I fled in opposite directions as the bull rammed into the wall. Lucius and I sprang onto its brawny back. It bucked and heaved and snorted, but we held on for dear life. Then it stood up on its hind legs and attempted to shake us off.

Meanwhile, the Green Pig's throne darted to and fro, and we heard him shrieking after us, "To struggle is vain, little ones! Sooner or later the Lacotian Minotaur will get you!"

At that moment, Lucius started sliding down the bull's rump. The minotaur gave a sort of shimmy that sent Lucius crashing to the floor. I pulled out my scalping knife and jabbed it hard into the buffalo-man's back. It roared and bucked again, got back on all fours, and trotted toward Lucius. I was sure it was going to trample him. Blood was running down my hands and arms. I didn't think I could hold on much longer. Just then, the knife slipped from my fingers and clattered to the ground—

—And me with it! I hit my head hard against a marble column. Blood ran into my eyes. The bull was running around crazily, Lucius' tunica still partly draped about its eyes. "Lucius, where are you?" I cried, as the Green Pig cackled somewhere in the background.

I heard him groan. I started to crawl in his direction. I was smarting all over. Opening my eyes, trying to make something out through the haze of blood, I saw Lucius huddling behind the buffalo robe cloak. I made my way toward him. The minotaur, distracted for a moment by the throne whizzing over our heads, didn't notice me.

"Give me the robe," I said.

Lucius just sat there, quivering like a calves' brain omelette.

"Hurry up," I said. "I may not know anything about Greek mythology, but I *can* stalk and kill an aurochs."

"But you're not even on horseback," Lucius stammered. "And that thing's angry, I mean *angry*."

"Horses be damned," I said. "We Lacotii hunted the buffalo for a thousand years without horses, before you conquering Romans showed up and bestowed the bloody creatures upon us." I knew this because Aquila had told me all about the ancient ways of the Lacotians. Of course, I had never actually practiced any of these ancient ways—I mean, whenever I'd gone hunting aurochs, it had always been in a group with plenty of horses and bows and arrows and whatnot—but I knew all about it, in a theoretical sort of way. "That's why I need the robe. And I need you to distract him."

"How?"

"Oh, you know. Jumping on his back, goading him, that sort of thing."

"I'm not getting near that bull again."

"Oh, come off it. You and I did the vow to the sun together. Surely you must have experienced something when you danced—you must have seen some kind of vision. Draw strength from it. We've endured all that pain together."

"Yes, well that was *controlled* pain. It's one thing to have your chest carved up by a homo medicinae, but it's quite another to offer yourself up to the horns of an unreasoning beast. One's got to draw the line somewhere."

"Lucius—"

"Oh, very well, very well. You know I'm just complaining for the sake of it." He handed me the aurochs robe. He wasn't shaking anymore...much. He didn't have time to, because the minotaur was already advancing steadily toward us, its hooves pounding on the marble floor, its nostrils positively smoking.

I threw the robe on my back, clenched the knife in my teeth, and starting crawling in the bull's direction, singing a song to myself: "I am a harmless buffalo cow. I am a harmless buffalo cow." I tried to move as an aurochs moves, from side to side, swaying, lethargic.

Meanwhile, Lucius jumped up and, putting on an admirable show of bravery, began to shout at the creature, "Here, buffalo. Nice buffalo. Come and get me, buffalo!"

Nothing loath, the minotaur charged.

Since I had transformed myself by my song into a harmless buffalo cow, the minotaur ignored me. I was directly in the path of the charge, with Lucius prancing around wildly behind me. I cried out to the pterodactyl spirit that had come to me in my vision, and I prayed that the bull would forgive me for taking its life. The bull sprang, and I simultaneously seized my knife and thrust upward with all the strength that yet remained to me.

I don't think I could have killed a full-sized male aurochs, but this thing was half human, and in its hybrid form considerably smaller, as well as clumsier. My scalping knife ripped into its chest and it fell on top of me. I managed to roll out from under it. Then I staggered up, sliced open its abdomen, and cut out a chunk of the steaming liver to gulp down on the spot, as was my right.

"Bloody good show," Lucius gasped.

"So," the Green Pig said, bringing his throne nearer. "You think you've won, do you?"

Blind fury gripped me. I ran at the throne and managed to grab hold of the lowest step, then I hauled myself up as the Pig pushed a lever to make it rise. "Grab on to my ankles!" I screamed out to Lucius, who did so. I pulled myself up and so did he, and we were both perched on the side of the control panel, glaring at His Viridiporcine Majesty and ready to scalp him at a moment's notice.

The Green Pig caused the throne to carom madly around the chamber, hoping, doubtless, to dislodge us.

Just at that moment there came a tremendous commotion from just outside the chamber. The three of us stared at the staggering spectacle. Titus Papinianus, C. Lentulus Fortunatus, my group of braves, and several other Romans and Lacotians unknown to me were all fighting off a veritable army of *android* warriors. Now and then several of the *androids* would disintegrate. I took this to mean that some of our gang were still downstairs trying to disable the remaining green men by releasing more captives from their glass amphorae. The number of simulacra seemed inexhaustible, though. More and more of them kept pouring in. Some were even popping in out of thin air, probably using one of those teleportation passwords that seemed to be the most convenient way of getting around the place. About a dozen Olmecs in funny headdresses were there, too, controlling the green men with black boxes into which they uttered commands.

"As long as even one captive remains," the Green Pig gloated, "I shall be able to run off copy after copy of him—enough to overwhelm any forces you might consider throwing at me!"

I grabbed wildly at him and caught his arm. A powerful shock racked my whole body, and blue bolts of lightning ran up and down me, making my hair stand on end.

"You see how foolish it is to try to attack me," the Green Pig said. "Now relax and watch the show, and I'll dispose of you later."

I tried bashing the controls, but the same thing happened. The whole throne was protected by some kind of mechanism that inflicted pain on prospective saboteurs . . .

We soared around the room while the conflict raged below. My braves screeched out their war cries. Fortunatus bobbed up and down through the tumult like a wineskin in the waves. My stepfather was fighting quite creditably; he was, after all, a general. He was bashing in heads and lopping off arms and legs with gusto, and I could not but admire his skill.

But how to attack the Green Pig without actually touching anything? Of course! I took the robe off my back. Lucius saw immediately what I was doing and took one end of it. Spreading it out as widely as we could, we threw it over the Green Pig's face.

The throne began to veer out of control.

"Now what?" Lucius screamed above the tumult.

"I'm not quite sure," I said.

Muffled sounds of protest came from behind the buffalo robe. The Green Pig's hands groped randomly about the console. At last they seemed to seize upon something. A lever was pulled. Crimson light irradiated us, and various buttons began to blink and glow.

I heard a rumbling.

The walls were shaking around us, and the floor was tilting to and fro. Green men, Lacotians, Olmecs and Romans alike were sliding up and down, colliding into each other, screaming, lashing out randomly with their weapons.

"You'll never win!" the Green Pig screamed from behind the aurochs hide. "This entire city is a self-contained, sealable environment, and I've got enough of your rogue universe gold to power a joyride through a trillion alternate realities. I'm taking this whole kit and kaboodle into space!"

The palace was moving into the air. But the throne had been flying around under its own power. The throne and the palace weren't moving at the same speed, so we went smashing down to the floor right next to the staircase, denting the marble and drenching ourselves in yet another shower of that ubiquitous green slime.

Lucius and I were thrown clear by the fall, about halfway up the stairs that seemed to lead up to the roof. The battle was following us; as the far end of the hall became cluttered with dead *androids*, the conflict seemed to move closer and closer to the stairs. "We'd better get some air," Lucius said, and we raced up to greet the rising sun.

It was a kind of rooftop garden. There were exotic plants everywhere, including the man-eating ones I'd seen in my dream of the dinosaur age. There were also cages full of the strangest animals you could imagine . . . composite beasts of legend. Cerberuses and manticores and chimaeras . . . each one, doubtless, a product of one of the Green Pig's genetic experiments. There was even a half man, half brontosaurus.

We hardly had time to take in everything when the flying throne came barreling up from downstairs, followed by dozens of furiously battling warriors. It was a free-for-all. I don't think anyone knew who or what they were fighting anymore.

Lucius and I ran to the edge of the roof, which was bordered by a low wall. We looked below and saw that the whole city had taken to the air with us. In the streets below, Olmecs and *androids* were dashing around in panic.

"Someone's got to help us," Lucius said. "Can't you summon Aquila or something? Or the Dimensional Patrol?"

"We're going to hit the side of that hill!" I shouted.

Sure enough, a peak of the Montes Negri loomed up to the east. Just as I was certain we would crash, the entire city turned on its side, causing all the combatants to roll around helplessly on the rooftop, grabbing each other for support, and began to climb steadily skyward.

"Do something!" Lucius said to me.

"What do you want? A rain dance?"

"It's better than nothing."

"I think I'll just go off somewhere and sing my death song."

Suddenly the city righted itself. We were over the crest of the hill. We were thrown against the wall. "If this isn't a good day to die," I said, "I don't think I can stick around for another one."

Just then—

Lucius was yanking my arm and pointing across to the east, where I saw, floating serenely in the sky—

A convoy of hot-air balloons! Each bore the legend SPQR. The frontmost balloon contained, in its basket, a tuba player who was vigorously sounding the charge. Beside him stood a tall and hairy figure who could be none other than Abraham bar-David, and next to him was the Egyptian. And suspended by ropes from the entire convoy of balloons was a familiar railway car—the car that had borne our fighting troops on the ferrequus ride from Iracuavia to Lacotia—laden with scorpiones, ballistae and catapultae—and a couple of dozen Lacotian braves and Roman troops on horseback!

"By the phallos of Priapus and the maidenhead of Venus!" Lucius whispered, thunderstruck. "It's the cavalry!"

CHAPTER
XXVIII

A PORK ECLIPSE NOW

N O SOONER HAD LUCIUS VINICIUS UTTERED THOSE words than the barrage of missiles began. The first convoy of hot-air balloons was now positioned just to the east, and fireballs were whizzing through the air at us. Everyone ran for cover—except the *androids*, who continued to fight anything that happened to be around, heedless of their impending destruction.

One flaming missile landed inside one of the bestiary cages. Small dinosaurs and chimaeras became tremendously agitated, and a fair-sized baby brontosaurus became so maddened that it crashed through the cage and began stomping about the rooftop garden, squawking all the while; a couple of hairy elephants charged out behind the brontosaurus, trumpeting and waving their tusks. *Androids* tripped and fell in all directions, and pretty soon the familiar old green slime was flowing like water.

Lucius and I ran for cover behind a huge plant . . . an astonishing species, for its enormous leaves, each longer than a man, appeared to possess mouths with rows of sharp, drooling teeth. The Green Pig seemed somewhat nonplussed at the appearance of the balloon-borne cavalry, and was causing his throne to dart hither and thither, dodging the missiles, as he gave commands to his lieutenants through some kind of amplifying tuba that he held to his lips. Part of the roof gave way, and several dozen Olmecs emerged. They wheeled before them a tubelike machine, bright silver in hue, about which glowed a pale blue aura. At a word from the Green Pig, the tube ejected a bolt of blue lightning which transfixed the nearest balloon, punctured it, and threw the railway car wildly off balance.

"Fire again!" the Pig cried gleefully, and another balloon popped. It must not be forgotten that all this while the entire city was rushing through the skies, skimming the hilltops, at breakneck speed.

"Fire! Fire!" the Green Pig shouted, as the railway car swayed precariously and I could see the catapultae slamming into each other.

The railway car was now only a few cubits over our heads, and I could see Ursus Erectus, on horseback, waving a war lance, his eaglefeather war bonnet streaming behind him, at the head of the Roman and Lacotian horse soldiers. At a signal from him, the horses started leaping down onto the roof, and then the spectacle *really* started. Balloons exploded above our heads. Balls of fire filled the sky. The stench of burning sulphur filled our nostrils. I could hear Lucius retching behind me.

"Isn't it about time someone rescued us?" he choked.

"I think this is about as close to a rescue as we're going to get," I said, kicking a flailing *android* out of the way. The Roman cavalry was bearing down on the *androids* now, trampling them as they wove in and out of the stampeding brontosaurus, hairy elephants, and mythical beasts.

I could hear Viridiporcus' commands over the tumult. "Get that damn lasercannon in gear, you idiots! You're supposed to be aiming at the enemy, not at yourselves!"

More blue lightning ripped through the air. Lucius and

I were in a relatively safe spot, though now and then it was necessary to dispatch the odd *android* that got in our way. Though our clothes and our faces were drenched in green slime, the supply of green men seemed endless indeed, and none of them were exploding wholesale anymore, so I could only conclude that the Green Pig had at least one more supply of those human templates salted away somewhere else in the palace.

It was at this dramatic juncture that a flying saucer appeared. What I mean is, it actually materialized out of nothing. It seemed to fill the entire sky, and the air reverberated with familiar, celestial music . . .

"Lucius! Everything's going to be all right!" I cried. "It's my father!" The music welled up, a throaty chorus of Lacotian voices punctuated by a soul-stirring drumbeat. Shimmering, rainbow-fringed light suffused the sky. "We're going to be all right, we're going to be saved," I said again, for I knew who it was that flying saucer carried.

"All right, my arse!" said Lucius. "I'd like to see him pluck us out of this singlehandedly."

"My father can do anything," I said confidently. A flock of pterodactyls soared and dived about the flying saucer, so I knew that these things were true to my vision.

Olmecs, *androids*, Lacotii, and Romans alike stopped in their tracks to gaze at the approaching saucer, which rotated slowly and cast a greenish glow over the entire rooftop garden. Dinosaurs screeched; elephants fell to their knees and trumpeted. The belly of the saucer opened up, and my father emerged, riding on a painted stallion, his lance held high. His voice rang out, "In a sacred manner I come!" His face glistened with war paint. Withered though it was, it seemed somehow rejuvenated, full of manhood.

His horse reared up. Then he literally came charging down out of the sky. I couldn't see how it worked until he was practically on top of us. Then I saw that there were these devices strapped to the horse's legs that sent out little spurts of blue flame. It was the same thing that had enabled the androids to fly around when they were trying to pluck us out of the trees.

The Green Pig's throne came flying straight at Aquila. But my father merely raised his hand. The throne was stopped by some invisible force.

Then Aquila said, "In the name of the Dimensional Patrol, I order you to desist from your illegal dimensional tampering this instant, and take you into custody by the powers vested in me by the Department of Interdimensional Stability of the United Universes."

"Don't be ridiculous," the Green Pig said. "You haven't got any authorization from the Dimensional Patrol. This is a rogue universe, and I can do anything I want here. Your action in arresting me is just as illegal as anything I might have done . . ."

"Perhaps so," my father said. "But now that I've taken it upon myself to capture you, I might as well see this thing through to the end. I mean, for you to throw a few legal niceties at me seems to be a case of the pot calling the kettle black, if you see what I mean."

"You can't possibly defeat me without your Dimensional Patrol colleagues anyway," Viridiporcus Rex said, rearing himself up on his trotters and running through his repertoire of imperial gestures, grimaces, and cloakflingings. "It's all an empty bluff. Why bother? We could go halves on the rogue gold on this world; there's plenty for everyone. Join me, and we'll be time criminals together—and rule the universe!"

I looked around. Most of the *androids* lay writhing about on the ground. The others stood completely still; presumably, without the controlling commands of the Green Pig, they were deactivated. The Olmecs had all gathered together at one end of the roof; clearly they couldn't quite make up their minds what was going on.

Ursus Erectus, the Sasquatius, and the Egyptian had joined my stepfather and fat old Fortunatus. Each was explaining the goings-on to all the others at the same time and completely ignoring the present spectacle. The ferrequus carriage and its contents—the most sophisticated in Roman weaponry—lay in shambles around them. Weird animals roamed about.

Aquila and the Green Pig faced each other, the one on his hovering throne, the other on his jet-propelled horse.

For a few moments they remained that way, glaring at each other, each waiting for the other to make the first move—

A crack appeared in the sky! Horrified, I saw the heavens appear to shatter into millions of pieces . . . and through the cracks I glimpsed a terrible blackness . . . a starless darkness . . . even the sun was rent by a thousand hairline fractures.

"Oh, no!" the Green Pig cried out, for the first time displaying a certain desperation. "You fool! You should not have intervened, Aquila. Your appearance here has upset the causality paths of this universe to the breaking point! Now you must bear responsibility for the fact that the infamous Third Law is about to come into effect . . ."

I looked from Viridiporcus Rex to my father. His face, too, seemed touched by momentary consternation, though it was hard to read his emotions through his bold red and ocher war paint.

"I care not for the Third Law of Conservation of Multiplex Universes," Aquila said at last, "though it is true that my interference may have been the last straw . . . that I may have triggered the self-destruction of the universe. But if you were Lacotii, like my son, or even like his friend Lucius Vinicius, who has become Lacotian by adoption, you would not fear the end. None of us is immortal. There is no reason for a universe to be immortal either. It is not the length of one's life but how well one has lived that matters. Far better to go now, flushed with the joy of battle, than to wait for a slow, dishonorable winding down."

"That may well be," the Green Pig said, "but, damn it, I'm a villain, and your noble sentiments just sound a little too goody-goody for me. So I might as well have the pleasure of killing everyone before we all go out like candles!" He turned to the Olmecs, who were cowering beside their infernal lightning-bolt machine. "You may fire when ready."

Enormous chunks were disappearing from the sun! Although we were still zooming through the heavens, there weren't really any heavens to zoom through anymore . . . for the blue sky was eroding into darkness. The Montes Negri were dissolving into blurry whorls of color.

The Olmecs looked at each other in consternation; then one, whose plumage seemed taller than the rest, came forward. "If it please Your Viridiporcitude, we can't fire right now."

"Why not?" the Pig asked. "We still have, I'd say, a good thirty seconds before the destruction of the universe."

"Your Magnitude . . . we've had a long discussion amongst ourselves, and we've come to the conclusion that this isn't an eclipse of the sun that any of our astronomers have predicted. Since the Olmecs are the wisest stargazers in the world, we would surely have known from our observations that an eclipse would occur around now, and performed the appropriate rites. Since this is an unforeseen eclipse, it seems clear that the world is coming to an end."

"But that's precisely what I've been saying for the past five minutes!"

"Well, your superscience may be all very well, but we Olmecs have dealt with the end of the world before, and you know, in times of trouble, it's best to stick with the good old-time religion. There's a perfectly normal way to avert the end of the world, and that's by sacrificing a couple of dozen people and ripping out their hearts. Every schoolboy knows that. Well, I don't know about any of you heathens, but I am personally honored to be the first to go. And now, Atahualpe, if you'd kindly wield the obsidian blade..." He pulled a black knife, carved from some glassy dark crystal, out of his panther-skin loincloth. He handed it to a second Olmec, a particularly colorful fellow in a cloak of turquoise feathers, with colored stones embedded in his nose. Then he lay down on the low wall at the edge of the roof garden, oblivious to a curious baby brontosaurus who was padding by, and allowed himself to be sacrificed without uttering a single cry.

"Now that's bravery," Aquila said.

"Superstitious rubbish! What a waste of time," the Green Pig said. "I'll never manage to get another dastardly deed into the last fifteen seconds of my existence if those idiotic primitives don't shape up."

As the officiating priest raised the bloody heart up to the sky, a moan went up from the other Olmecs.

I heard Aaye the Egyptian muttering to the sasquatch, "Fascinating, isn't it? We used to do stuff like this at home, a few thousand years ago. These Olmechii have pyramids, too, did you know that? Why, they're almost civilized."

Calmly, a second sacrificial victim took the place of the first. He, too, died without a whimper.

"You can see," the Green Pig said, "that this is all useless."

"We know what we're doing," said the knife-wielding priest.

"Look at the sun!" the Pig said. "It's just getting darker and darker every second."

Colder, too, I would have to add. And there was a distinct thinness about the air, as though it were being sucked away. I could barely breathe. We all turned to gaze at the sun ...

A little piece of it was coming back! A tiny patch of yellow glistened like a jewel ...

"Told you we knew what we were doing," the High Priest said, as he raised his blade to despatch another victim.

The sun was coming back very quickly now ... the fractures in the sky were healing ... the Montes Negri were rapidly reforming out of the shifting rainbow haze ...

And then, without warning, an entire fleet of flying saucers became visible, falling upon us out of the sun!

"I should have known!" the Green Pig said. "This time it really *is* the Dimensional Patrol. They're going to have one of their silly trials again. Well, *your* arse is on the line as much as mine, Aquila, but I'm not going to hang around for one of their interminable judiciary committees. I'm taking advantage of this temporary dimensional rift to—"

He didn't finish his sentence. Threads of darkness began spinning about him, and in a moment he was completely englobed by a cocoon of darkness. Then he vanished.

Only his mocking laugher remained.

The Dimensional Patrol bore down on us as light filled the world once more.

"I guess we've been rescued, Lucius..." I said. Then, hearing no response, "Lucius? Lucius? *Lucius?*"

"G-g-g-et me out of this th-th-thing—"

I jerked around to see Lucius' torso poking out from the mouth of one of the leaves of the plant under whose shade we had been hiding.

"I've been t-t-trying to attract your attention for horae! This thing's trying to eat me alive!"

I grabbed hold of his arms and began to pull. A fearsome tug of war ensued. The plant was drooling all over me. I called for help. It took a sasquatch, my stepfather, Ursus Erectus, and several others to drag Lucius out of its slavering maw.

"Thank Jupiter," he said. "It only succeeded in devouring the rest of my tunica and a few leg hairs . . ."

The Olmecs were jumping around for joy at one end of the roof. They were going to take all the credit for saving the universe, I suppose. "We'd better figure out how to land this thing," I said.

"Too late," my father said. "The time for judgment is at hand!"

The entire city was snatched into the belly of the nearest flying saucer. I didn't see or hear anything more for the next few hours. I must have passed out.

CHAPTER
XXIX

MARTIAN ODYSSEY

WHEN I RECOVERED CONSCIOUSNESS, I WAS alone in a cell. At least, it seemed like a cell to me, although there were no rats running around, no foul stenches, no manacles, and no guards. It was a completely featureless white room. There didn't seem to be any doors or windows either.

There was a device in the middle of the room, one of the usual whirring, buzzing, beeping, flashing things that I had come to expect of our guests from the future. Sensing, perhaps, that I had come to, it started whirring, buzzing, beeping, and flashing at an absolutely frantic pace, and pretty soon a raw aurochs liver on a silver platter popped out. It smelled pretty good, even though it was green.

I ate greedily.

"Thank you for eating," the machine said. "I was beginning to get worried. You've had a most trying day, I understand—what with the universe coming to an end and all that." I couldn't quite tell where the voice was coming from, but it was speaking Lacotian pretty well—with perhaps a trace of a Greek accent.

"Where am I?" I asked. "And I thought that the universe had been restored—at least, it looked like it was all coming back into being just before I passed out."

"Fat lot you know," the machine replied.

"Wait a minute. I don't really feel right being insulted by a glorified oven, no matter how advanced. You'd better be a little more polite."

"What are you going to do, give me fifty lashes, you neolithic nincompoop?"

I threw my hands up in the air. "Just explain."

"Very well, Master Equus Insanus. As you know, the Third Law of Conservation of Multiplex Realities—"

I could see that we were about to be launched into yet another of those expository lumps so beloved of the writers of *scientifictiones*. "How many of those laws are there anyway?"

"Just as many as are needed," the food dispenser said in an injured tone. "In words of one syllable, a condition of extreme causal ambiguity was created by all that transdimensional interference, which precipitated, as you so astutely observed, the end of the universe. However, that moment of ending was pregnant with causality paradoxes. Thus, it was possible, by using tachyon surges permissible within the limits of the uncertainty principle, to propel your entire solar system into what's called a holding universe until certain legal matters can be settled."

"And the Green Pig?"

"Alas, he too took advantage of the causal ambiguity to engineer his own departure from the universe. He could be anywhere."

"Well, what are these legal matters you're talking about, and where are we going, anyway?"

"Well, we're going to Mars. That's where the district court is. Very boring place, Mars—a dump, really. And people have been throwing their junk into those canals for so long they're nothing but filth. But the trial's got to be there, so there it's going to be."

"Whose trial?" I had a horrible feeling . . .

"Why, yours, of course! Well, you're a material witness, anyway. But it's mostly that father of yours, Aquila. It seems he's been taking the law into his own hands . . ."

The machine was absolutely right. It corroborated what Lucius had told me about his previous saucer voyage: Mars was a total slum. The buildings were all metal cubes; they had neither the grand ostentation of Rome nor the natural simplicity of the Lacotian dwellings. Outside the one city, the entire landscape was red. The sky wasn't blue, and on the one occasion they took us out of the city, we had to wear funny suits that covered us from head to toe.

There were a few tourist attractions: signs everywhere pointed to the "famed canals," for example—the signs were in alien scripts on the whole, but now and then there was one in Latin or Greek. We went past the canals in a sort of horseless chariot, and I must say that the Roman aqueducts were far more interesting. There were also a lot of shops selling tawdry, mass-produced souvenirs, including copies of the Flavian Amphitheater, which, for some reason, they referred to as the Colosseum, and the Statua Libertatis. I gathered that Mars was a sort of stopping-off place, a resort for alien beings and a watering hole for members of the Dimensional Patrol. People weren't actually allowed to come to Earth itself because it "wasn't ready for the tourist trade." Well, I'd seen what the trade had done to the eastern ports of Terra Nova, and I can't say I objected to the exclusion of visitors from outer space to our world.

I, Lucius Vinicius, and my other companions were wined and dined for several days, in a small palace that was supposed to remind us of home—full of baths, a couple of tipis in the atrium, fountains, and *android* dancing girls. We all got a chance to devour our favorite foods: Lucius had all the larks' tongues he could eat and I had nothing but roast aurochs. All the food was produced by talking machines, and it was all green.

I didn't see my father for several days.

At last, they—"they" being our guards, who were all enormous green lobsters in armor—brought us to the court, which was really much the same as a Roman tribunal. My father stood behind a sort of pulpit, and the judge, a sort of green elephant in a toga and an Egyptian wig, sat on a couch at the back of the room. There were galleries all around us, making me feel somewhat as though I were in the Circus Maximus about to engage in gladiatorial combat. The stands were packed with green lobsters, green were-jaguars, green walruses, green horses, and machines in costume, who all scrutinized us through tubelike, extensible metascopes. There were the usual futuristic devices; I no longer paid any attention to them, because I had long since learned that in the far future these devices outnumbered people by at least a hundred to one.

The sasquatch gave evidence. The judge showed great interest when he discussed the uranograph, and the audience laughed uproariously as Abraham bar-David explained that it was used for finding politically correct sacrificial animals. Lucius, who was sitting next to me on the benches before the judge, nudged me and said, "I don't see why that's funny."

"Silence!" said the lobster who guarded us. "This is serious business."

"Why?" I said. "What's going to happen if Aquila is condemned?"

"Well, first there'll be the old brainwipe. *Then* they're going to have to figure out what to do with your world."

"What to do with it?" I asked. "What do you mean, what to do with it?"

The lobster peered at me smugly and said, "Your entire universe has already disintegrated. Only your immediate Solar System remains, and the holding universe won't hold it forever. Every universe has slightly different physical laws, you see, and it tends to reject transplanted segments with the wrong laws. We have to constantly barricade your system from the self-protecting instincts of the host universe—the immune system, if you will."

"Speak Latin," I said, "I'm tired of all this double-talk."

"It's simple enough," the lobster said. "It costs a lot of energy to keep your little segment from being eaten alive by the host universe. Now, the Dimensional Patrol is compassionate, but it doesn't have unlimited resources. If we can't find a good reason to maintain the barrier around your system... then, I'm afraid, *delenda est Terra vostra.*"

"What? You can't destroy our Earth!" I said.

"Oh, yes we can," the green lobster said grimly. "Oh, don't worry. You people will be fine. We'll evacuate you and your immediate family and whatever friends you can't live without, and set you up in a smaller-scale, physically anomalous environment in some other universe. In other words, you'll be safe, and your needs will be completely provided for."

"Sounds like life imprisonment to me," Lucius said bitterly.

"It's an outrage! A small-scale environment indeed," I said. "You mean we won't be able to roam across the great plains, or even to ride that stupid ferrequus across the continent... or hunt, or make war, or watch the sun and moon crossing the sky."

"Don't worry," the lobster said. "There'll be some kind of surrogates... highly realistic illusions... you'll not notice a thing."

"But I'll know. In my heart I'll know." I turned to

Lucius and sighed. And I knew that, although he was sitting quite still and had set his face into a mask of enviable Roman stoicism, that he suffered the same torment in his heart that I did.

The trial droned on and on, with my father being cross-examined in detail over his decision to intervene with the rogue universe. They interrogated Lucius for a while, too, and Titus Papinianus gave his own idiotic account of the whole affair. At last, they called my name. "Equus Insanus, also known as Titus Papinianus the Younger—come forward!"

I did so, and, after being attached to yet another of those infernal devices, this one supposed to reveal whether or not I was lying, I proceeded to relate the entire tale of my adventures, beginning from my flagellation at the hands of the pedant Androcles, all the way up to our abortive attempt to defeat the Green Pig in his citadel.

My tale provoked much merriment in the audience, often for reasons I didn't quite understand. But during my description of the vision of the pterodactyl, and the sun dance that brought hope back to my dispirited people, they listened in profound concentration. The judge nodded sagely during it all, and I thought I saw him wipe a couple of fat, emerald-colored tears from his beady elephant's eyes.

At length, my testimony was done. But I didn't leave the stand. The judge looked at me and said, "Well, have you anything to add, my child? If there is nothing more to say, you may as well retire. We'll be delivering our verdict soon, but either way you'll be living happily ever after."

It was at that moment that I started yelling at them all. I couldn't stand it anymore. "Happily ever after? Happily ever after? It's a foregone conclusion, isn't it? You're going to let the world be destroyed, and you're going to put my friends and me in prison for the rest of our lives. Don't try to fool me, O Judge!"

"I would hardly call it a prison, young man—"

"Worse than a prison then. More like a zoo. That's what we primitives are to you, isn't it? Nothing but animals, to be petted and cooed over, but hardly to be taken seriously!"

"Taken seriously? My dear young man," the judge said, his trunk fibrillating furiously, "we *do* take you seriously. After all, you almost caught the greatest criminal of all time . . ."

"And if we'd caught him for you?"

"Well, things might be a little different."

"I'll say!" I screamed. "We wouldn't be in this pickle if we'd managed to capture him. After all, your Dimensional Patrol was pretty bloody grateful to us last time, weren't they? We savages went and handed him to you on a silver platter . . . and it was *you* who went and bungled it by not knowing about the effect of those Laws of Conservation of Multiplex Realities. I'm sure you have the power to destroy us—for *your* mistakes—but it's just not fair. It's an infernum of a way to run a ferrequus, if you ask me."

They dragged me to my seat. I screamed. I spat at the green octopus who held onto me with four or five of his arms while I struggled. I knew we were doomed now. I watched my stepfather and the others; they seemed frightened. Only Aquila's face held no fear. I was proud of him and proud to be his son.

Lucius smiled at me. "Bonum est, hac die mori," he said softly. I knew at last that we understood each other. Though we could never belong entirely to the other's world, I knew that Lucius was my friend as well as, by accident of fate, my brother.

"Yes. It is a good day to die."

* * *

Then came time for the verdict. Aquila stood before the judgmental seat. Impassively I watched as the judge rose and addressed the throng.

"We find that Aquila has acted illegally in his attempt to intervene in the foreclosure of universe X-928301-NB-29371ΩΩΩ," he intoned. "But inasuch as he was motivated by compassion and love for his home world, we hereby commute the sentence of brain erasure. However, since he is obviously unready to assume the great responsibilities that the guardianship of the Dimensional Matrices requires, we hereby reduce him to the state wherein we found him, videlicet, that of a normal human being incapable of interdimensional travel. We suspect that he would prefer this state of affairs anyway."

"Absolutely!" Aquila said. "I am a Lacota, not a green-faced, meddling busybody from the future."

"As for the future of your universe . . ."

The crowd was tittering now, obviously bored. The fun part of the trial was over with, and they were about to hear a routine sentence of absolute destruction. I gritted my teeth.

"Young Titus," the judge said.

I started at being addressed directly, then stood up. No green elephant was going to scare me. I knew who I was.

"I have one question to ask you before I decide upon the fate of your world," the magistrate said.

"Ask me." I spoke not as a humble slave, but as a free man to another free man.

"If you were given an environment that simulated your home reasonably well . . . and the opportunity to live an idyllic existence for the rest of your days . . . would you not be happy?"

"Sir," I said, "if that were my only choice, I would find a corner somewhere in that simulated environment, and I would sit there and think of the sacred burial places of our people for some time; then I would sing a death song, and my spirit would leave me forever. My spirit would seek out the Land of Many Tipis. You say that my entire universe has destroyed itself, but you don't know everything. My spirit will be able to find that land."

"You're saying you would rather die?"

I shrugged. "My people think little of death."

"You may sit down now."

I returned to my seat. After a time of deliberation that seemed to last forever, the judge resumed addressing the people. By that time most of the onlookers had disappeared. Only the machines remained behind in the tiers that surrounded us. I suppose they were strapped down or something.

"All right, boy," the judge said. "We're going to keep the hold on your Solar System for as long as we can. For one thing, you came *this* close to catching the Green Pig... and he is one of those criminals who likes to return to the scene of his crime. Perhaps, next time, you *will* catch him."

I turned around. My stepfather let out a wild whoop. Fortunatus laughed. Ursus Erectus smiled a little. I said, "What about the rest of our universe? After all, we humans are not going to be confined to one world forever. We have to have somewhere to go..."

"You drive a hard bargain, child!" the judge said. "But, although your universe has already destroyed itself, it may be possible to perform a time-reversal... it will require *vast* amounts of energy, of course, but... nothing is ever completely lost, you know."

"You mean, you might be able to restore everything to the way it was?"

The judge looked at me. There was much laughter in his eyes. "We've never done it before," he said, "but there *are* some theoretical ramifications within the *Fourth* Law of Conservation of Multiplex Realities..."

CHAPTER
XXX

THE MARCH OF PROGRESS

AND SO IT WAS THAT MY FATHER AND I WERE REUN-
ited; and that he and I, decked out in our eaglefeathers and our togas, were sitting together, under the
wide blue skies of our native Lacotia, on a Roman couch
flanked by centurions, watching the laying of ferrequus
tracks and having roasted aurochs served to us by doe-
eyed Scythian slaves.

My other father was off in the distance, barking orders to his overseers and becoming visibly apoplectic.
He and Fortunatus were no longer at odds, for they had
decided it would be better to cooperate on the ferrequus
than to build at cross-purposes. Fortunatus had returned
to his procuratorial seat in Caesarea-on-Miserabilis, presumably to sit in judgment over the usual wretches and
petty criminals.

Aquila laughed. "What an idiot," he said. "And yet,
there is something about him . . . one cannot help liking
him. He's like a mangy old dog that farts and smells and
hangs onto one's legs and yet one would never get rid of
him because of all we have been through together."

"It's only an hour or so to nightfall, father," I said. "What shall we do?"

"Eat, my son, and sleep. Away from war, these are the only occupations fit for a man." He laughed again.

"I'm glad you're never going away again," I said.

A troubled look crossed his face. I thought, Perhaps he knows more than he's telling me.

"My only regret," I said, "is that, since they've taken away all that the Green Pig created, I shall never see the lizard-bird of my vision again . . ."

"You're unique, my boy. You're the only one who ever went on a vision quest and was visited by a spirit animal from a parallel universe. I'm sure that your experience has been much discussed by xenoanthropologists all over the known universes by now."

I would always love my father, nay worship him; but I knew he had touched and seen many things beyond my comprehension, and that we would never share the same vision . . . not completely. Perhaps this realization was merely a part of growing up. I was thinking about that rather a lot, since my birthday was coming up soon, and this time I would be asked to doff the toga praetexta of childhood and put on the pure white toga of a man. "I don't really care about that," I said to him. "I have become a man in the way of the Lacotii."

My father said, "It is not the ritual, son; it is what you carry in your heart."

I looked across to where the Egyptian Aaye was sternly overseeing the uranographic analysis of a herd of white heifers. Soon the hour of evening sacrifice would be upon us, and the augurs would be proclaiming the future once more—a future made more certain by the scientific advance of the uranograph.

Below us, beside the ferrequus track, slaves were erecting a tower. Not much of one, actually; it was more of a pole, with climbing footholds, and a platform on top.

On the platform there was a Lacotian brave who tended a fire. "That's something new," I said.

Lucius and Abraham came up the hill. The Sasquatius was full of himself; I knew he was about to come up with some tremendous discovery. Lucius was wearing full military uniform; for the first time, I thought, it did not seem to dwarf him. He looked splendid as a tribune of the Imperium Romanum.

"Have you seen the latest invention?" Lucius shouted. "It's phenomenal!"

I looked at the tower. The brave was damping the fire now, and a trail of smoke rose into the afternoon sky. I looked far to the east and saw, at the very limits of my vision—which were great, for I saw with the eyes of a pterodactyl—another thin line of smoke.

"Isn't it wonderful?" the Sasquatius said. "Once more, the vision of Lacotia wedded to the technology of Rome . . . a system for sending smoke signals all the way across the continent . . . a tower every couple of mille passuum . . . I call it the telegraph. We are going to put telegraph poles all the way down the ferrequus tracks . . . for instant messages to be sent from Lacotia to Iracuavia. And eventually . . . a line of ships, perhaps, stretching across the Oceanus Atlanticus, each capable of sending up such a signal . . . given ideal weather conditions, the emperor should be able to communicate with his most distant subjects in a matter of days!"

"Magnificent, O hairy one!" Aquila said, knitting his brows. "I suppose, now that we've been deprived of all flying saucer technology, we will have to rely more and more on the ingenuity of such as you."

I looked at my friend and brother. Suddenly I realized that he must be about to tell me something . . . that he'd been trying to tell me ever since we returned from Mars.

"You're going back, aren't you?" I said to him.

He nodded.

"We had so much fun together," I said. I made as

though to bid him remain with us, but he stayed my hand. Together we walked down the hill, not talking to one another.

I overheard Papinian, shouting enthusiastically at no one in particular, "In a year we'll have ferrequi hurtling across the land! We'll have telegraphic messages smoking their way from shore to shore of this great continent! Civilization is coming to these barbarian lands at last!"

"Let's go for a ride together," I said to Lucius Vinicius.

He saddled his horse. I rode in the style of the Lacotii.

We rode for a long time, westward, across lands untouched by the iron tracks. The afternoon darkened into evening. We rode with the wind in our faces. The sky had reddened now. It was cold; summer would soon be fading, and the trees would become the color of blood. There was no one but us out here: the land stretched on and on, vast, imponderable, untameable. I did not think the Romans would ever civilize it; for beyond their cities and their aqueducts and their gore-drenched circuses there would always be the infinite plains.

We came to a stop on a low promontory overlooking more endless plains, and Lucius said to me, "Let's turn back now. I've got to pack. There was a message from the emperor waiting for me when we got back; he wants me in Rome; thinks my escapades in Terra Nova are not good for me. Besides . . . Rome is my country, not Lacotia . . ."

"And that's why I must stay here," I told my closest friend.

"But Rome will creep up on Lacotia, I think, eventually. And then where will you be? Who can escape the hand of Rome?" Lucius said. He spoke like someone who would one day be Emperor, and I thought, He will be a good ruler, and truly love his subjects.

"I'll escape somehow," I said. "Even if Rome should

conquer all of Terra Nova, and put up baths and race-courses on every hill of the sacred burial grounds...I'll find a place that's free of her. Perhaps I'll cross the Oceanus Pacificus...and find that mysterious China everyone's been looking for...or who knows, even light out for Indian territory, like Alexander the Great did, and see for myself the land of saffron and swarthy-skinned princesses."

"By Jupiter!" Lucius said. "You've certainly got a bloody lot of ambition, haven't you?"

"You don't know how much," I said softly. Then, "You go on ahead. I'll follow."

At last I was by myself. Soon the stars would come out. They wouldn't be the right stars, of course, because, even though our world was as it had been, I knew that we were hostages in an alien universe that might at any time spill over and engulf us.

Unless I could catch the Green Pig...

Lucius was right. I *was* ambitious. I was going to save the universe. Singlehandedly, if necessary.

A huge bird flew across the crimson sun...no! It was no bird! It was...dared I hope?...yes, it was indeed ...the lizard-bird of my vision! The pterodactyls had not gone from my world altogether, then...and that meant, perhaps, that the Time Criminal had already returned to the scene of his crime...

I gazed out to the west. Away from Rome.

Then I rode into the sunset.

Alone.

About the Author

Somtow Papinian Sucharitkul (S. P. Somtow) was born in Bangkok in 1952 and grew up in Europe. He was educated at Eton and Cambridge. His first career was as a composer, and his musical works have been performed, televised and broadcast in more than a dozen countries on four continents. He was artistic director of the Asian Composers EXPO '78 in Bangkok and was chosen Thai representative to the International Music Council of UNESCO. In the late 1970s he took up writing speculative fiction and won the 1981 John W. Campbell Award for best new writer, as well as the Locus Award for his first novel, *Starship & Haiku*. His short fiction has twice been nominated for the Hugo Award.

Somtow now lives in Los Angeles. He is working on more satirical novels, a serious, ambitious horror novel, and has recently written the script for a forthcoming motion picture. *Aquila and the Iron Horse* is the second volume in *The Aquiliad*.